THE SAVAGE END

THE VAMPIRE WORLD SAGA BOOK 6

PT HYLTON
JONATHAN BENECKE

Copyright © 2019 P.T. Hylton & Jonathan Benecke

All rights reserved.

This is a work of fiction. Any resemblance to actual persons living or dead, businesses, events, or locales is purely coincidental.

Reproduction in whole or part of this publication without express written consent is strictly prohibited.

Thank you for supporting our work.

WHAT CAME BEFORE

ALEX GODDARD is the captain of the Ground Mission Team, an elite task force that supplies the ship *New Haven* with resources recovered from the vampire-infested Earth's surface.

After releasing a virus designed to kill all the vampires on the planet, the humans learned of an unexpected side effect. All vampires directly created by JADEN were not killed by the virus. Instead, they were transformed into Twisted—deformed creatures with all of the vampires' strengths and few of their weaknesses.

Among these Twisted is MARYANA, the vampire who brought down civilization.

Alex and Jaden team up to stop Maryana's assault on Agartha, but when the battle is over they realize it was just a distraction. Maryana's real target was *New Haven* all along. By transforming the city's badges into Twisted under her complete control, Maryana is able to quickly take *New Haven*.

Alex and the GMT attempt a rescue mission, but they

are forced to retreat, leaving behind JESSICA, CB, and forty-thousand helpless humans.

As they fly away from the city-ship, Alex makes a solemn vow. "I'm coming back for you."

1

THE WHEELS of the transport ship touched down with a jolt, shaking everyone inside. Alex kept her balance, but Felix teetered awkwardly. She grabbed the back of his vest, steadying him, and wondered how long it would take for Owl to recover enough to fly the ship. She wanted the best pilot at the helm when they returned to *New Haven*. She hit a button and the cargo door opened, revealing Agartha's hangar bay. Ed, Chuck, Jaden, Felix, Brian, and a handful of techs followed her off the ship and into the city.

"As much as I'd like to let you get settled in, there's no time for that." She marched through the hangar, not looking back as she spoke. "We need to work with the people of Agartha to get the defenses restored as quickly as we can. Maryana could be launching an attack as we speak."

"I'll go see what George needs," Brian replied. "Maybe I can come up with something that will buy us some time."

"Perfect. We could really use a Twisted-killing weapon." Alex walked briskly through the open area, heading for the control room. She knew the leaders of Agartha would be gathered there. She wanted to be involved in planning how to defend against the attack they all knew was coming.

Jaden trotted alongside them. "Brian, I need you on something else." He sounded annoyed, and Alex detected a slight shake in his voice.

"Something else?" Alex didn't bother trying to hide her surprise. She kept talking as she marched into the hallway that led to the control room. "What's more important than defending the city?"

Jaden moved in a flash. He put a hand on each of Alex's shoulders and pushed her against the wall. He didn't press hard enough to hurt her, but she still felt the strength in the fingers gripping her. The cold metal wall touching her back sent a chill up her spine.

"You have my attention," she said, her voice hard. She didn't know what was happening, but Jaden was clearly upset. Though it wasn't exactly pleasant to be shoved against the wall by a creature with superhuman strength, part of her welcomed the passion she saw in his usually stoic eyes. "Tell me what's more important than preparing your city to survive the next attack."

"How quickly you forget the sacrifice we've made." He forced his words through gritted teeth. "The city's best defense is the vampires that reside within its walls. The same vampires that saved your life and the lives of everyone here. Their reward is death. The virus crawls through their bodies now. If you want to save this city, we have to save those vampires. Brian may be the only person capable of the task." As he finished, he let go of Alex's shoulders. The anger disappeared just as quickly as it had flared up, leaving a hollow sadness in his eyes.

Alex pushed down the urge to strike back at him for laying

hands on her. The truth was, he was right. She hadn't given one thought to the virus infecting the vampires of Agartha. It hadn't even crossed her mind since she'd discovered that Maryana was headed to *New Haven*. "I'm sorry. You're right. They are the city's best defense, and we do owe them a great debt." She turned to Brian. "I'm sure George will be able to get you set up with a lab and some equipment. Their techs have been working on a cure. Maybe you can help them figure it out."

The group hustled to the control room. When they reached it. Alex walked in first. Every eye in the room looked up as they entered.

George stood near the front of the room, Natalie on one side and Cynthia on the other. "What happened?"

"Maryana reached *New Haven*." Jaden's voice was calm and even. "She was able to get inside the city and turn a large force. She has control of the ship and all of its inhabitants." He looked Natalie in the eyes. "There are forty thousand people on *New Haven*. We need to consider all of them her army, now."

Alex bristled. "The people of *New Haven* are not her army. They're her prisoners. We need to save them. That's the plan. First, we secure Agartha, and then we figure out a way to get back on *New Haven* and take her out." Alex looked from Jaden to Natalie as she spoke, but neither returned her gaze.

"Yes," Jaden said slowly. "Killing Maryana and releasing those under her control is the plan. But until we do, everyone that she turns is the enemy. That monster destroyed a world full of people to get what she wanted. She will not give a second thought to turning every person on *New Haven*. For now, we must consider the possibility that she has an army forty thousand strong. We lost the world to her once. If the vampires of Agartha die, we will lose it again."

As Jaden spoke, Alex had a terrible realization—he was afraid. Maybe not of losing to Maryana, but of losing his family. He had spent lifetimes with these vampires and their bond was something she could never hope to understand. She turned to George. "Could you point Brian in the direction of your lab? He has work to do."

ALEX SLID THE CURTAIN BACK, revealing the hospital bed, and its occupant groaned in response.

"I'm awake. Did you get her?" Owl lay in bed, two empty blood packets next to her. The burns from the explosion still marked her face and arm, but Alex was shocked to see a noticeable improvement in the condition of her wounds.

Alex sat on the bed next to Owl, and the springs of the uncomfortable mattress squeaked. Sitting down made her aware of just how tired she was. The adrenaline of battle was fading and exhaustion was starting to set in. Alex looked up with tired eyes, trying to find a way to tell Owl that she had failed. The words didn't come.

Owl looked down at her lap. "How bad is it?"

"Bad. She has *New Haven*. It looks like she turned all of the badges."

Owl's head shot up and there was fire in her eyes. "When are we going to get her? What about CB? What about Brian?"

"We got Brian out. He's working on saving the vampires of Agartha right now." When Alex tried to say CB's name, her breath caught in her throat. She focused, drew a breath, and tried again. Tears crawled down her cheeks as she spoke. "I talked to Jessica for a second. She thinks that CB is dead. I failed, Owl. We didn't get there fast enough and there were just too many Twisted. God knows what Maryana is doing to our home right now."

Owl leaned over and put her arms around Alex. The room was silent, neither Alex nor Owl making a sound as tears rolled from their eyes. Alex could smell the charred skin on Owl's face and felt the misshapen spine that ran up her back, another reminder that the world was no longer what it had been.

She drew a breath and wiped the tears off her face with the back of her hands. "This isn't over yet. I'm going to find a way to finish this once and for all." She was surprised to find she felt a bit better after shedding a few tears.

"Putting a sword through Maryana's chest would be a good start." Owl gave a small smile.

"I like that idea. Although that may be the finish, not the start. We need to figure out how to get there."

"We will get there. We're the GMT. If anyone can pull this off, it's us."

ALEX WOKE WITH A START, and her eyes immediately went to clock on the wall. When she saw the positions of its hands, she sprang out of bed. Somehow, she'd slept for eight hours. She had agreed to lie down for a minute when Jaden pointed out how exhausted she looked. She hadn't thought she would be able to sleep, but once she laid down, fatigue did the rest.

The room they'd given her was small, featuring a narrow bed that left little room for anything else. Her clothes were still in a pile where she had thrown them before climbing under the sheets. She dressed in her dirty fatigues, grimacing as she noticed the blood splattered on them. She made a mental note to see if George could get her some clean clothes, or at least get these washed.

Ten minutes later, Alex opened the door to the lab and found Brian exactly where she'd known he would be. He sat at one of the room's many tables, his eyes darting back and forth between a monitor displaying a microscopic image and another one displaying charts of data. As expected, he was completely lost in his work, and he didn't notice when Alex entered.

A woman at the desk next to Brian stood up. "This is a restricted area. You can't be here."

Alex raised an eyebrow, amused. "I'm pretty sure I've got as much clearance as you can have. I'm Alex Goddard, captain of the GMT and lifelong friend of Captain Unobservant, there." She pointed a finger at Brian. "Brian, help me out."

Brian shook his head like he was waking up from a dream. He looked away from the monitors and saw Alex. "Oh, hey, Alex. Sorry, I didn't hear you come in. Did you get some rest?"

"Yep. More than I intended. How are things going in here? Have you figured out a way to kill all the Twisted while changing Owl back to her original self, and saving the vampires of Agartha? It has been almost eight hours, which is like a year in genius terms." Alex gave him a little smile as she spoke.

Brian attempted to return the smile, but the strained expression only brought out the dark circles under his eyes. Alex wondered if he had eaten anything since they arrived. "It's not going well. I don't know if I will ever be able to solve this one. Maybe, given enough time, but I'm in the early stages of a long process."

The woman who'd tried to stop Alex from entering spoke again. "Your work is amazing. You have made more advancements in one night than our team made in the last few weeks working the problem." She looked at him with true admiration.

"Yep, he is the best and the brightest," Alex said, turning back to Brian. "I thought that you may be able to pull this off, since you cracked the virus in the first place."

He looked down and shook his head "That was different. Ten years of data was just sitting there waiting for me to find it. I had the entire puzzle; I just had to piece it together. I don't even know which direction to go with this one. Even if I did, I'm starting from scratch on a project that has no precedent. I'm sorry, Alex. I just don't think I can pull this off."

Alex knew it was crazy, but she'd hoped that Brian would come through with a miracle. She tried not to let the disappointment show on her face. "You don't need to be sorry. I know that you're giving it everything that you have. Just keep trying and let me know if I can help in any way." She looked him up and down. "Have you eaten yet?"

Brian looked confused "Why? Is it lunch time?"

"I will never understand how you can be so smart, but you still can't take care of your basic human needs." She turned to the woman. "What's your name?"

"Stephanie. I run this lab."

"Stephanie, it's nice to meet you. I can tell you already get what Brian means to all of us. Could you do me and the rest of the world a huge favor and make sure that he takes time to eat and sleep? I'd hate to lose the war because Brian starved to death at his desk."

Stephanie paused for a moment, not sure if Alex was kidding. Then she looked at Brian. "I'll help him out in any way that I can. Even if that means keeping him fed."

"Thanks. Just let me know if he gives you any trouble. He can be stubborn as hell."

Brian laughed at that. "You are the last person who should be calling someone out for stubbornness."

The door to the lab opened and Natalie marched in, her expression hard. "George told me that you need something."

Brian nodded. "Yes, I need a sample of your blood to see how the virus is progressing."

"Of course. Take what you need." Natalie took a seat across from him at the table.

Alex watched as Stephanie went to work, grabbing the supplies needed for the blood draw. She looked back at Natalie and her smile faded.

Natalie noticed the change in Alex's expression. "What is it?"

"Your nose. It's bleeding."

2

THE FIRST VAMPIRE died three and a half days later. His name was Toby. According to George, Toby had been one of the last humans turned into a true vampire shortly before Maryana's infestation. He'd spent his century and a half in Agartha preferring to live a peaceful existence, only going out with scout teams when absolutely necessary. Instead, he'd run the stockroom, keeping careful tally on the supplies for the city.

Alex had gotten all this information from George, because the vampires—even those showing minimal sickness—had become withdrawn. Jaden had retreated with them, only occasionally leaving the vampires' enclave to berate Brian on his lack of success in finding a cure. George was one of the few humans who dared to enter their area to occasionally check on them.

According to George, Jaden had sat by Toby's side as he died, and he'd vowed to do the same for each and every vampire who fell to the virus.

Alex walked the halls of Agartha, her heart in two places

at once. On the one hand, she could hardly blame Jaden for circling the troops as they faced the virus. The virus *she* had released. The fact that Agartha had allowed her sanctuary and none of the vampires had torn her throat out was a testament to their restraint; although, she wasn't about to press her luck by going into the vampires' section of the city.

On the other hand, a good portion of her mind was on *New Haven*. By all measures, she'd lost the battle to Maryana. She'd been outplayed at every turn. Maryana had maneuvered her and Jaden to exactly where she'd wanted them, toying with them, getting them to destroy their own away ship, having them fight her troops at Agartha, while she flew their ship to *New Haven*.

And now just about everyone Alex cared about was dead or under her control. Jessica. Wesley and his family. CB, if he was even still alive. Maryana could be torturing them right now, and there wasn't a damn thing Alex could do about it.

Alex found herself in the lab, where Brian had holed up with the few lab techs they'd been able to save from *New Haven*, along with a dozen or so from Agartha. Brian was pushing them hard, teaming with Stephanie, the head of Agartha's lab. The two of them sat side by side at a long table, each staring into microscopes.

"Hey, guys," Alex said. "How are things in genius-land?"

For a long moment, neither of them responded. Then, as one, they both looked up.

"Oh, hey Alex," Brian said.

"You got a minute?" she asked.

"Sure." He stared at her for a long moment before realizing she wanted to speak with him privately. Brian had come a long way since his early days as the head of the

GMT's lab, but he still struggled with basic social cues much of the time.

The two of them walked to a quiet corner of the lab and sat down at a table.

"So, what's up?" he asked, quietly.

"I was just wondering how things are going. Any progress?"

He shrugged. "The two teams are working well together. There's progress, but…"

"Not enough progress," Alex finished.

Brian hesitated, then shook his head. "No. Not enough to save them. Every vampire in this city will be dead in two days. The chances of us cracking this thing before then are slim to none. With a heavy emphasis on none."

Alex looked down at the scratched, metal table. She hadn't expected a miracle cure, but it was still tough to hear. Guilt rose up inside her. Not guilt that she'd released the virus. She still felt like that had been the right call, even after all of this. They'd succeeded in wiping the Ferals out. In fact, her guilt was sort of the opposite. Her lack of concern for the vampires was what was bothering her. She knew she'd feel the pain of each one of their deaths, not because a life was being snuffed out of existence, but because each vampire who died meant one less weapon in their struggle against Maryana.

Abandoning *New Haven* had been the toughest decision of her life, and she'd made a vow when she'd left. A vow to come back and take Maryana out once and for all. That would have been a nearly impossible task with one hundred vampires by her side. With only two Twisted, she couldn't even imagine a path to victory.

Brian sighed. "We're not going to give up. We have some

promising leads. We've been studying Owl's blood, and I think there's a chance we can isolate what makes her immune. In theory, it could be replicated and spread to the other vampires. It's just the time element."

Alex nodded. "I know it's not fair to ask you to come up with a miracle yet again, but you're the only shot we have. If there's anything I can do to help, just say the word."

Brian swallowed hard. "Actually, there is one thing. Do you think you could ask Jaden to quit coming by every two hours?"

"Yeah, of course. Is he distracting your people?"

He nodded toward a table across the room. Its metal surface featured a fist-shaped dent. "Distracting. Terrifying. Take your pick."

"No guarantees. The guy's going through a lot right now. But I'll see what I can do." Alex crossed her arms and frowned. That was a conversation she was not looking forward to having.

Claude lay on the floor, flat on his back, gazing up at the ceiling. Jaden sat by his side, resting a gentle hand on his shoulder.

"Jaden," Claude muttered, his voice a weak croak that might have been difficult to hear if not for Jaden's vampire senses. "Tell me you remember Mumbai."

Despite everything, Jaden couldn't help but smile. Of course Claude would bring up Mumbai. "I remember, old friend."

Claude let out a weak cough, sending a spray of black blood into the air. "I resisted the urge to say I told you so for three hundred years. Now, I figure, what's the point? So... I told you so."

Jaden patted his friend's mouth with a cloth, wiping away the blood. "That you did."

The incident in question had taken place in the late nineteenth century, when the city had still been called Bombay. They'd been after a rogue vampire who'd broken the rules of the one hundred and seemed intent on starting his own rival clan of vampires. Compared with Maryana, the rogue vampire didn't seem very ambitious, but it had been quite the scandal at the time. Claude had scouted the situation and believed the vampire was hiding somewhere in the city. Jaden had disregarded Claude's intel, believing the rogue would try to escape via boat. After a long night spent futilely searching the rugged Konkan coast for any sign of the vampire, Jaden had eventually relented, and they'd found the rogue hiding in the city.

There was a sparkle in Claude's eyes when he spoke again. "Just wanted to remind you that no one's right every time. Not even you."

Jaden's face darkened. "I know that all too well, old friend."

He watched for another hour after Claude's eyes drifted shut, and he kept a hand on the vampire's arm until he spasmed, expelling another spray of blood out of his mouth and nose. Though the life in a vampire's body couldn't be judged by a heartbeat or breath, Jaden had gotten quite good at measuring the subtler signs of life; he knew Claude was dead.

Jaden pushed his rising emotions aside. He picked the vampire up off of the floor and moved him to the room with the other thirty-seven bodies. He would have preferred to spend his time talking to the other vampires currently experiencing their final hours, but there was no one else to do the work. He'd only allowed vampires into this area, and he was the only vampire not currently dying. The only vampire but for one.

The past couple of days had tested him in ways he'd never imagined possible. Watching his friends, his family, die had wrung him out like a wet towel. Even for a creature so accustomed to death, this was almost too much to bear. He held it together, ignoring the rage and sadness, for the sake of the dying. There would be time to mourn later, but his vampires needed him now.

Owl's face still bore the wounds from the recent battle, but she sat near the dying vampires, same as Jaden, doing her best to provide them a bit of comfort in their final hours. And Jaden had to admit that she had been a great help. It had been her idea to forgo the beds and set the vampires on the ground. The cool rock seemed to alleviate their raging fevers a bit. Besides, the way they bled had caused them to run out of clean bedding some time ago.

Jaden returned to the open area where the sick vampires lay and quickly scanned it, looking for another vampire who looked close to the end. There was no shortage of them. He imagined that by the end of the night, at least half of his vampires would be gone.

Near the south end of the room, he saw someone spasm. It took Jaden a moment to identify the vampire, and when he did, he frowned. But still, he moved to the vampire's side and placed a hand on his arm.

"Hello, Frank," Jaden said. He hadn't known Frank long, and his interactions with the vampire had been limited. But he couldn't help but respect the sacrifice Frank had made for *New Haven*, agreeing to give up his life

The Savage End 15

to act as the canary in the coal mine for the vampire lifecycle. It still irked Jaden a little that the leaders of *New Haven* had been so bold as to create a vampire without Jaden's knowledge. Jaden wasn't even sure exactly how they'd managed to do it. But that seemed like small potatoes in the greater scheme of things. Frank was just like the others—a dying vampire who deserved comfort in his final moments.

Frank opened his eyes, and thick blood seeped out. It seemed Frank was dying even harder than most. Still, his gaze focused on Jaden. "*New Haven...*" His voice was thick with emotion. "Is it safe?"

Jaden met his eyes, resisting the temptation to lie to the dying vampire. Frank deserved the truth. After everything he'd been through, he'd earned that right. "No. But it will be. You have my word."

Frank shuddered, and the shudder quickly became another spasm. Jaden assumed it would be his last. But instead of stopping, the shudder changed. It grew in intensity. His limbs stopped moving, even as something deep inside him began to shift. His body changed with a series of audible clicks and pops as his very bones twisted beneath his flesh.

Jaden looked on in horror, his eyes wide. What he was seeing was impossible. He understood what was happening, but his mind couldn't quite accept it. He'd never seen this process, but he'd lived it. He'd felt his own body change in exactly the same way. At the time, he'd assumed he was dying. Now he knew better.

He sensed Owl standing behind him, watching in equally horrified silence.

The process only lasted a minute and a half, and then Frank lay still. His eyes slowly opened, and he sat up, wiping the blood from his face with the back of a deformed hand. He blinked hard as he stared down at his new body.

Jaden didn't understand how this had happened, but there was no mistaking it, now. Frank had survived the virus. He'd become Twisted.

3

FRANK SAT on a table in an examination room, his shoulders hunched forward even more than his newly curved spine demanded. He gently moved his fingers across his elongated mouth and deformed jaw line like he was touching a land mine that he didn't want to detonate. The techs in the lab bustled around him, some taking blood, others measuring various parts of his body and jotting down notes. Frank let them do their work without making a sound.

Alex, Owl, and Brian watched Frank through a glass window in the next room. "How did this happen?" Alex asked.

Brian held his tablet so Alex and Owl could see it. "I can answer part of that question. Take a look at these samples." He opened two windows on the tablet showing rows of dashes with slightly different shades of colors. "These are samples that we took from Owl and Jaden." He overlaid the readings from Owl and Jaden's blood. "You can see the similarities between them. Her cellular structure changed to match his."

"Right, because he turned her. It's kind of like making a

copy of himself, right?" Alex hoped that she understood the basics.

"That's right. The relationship between generations of vampires is similar to the parent-child relationship. The genes get passed on, but some changes occur. Now, look at this." Brian overlaid another sample onto Jaden's. It was almost exactly the same as Owl's. Brian looked up at Alex like he had just explained everything.

"Just spell it out for me, Brian," she said with a frown. "What are we looking at?"

He gave the slightest eye roll. "That is Frank's sample. He was created by Jaden."

For a moment, Alex didn't know how to respond to that. Then she turned to her friend. "Did you know about this, Owl?"

"No. I don't think Jaden did either. He seemed shocked when Frank turned into a Twisted. I was in the room when it happened."

All three of them stared at Frank.

"So how the hell did Jaden make a vampire without knowing about it?" Alex said.

"That's the part I can't answer. I mean, I could make some guesses, but they would all be in the hypothesis category. We will have to do some—"

Alex cut him off. "I got it. You don't know, but *he* might."

She walked out of the observation area into the examination room. Frank looked up at her when she entered, but stayed quiet.

"Hey Frank, how are you feeling?"

"Alive." He stopped touching his face and his sad eyes met hers.

"This is great. You survived the virus. We are a little confused how that happened, but it is great."

Frank looked across the room to a mirror on the wall. He reached up and touched the corner of his mouth. "I know I should be glad that I am alive, but I've accepted my death a few times, now. I just wasn't ready for this. That may seem crazy to you, but I thought I was done being a monster."

Alex put a hand on each of his shoulders. He straightened up a bit but was unable to meet her gaze.

"You are a hero and a badass," she said. "You answered the call when the world needed you, without any concern for yourself. You helped us save *New Haven* and you have suffered more than most men could take. Even after all of that, you have remained honorable and kind. You're not a monster; you are an example of what every person should be." She spoke in the clear, controlled voice she used when commanding her soldiers. Frank started to lower his head, but Alex took a hand and raised his chin so that their eyes met. "Do you hear me? You still have purpose, maybe now more than ever. I know that you still have the spirit it will take to continue the fight. Can I count on you, or are you going to lay down and die?"

The techs in the room had stopped what they were doing to watch the interaction. Alex's presence commanded their attention and changed the atmosphere of the room.

Frank straightened up a little more. "I guess I'm not fully dead yet." A slight smile formed at the corners of his mouth. "Thanks, Alex."

Alex let go of Frank's shoulder and took a small step back. "Hey, we all need a little reminder or a kick in the ass every once in a while." She paused, then asked the questions that had brought her into the room. "Do you know who turned you? Or where they got the blood that made you a vampire?"

Frank thought in silence for a few seconds before

responding. "We had only been in the air for a few days when they injected me with the blood. I did ask where they got the vampire blood, and they told me they'd collected it from a vampire while treating his wounds. I'm guessing that it wasn't just any random vampire blood."

"Nope. It looks like Jaden is your 'dad'."

THE SOFT GLOW in the room might have been considered romantic under the right circumstances. A wall of monitors behind George cast their light onto the stainless steel surfaces of the otherwise dim room. Alex listened as he dryly spoke about the current state of the city's external defenses. She'd always hated meetings, especially when they involved presentations, but today was different. Rebuilding the city's defenses was their one clear purpose at the moment, and it was going as well as it could. They were succeeding in fortifying the city. It felt good to have even this small success.

Chuck and Ed sat on either side of Alex. Both had spent the last few days working with the citizens of Agartha to get the defenses working again. Owl and Felix sat on the other side of Ed. Jaden was notably absent.

George pointed at the monitor to his left, which showed a map of the area outside Agartha. It had green dots wherever there was a functioning turret and red dots over the ones that still needed repair. "As you can see, we will still need to add four more turrets to be back at full coverage to the main entrance, but we are at eighty percent of the original defenses."

"How long until we are at one hundred?" Alex scrolled through her tablet, checking other data while she spoke.

"We should be fully repaired in two days."

Ed let out a soft whistle. "Damn, you guys really are good at fixing stuff. Maybe we will stand a chance of defending this place after all."

George shook his head, "We had redundant parts for all the weapons, in case they were even damaged. If we suffer another attack, rebuilding the defensive systems will take much longer. Normally, we would send the vampires out on supply missions already, but... but that will never happen again." He looked at Alex. "Why hasn't Maryana come for us yet? She has the numbers, and she must know that our vampires are dead by now."

All eyes shifted to Alex. She pushed her chair back and stood. "I've been thinking about that ever since we got here. There are a couple of logical possibilities. Chief among them, *New Haven* doesn't have a transport ship to get troops down to the ground. She may be working on that problem. It's possible she wants to wait until she is sure that all the vampires in the city are dead. She may also be preparing a large-scale attack. Something with several thousand Twisted that we couldn't have any chance of stopping." Alex paused. They had all been thinking it, but hearing it out loud made everyone realize how hopeless their situation really was. "Remember, we're not dealing with a logical enemy. Maryana is unpredictable. She may just spend the next week, month, or year torturing the citizens of *New Haven* before she decides to attack. There is no way to be sure when the attack will come, but it will come."

Owl spoke up. "Has *New Haven* moved?"

"No," George said. "It has held a constant position above Agatha since shortly after Maryana took control of the city. I'm glad that we know where she is, but if we send a ship up, she will see it right away." He tapped on his tablet and the radar showing *New Haven* came up on one of the monitors behind to him.

Chuck stood up. "I've been working on a grid design for explosives around the perimeter. I think we can set something up so that we can remote detonate sections and then set off a second wave when more forces come through. It should help against a large-scale attack." He pointed out locations on the monitor while he explained the formation of the explosives.

"That's great! Let's make it happen as quickly as we can," Alex said. "What about our troops? Without the vampires, we are down to the remaining members of the GMT and Agartha's security force. We are sure that Maryana has at least five hundred Twisted. That's more than we can handle without more soldiers of our own."

George grimaced. "We have enough gear to arm about six hundred fighters. We could pull people from the mechanical systems department. They will probably be in the best condition."

Ed scoffed at the idea. "Workers are not soldiers. They don't have the training to go against the badges, let alone Twisted. Six hundred pipe fitters would be about the same as six members of the GMT." He glanced at George and added, "No offense."

Felix spoke up for the first time since the meeting began. "We still have three Twisted on our side. Jaden and Owl are worth twenty of Maryana's soldiers each, and now Frank can walk in the daylight. That has to count for something."

"Yeah, it counts for a lot less than five hundred," Ed barked. "That's assuming Maryana only has that many. She may have turned everyone in New Haven by now."

"We could have more," Chuck said, his voice contemplative.

"What do you mean?" George asked.

Chuck looked around the room at the others and spoke quietly. "Maryana isn't the only one who can turn her soldiers into Twisted. What if we asked for volunteers from Agartha? Jaden could turn them."

The room fell silent. Ed took in a breath to respond, but the words didn't form, and he looked to Alex for an answer.

Owl spoke first. "That can't be the way. Turning people into whatever I am can't be the path to victory. They would be sacrificing everything. The price is too high."

There was a long silence before Alex spoke. "The price is high, but it may be exactly what it takes to kill Maryana. If people are willing to volunteer, we should consider it." She looked at Owl. "This is not the time to hold back any weapons we might be able to use. This may be humanity's last battle, win or lose. I don't like the idea of turning humans into Twisted, but it may be the only option that we have." She looked around the room. "Anybody have a better idea?"

George looked down at his feet. The members of the GMT shook their heads.

Owl was still, but looked at Alex with pleading eyes. "You can't talk to Jaden about this right now. He's still grieving."

"We don't have the luxury of time. We need Jaden to make us an army."

4

Alex found Jaden where he'd been almost since the moment they arrived in Agartha—in the vampire's enclave. He knelt on the stone floor, a brush in his hand. It took Alex a moment to figure out what he was doing. He was scrubbing the blood stains off the ground.

He stopped his frantic scrubbing when she walked in the room, but he didn't look up. "What is it?"

"Just wanted to check if you're okay. Owl said there were only a few vampires left."

"There were," he answered. "Until about twenty minutes ago. Now it's just me."

"I'm sorry." She let that hang in the air for a moment before speaking again. "You don't have to clean this whole place alone. We can get someone else."

He looked up at her for the first time since she'd entered, and she saw his eyes were ringed with red, whether from sorrow or exhaustion, she did not know. "Who else is there? This is vampire blood! If it gets in your system, you will be turned and the virus will kill you. Is that how you want to go out? Scrubbing a damn floor?"

"There's Owl. And Frank. You don't think they'd help you?"

Jaden scowled and turned back to the floor. "They didn't know these vampires. Not really. Not like I did. For more than a thousand years, the one hundred true vampires protected humanity, and now they're gone."

Alex drew a deep breath. This was the best opening she was going to get. "Maybe they don't have to be."

Jaden's brush paused. "If Brian's succeeded in creating a cure, he has very bad timing. Unless this cure also brings back the dead."

"That's not what I meant." She squatted down next to him. The thick, pungent smell of vampire blood hung thick in the room. For so long, that smell had meant battle; it was all Alex could do to calm her racing heart. "It's like you said, Jaden. Humanity needs vampires to protect them. Now, more than ever."

Jaden let out a joyless laugh. "*Now* you believe the vampires should live?"

She considered that. "I don't see how we have a choice. We can't beat Maryana with what we have. But you have the power to change that. You could make one hundred new vampires. Put things back the way they were meant to be."

In a flash, Jaden hopped from his knees to a crouching position. His elongated nose was an inch from Alex's face, and she felt his hot breath on her skin when he spoke. "You really don't understand her, do you?"

Alex flinched backward a little, in spite of herself. "Maryana? I understand that she has the badges of *New Haven* under her control, and who knows how many others. Ed, Chuck, Felix, and I aren't going to get the job done by ourselves. That's why you talked me into retreating, right? So we could come up with a better plan. This is that plan. We have to fight her army, so let's make one of our own."

Jaden shook his head, an expression of disappointment on his face. "If I make a hundred vampires, she'll make a thousand. Once we start down this path, she'll keep coming at us with larger and larger armies, forcing us to change the people of Agartha until there's no one left. She'd do it just for the sport of it."

Alex pushed herself to her feet and glared down at him. She couldn't believe what she was hearing. It almost sounded like Jaden was giving up. "Not if we catch her by surprise. We take one hundred Twisted, and we assault *New Haven*. I know the layout better than her, and we can—"

"I said, no!" Jaden snarled. He paused, looking down at the half-cleaned blood-stain on the stone between his feet. "Listen to me, Alex. You made a choice back in Puerto Rico. You released the virus. I'm not angry with you for making that choice, not anymore. But the price was high. You can see that cost in the splotches on the stone around this room."

"I know you paid a high price. And once we defeat Maryana, it will all be worth it."

Jaden shook his head. "You're not listening. The choice you made was to end the vampires and let humanity guide its own fate. I'm going to help you stop Maryana. I'll do everything I can, but I won't create new vampires. If we change a hundred Agartha citizens, it will be like my friends died for nothing."

Alex stared down at him. There was no malice in his voice. He wasn't saying this out of spite. But there was an expression of steely conviction on his face; she knew he wouldn't change his mind.

"The time for vampires to protect humans has passed.

You have to forge your own path now. I'll help you defeat Maryana, but it will have to be another way."

With that, he turned back to the floor and started scrubbing.

ED AND CHUCK led Frank to the armory, keeping one eye on the new Twisted.

"Do we really have to do this now?" Frank asked. "I've been a Twisted for like twelve hours. Don't I get some sort of an orientation period?"

Chuck shook his head. "Afraid not. Ed and I were on the surface a couple days after we joined the GMT, clearing out an old prison. And Felix faced Maryana on, like, his second mission. Alex is a big fan of what you might call on-the-job training."

Frank paused. "Is that what I am now? GMT?"

Chuck and Ed exchanged a glance.

"Um, yeah, didn't Alex mention that?" Ed said. "You kinda got drafted the moment you didn't...err...die."

Frank frowned. "And I don't get any say in this?"

Ed rolled his eyes. "The guy gets a free ticket to join the most elite fighting force on the planet, and he wants to know if he gets a say."

"You know how many badges on *New Haven* would have killed for this opportunity?" Chuck added.

"Yeah, even before they were murdered and turned into vampire slaves." Ed clapped Frank on the back. "Look, man, you want to have an existential crisis, I'm sure Alex or Jaden will be around later. Even Owl has had her share of moody outbursts lately. Any of them would be happy to talk about the great burden of immortality or whatever. Chuck and I are just here to show you the guns."

Frank cracked the slightest of smiles. "All right, message received. I'll lay off the drama for now. Let's talk weapons."

Ed let out a boyish laugh as he held his keycard up to the door. "I can't believe they gave us free reign over this place."

Chuck pulled the door open and stepped inside. "Now, traditionally you vampire types tend to carry swords. Your speed and strength pair nicely with the whole hack and slash thing."

Frank stepped up to a rack of swords and took one down, testing its weight in his hands. "Seems sensible. I've actually been doing a little training with swords. When I get time away from the stockroom, which isn't often. That place is always hopping."

Ed and Chuck exchanged another glance.

"They had you working in the stockroom?" Chuck asked.

Frank shrugged. "It was more interesting than it sounds. It took me a while to get the hang of it, but once I mastered pivot tables, I was able to increase our efficiency by simply documenting a lean process and tracking our results."

"I think I just fell asleep with my eyes open," Ed said. "Look, forget all that. What about back in the day? What kind of weapons did you use?"

Frank stared at him blankly. "Back in the day?"

"Yeah, during the infestation. Were you a rifleman? They may not have the exact model you used but we should be able to find something close enough to make you comfortable."

Frank cleared his throat. "I think you have the wrong idea. I was a janitor back before *New Haven*."

"A janitor?" Chuck carefully kept his face blank. "So your combat experience is—"

"Non-existent." He grinned sheepishly. "I mean, I've been sparring with the vampires here when I have time, but they always have me on the mat in, like, two seconds."

Ed sighed. "Well, like I said, Alex is a big fan of on-the-job training. Luckily for you." He grabbed a pistol and shoved it into Frank's hand. "Let's start with this. Run up to dudes and shoot them in the head at close range. If that doesn't work, chop off their heads."

Frank frowned at the weapon. "You're going to show me how to load this thing, right?" He paused until he saw Ed and Chuck's barely concealed looks of annoyance, then he smiled. "I'm kidding. I do know that much."

Ed shook his head. "A city full of ancient warrior vampires, and we get the janitor."

A burst of static cut through the air, followed by Felix's voice. "Chuck, you there?"

Chuck pulled the radio off his belt. "I'm here, man. What's up?"

"I hope you got the new guy geared up, because we've got trouble. A handful of Twisted just fell out of the sky, and they're headed for the north entrance."

"We'll be right there," Chuck said.

Frank looked like he might be sick as he stood there, a sword in one hand and a pistol in the other.

Ed grinned at him. "Good news, buddy. You're about to get your first training session."

5

THE COMMAND CENTER was alive with action when Alex entered the room. She'd run from the cafeteria after receiving George's call, and a small bead of sweat worked its way down the small of her back. George was flipping between tablet screens and pacing back and forth.

"Status update," Alex called out.

"They set off the outer perimeter alarm ten minutes ago. I'm sure there are at least fifteen of them, but there may be more. We caught some of them on the far cameras. They dropped in with parachutes. They came in hot and opened the chutes at the last moment."

"Have they engaged the defensive systems?"

"No, they haven't moved in yet."

"I want to know as soon as you get an accurate count on the number of Twisted out there. Get the turrets ready, but do not fire unless there's a large group in the kill zone, or if a turret is attacked." Alex grabbed the radio on her belt. "GMT, I need everyone ready by the blast door ASAP. Owl, make sure that Jaden is there."

"Copy that," Owl replied. "I think he'll be glad to have an enemy to help him work out his grief."

George pointed at one of the screens. "We have movement. I'm bringing up the feed now."

The monitor in the center of the room showed a Twisted running full speed through the trees. He moved in a zigzag pattern and seemed to be searching the forest.

George looked to Alex. "Should I engage the guns?"

"Not yet. We want more Twisted in range."

The vampire moved a little deeper into the forest. When he was a hundred yards from a turret, he threw a grenade. It landed at the foot of the turret and exploded, damaging the weapon.

"Take him out, now!" Alex watched on the monitor as two turrets sprang to life. One was in front of the Twisted and the other behind him. He tried to throw another grenade, but he was cut down by the weapons before he could make the throw. Bullets tore into his chest and legs, and the force of his momentum made him tumble over the forest floor. The turrets continued to track him as he came to a stop. Pine needles, dirt, and blood flew into the air as bullets tore into the Twisted and the earth around him.

The turrets stopped firing, and everything was still for a moment. Then one of the turrets on the monitor exploded in a hail of bullets. The report of more gun fire quickly followed. A moment later, the other turret that had engaged the Twisted was hit by long range fire.

"Shit!" Alex slammed her hand down on the desk in front of her. "They're going to pick apart our defenses. You're sure that there are only fifteen of them?"

George looked over the scan again, "No, there could be as many as twenty. I don't think there are any more than that. At least, not in range of our motion detectors."

"If those numbers change, let me know. We are going to engage them in the field. Cover us with the turrets when you can." Alex started out the door and then turned back. "I'd also appreciate it if you could make sure those turrets don't take out any of the GMT."

Before George could respond, Alex marched out and headed for her team waiting at the blast door.

THE TEAM WAS GEARED up by the time Alex arrived. She looked them over and felt a chill go down her spine. This team was not ready. Frank had a nervous look in his eyes as he checked his pistol for the tenth time. Felix was still green, although he had more experience than Frank. And then there was Jaden. Alex couldn't tell if he was even aware the rest of them were there. His eyes were so distant that it was hard to tell if there was anything behind them.

"You with us, Jaden?" she asked, cautiously.

Jaden slowly turned toward her and spoke in a soft voice "My body is a weapon. It will function as it has been trained."

"Your head is attached to the body, and it sounds like it's up your ass right now. Can we count on you?" Ed stood face to face with Jaden as he spoke.

Jaden eyed him coldly. "I'm ready." His voice still sounded distant and almost inhuman to Alex, but she trusted that he'd come through when the battle started.

She turned her attention back to the others. "Ed, Chuck, and Frank, you take the right flank. Owl, you go with Felix on the left flank. They have snipers, so move after you take a shot. Jaden and I will be in the forest. We will need your cover fire if they send in a big wave. Any questions?" After a moment of silence, Alex clicked on her radio. "Are we clear to open the door?"

George responded. "They haven't sent in any other soldiers yet. You're good to go."

The locks released and the thick steel door swung open on perfectly balanced hinges. The team spread out, as Alex had ordered. Alex hurried to the forest, her eye scanning for movement, Jaden at her side. Now that they were in motion and he had a blade in each hand, Jaden seemed more like himself. They stopped alongside a line of turrets. Alex crouched behind a fallen tree, a pistol in each hand, eyeing the forest in front of her.

George spoke in her earpiece. "There is a Twisted coming in fast, just like the last one. He's headed toward your position, Alex."

Alex spoke softly, her eyes still fixed on the forest ahead. "I'm going to try to take him out, but if he gets past my gunfire, use your swords." When there was no response, she turned and silently cursed. Jaden was gone.

The sounds of snapping twigs and pounding feet brought her focus back to the task at hand. The Twisted was coming in fast, making no effort to be quiet. The familiar surge of adrenaline filled Alex, and her senses heightened. Her heart pounded in her chest and the smell of the forest seemed to intensify. She raised her pistols, staying low to keep as much of her body behind cover as she could. The weight her guns seemed to disappear and the weapons became part of her.

She saw the first flash of the Twisted through the trees. He moved in a zigzag pattern, just like the previous Twisted. She drew a breath. The moment he stepped into a clearing in the brush, she fired, one hand aiming at where he would be, and the other aiming where he was.

The Twisted stumbled to a halt when the barrels flashed. One shot hit the tree in front of him, but the other slug tore into his shoulder. The force of the bullet knocked him off balance for a moment. Alex took advantage and she squeezed off two more rounds. Each shot was true and two red dots appeared in the Twisted's forehead, while a spray of red misted up from the back of his head. Alex still had her pistols trained on him as he fell, ready to fire again.

Wood splinters shot into the air as a bullet slammed into the log in front of Alex, quickly followed by the report of a sniper rifle. She ducked behind the log to avoid the next shot. An answering shot rang out from Chuck's position. He must have taken a shot at the sniper. A moment later, the Twisted fired again. Then another from Chuck.

Taking advantage of the distraction of the dueling snipers, Alex snuck out from behind the log. Staying low, she moved quickly from tree to tree, taking momentary cover behind each one as she checked her flanks. She grimaced at the thought of how much easier this would have been with Jaden watching her back, but he'd once again decided to turn this into a solo mission.

Shots continued to ring out from both sides. Based on the sounds of the reports, she guessed that there were at least three snipers taking shots at the GMT.

Alex spotted a six-foot-tall boulder just ahead, and she positioned herself behind it. As she readied herself, she heard gunfire rattle off from up ahead. She recognized it as cover fire and knew an assault was imminent. She peeked around the boulder and saw more than a dozen Twisted charging her position.

A turret opened fire, spraying bullets, cutting through several trees as it tracked the fast-moving creatures. It hit a target a moment before one of the snipers destroyed the gun. Another shot rang out from Chuck's position, followed quickly by a scream from a Twisted sniper.

More turrets came to life as the Twisted continued to advance through the forest. The turret closest to Alex tore through a couple of Twisted before being disabled by a hail of grenades.

Alex could see ten Twisted from her position. One sniffed the air and turned mid-stride, heading straight at her. Even though he was moving fast, his direct path made him an easy target for Alex. She fired off two shots, then targeted the next closest Twisted. The remaining Twisted had turned their attention toward Alex now, and were quickly closing the hundred-foot gap between them and the bolder where she crouched.

The Twisted charging from the left careened backward into a tree when a round tore into his chest. He paused, glancing down at the hole in his side as he regained his footing, then continued forward for a few steps until a round through his head finished the job. Alex made a mental note to buy Felix a beer for that shot.

Still the enemies continued to charge.

Adrenaline flowed through Alex's veins as a simple but devastating thought flashed in her mind—*There are too many*. She gritted her teeth and fired again. The expression on the lead Twisted's face went slack when Alex's bullet found his heart. A shot rang out from her right and another Twisted went down, courtesy of Chuck, but the seven remaining creatures were only twenty feet from her now. One of them raised a pistol, and Alex quickly ducked back behind the boulder a moment before a round slammed into the stone. She pressed her back against the rock and readied herself as bullets continued to ricochet off the boulder. She knew that at any moment the Twisted would reach her position, and she wanted to take one more of them out before she died.

Suddenly, the gunfire stopped and a high-pitched scream took its place. A body—or at least a body part—thudded against the ground. A few more shots rang out, but none of them hit the boulder. The Twisted had a new target. Alex slowly shifted her position, angling to see what was happening.

The sight before her caused Alex to freeze for a moment. Even with everything she had seen, this image would haunt her dreams.

A blood-splattered Jaden stood over a Twisted woman who lay on the ground, one arm missing and her legs removed at the knees. Her remaining arm was outstretched, the fingers clutching at the ground as she tried to drag herself toward her fallen weapon. Three more Twisted bodies lay separated from their heads on the forest floor.

The closest remaining Twisted stood ten feet in front of Jaden, a pistol raised in his shaking hands. Despite his Twisted form, Alex could tell he was a young man. He squeezed off a shot but Jaden moved like water, avoiding the bullet. He crossed the distance between them in a moment, his sword in motion, and sliced off both the man's arms.

Alex flinched as blood splattered across the forest floor. She'd seen Jaden in battle a dozen times now, and he always went for the clean kill. Brutal, but efficient. This time he'd avoided the quick kill, opting for pain. She regained her composure and rejoined the fight, finishing off the woman crawling for her gun and the man with the amputated arms as Jaden charged past. She was vaguely aware of distant reports of rifles, but she didn't know if they were from the GMT or their enemies.

Jaden's elongated mouth snarled, exposing his razor-sharp teeth to the gum line. Those awful teeth looked like they wanted to escape his mouth and drive themselves into his enemies. Four more Twisted raised their guns as he approached. One of them fired, and a bullet struck Jaden's right shoulder, but he barely seemed to notice. He ducked between the two nearest Twisted, who stood four feet apart. He let out a grunt as he brought his swords up in a flash, slicing through both soldiers at the waist. They screamed as they fell, but he'd already moved on. The last two Twisted stood frozen at the sight of the carnage. Before they could process what they had just seen, Jaden removed their heads.

Alex fired one shot into the heads of each of the Twisted Jaden had cut in half, silencing their screams. The breath seemed to leave the forest, and she was surrounded by silence. She slipped back behind part of the boulder for cover and spoke into her radio. "We're clear on the forest floor. What is everyone's status?"

Chuck answered first. "We are all clear. I don't see any other snipers. Owl went to check their position, to be sure we got all of them."

"There were a few shots that were too close for comfort, but I'm clear and unharmed," Felix reported.

"We are good," Owl chimed in. "All the snipers are down."

Alex stood up and walked to Jaden. She gripped her pistols tightly as she approached, unsure what he would do next. He slowly walked toward Alex. Blood dripped from his blades, leaving twin trails along the forest floor. The snarl left his face and he started to look like himself.

"What the hell was that?" Alex asked.

Jaden wiped his blades on his sleeves and then put them into their sheaths. "That was the beginning of vengeance."

6

THE GMT GATHERED in Brian's lab an hour after the battle. Alex had told her team to shower, get cleaned up, and meet to talk. Since Agartha's vampires were all either dead or Twisted now, the sense of urgency around finding a cure had dissipated. Brian had released his disheartened staff and told them to get some much-needed rest. The GMT had the lab to themselves.

Alex surveyed her team as they entered. None of them spoke at first, not even Ed. The battle had clearly shaken them. Owl seemed the least disturbed, but even she had a vacant look in her eyes. Frank was at the other end of the spectrum, his face screwed up in a mask of discomfort.

Jaden didn't join them, which didn't surprise Alex. She wasn't sure whether he still considered himself a member of the GMT, but even if he did, he was dealing with the death of nearly a hundred friends at the moment.

"You did well," she said to her gathered team. "Frank, I liked the way you carried yourself out there. I know you're inexperienced, but I have some thoughts on how we can use your skills without requiring you to be an expert soldier overnight. If we send Owl out as point, we can use you to—"

"Captain, are we really not going to talk about what just happened?" Chuck asked, his voice soft, but firm.

Alex glared at him, annoyed at the interruption. "What do you think I'm doing?"

"When you called us here for a debrief, I thought we were going to talk about Jaden's... um..."

"Slaughter," Felix finished. There was anger in his voice, barely hidden behind his usually unreadable face. "It was a slaughter. That woman whose legs he cut off? That was Christi Palmer. She worked behind a desk at badge headquarters. She had two kids."

Alex swallowed hard. "I know. I recognized her, too."

"And that man he chopped in half at the waist? Tyrone Merrick. He headed up that program that worked with the school kids on civic projects."

Alex said nothing. She hadn't known Tyrone.

"And how about Santiago Ramos? Jaden chopped off the dude's arms and left him there for two minutes before you finished him off."

Alex took a step toward Felix. "And what was he supposed to do? They were enemy combatants. Maryana sent them to kill us. You'd prefer he had a nice chat with them, maybe invited them inside for tea? He did what he had to do."

Frank shook his head, his sad eyes wide. "Taking out enemies is one thing, but that was a Quentin Tarantino movie."

Alex didn't get the reference, but she wasn't about to ask for clarification now. She turned to Ed. "Tell them. This is how battles go down, sometimes."

Ed thought for a long moment, then shrugged. "Alex,

I've seen some shit in my time. At least, I thought I had. But Jaden wasn't just trying to kill his enemies. He was trying to hurt them. It's not right. Especially knowing they aren't fighting of their own free will."

Alex sighed. She had to admit that she agreed with them. She'd tried to explain away what she'd seen, but it had bothered her. "Okay, I'll talk to him."

They went over the rest of the battle, and Alex gave the debrief she'd been intending. The Twisted were a new enemy, and they needed to take every encounter as an opportunity to learn and grow. And with Maryana's huge army, it seemed they'd have plenty of opportunities to do just that.

After the rest of the team dispersed, Brian called Alex over. "You talked to Jaden? About turning more vampires?"

She nodded. "He won't do it. He thinks it would cheapen the deaths of his friends, I guess. He believes it's time for humanity to stand on its own two feet."

Brian was silent for a long time, his eyes on the floor. Alex was about to leave when he spoke again. "It strikes me that Jaden may not be in the best mindset for proper decision making."

She raised an eyebrow. "You're saying we should go ahead and do it? Without Jaden's okay?"

Brian looked up, meeting her eyes. "I'm just raising the possibility."

"How, then? Owl?"

"Perhaps. Or, if we want to do it a little more cleanly…" He opened his hand, revealing a vial of dark liquid. "Frank's change made it clear that we don't need a vampire to turn someone. We just need a vampire's blood. Jaden gave us a few samples to use when we were working on the cure. I've got this one left."

Alex stared down at the vial in her friend's hand. Such a small glass tube, and so much potential to change the world. How many Twisted could they create from that one vial? Enough to catch Maryana by surprise and take her out? Even if they didn't involve other Agartha humans, she could turn herself and the other GMT members. How much more effective would they be with vampire powers?

"I don't know, man. Sometimes I think Jaden overdoes it with his whole wisdom-of-the-ages thing. But I think we can all agree he's an expert when it comes to vampires. I'm thinking maybe we should listen to him this time."

Brian carefully set the vial on the table and gave Alex a long look. "I marked it as used in the inventory. Do what you want with it, but I can't keep it."

"Well, shit." Alex put the vial into her vest pocket. It felt hard and cold against her chest. "We don't have to decide anything now. There's something else I need to talk to you about. Now that you're not working on the cure, I was hoping you'd help me figure out a way into *New Haven*. You spent time hiding in the underbelly of the ship during Fleming's reign, and I feel like you've got a pretty good read on the defenses."

Brian nodded. "I've been thinking about that since we left the ship, actually. And the way I see it, there's only one surefire way to get into *New Haven*."

ALEX WAITED outside Jaden's quarters for nearly two hours before he finally showed up, his normally alert eyes focused on nothing more than the floor three feet in front of him. He looked bone tired.

"I figured you'd have to sleep sometime," Alex said with a grin.

He glanced up at her. "It's strange. I'm used to daysickness telling me in no uncertain terms when it's time to sleep. Now that the daysickness is gone, sometimes I forget to sleep." He paused in front of her. "You need something, before I turn in?"

"I was hoping we could chat for a moment."

He glanced at the door to his quarters. "Can it wait? I haven't slept since *New Haven*."

"Then I'll keep it short. Brian has a plan, and I think it's a good one."

He looked at her blankly for a long moment. "A plan for what?"

"Are you kidding me right now? A plan to take out Maryana!"

He let out a soft sound that might have been a disbelieving laugh. "You still don't understand what's happening. We can't take her out. We should be looking for an exit strategy."

Alex looked at him, her eyes wide with shock. She couldn't believe what she was hearing. "You want to run?"

Jaden pointed at the sky. "She's toying with us. She has an army of forty thousand people, and she sent fifteen."

"They're not her army. Not most of them, anyway. They're her prisoners, and they need our help."

"She's going to keep turning them and sending them after us. Do you think I liked killing all those innocent *New Haven* badges?"

Alex took a step toward him. "I don't know. Did you?"

He broke his gaze away from hers and looked at the ground. "Perhaps I let my anger get the best of me during the battle. I apologize."

Alex didn't know what to say to that. She wanted to tell him that it was fine, but it wasn't. He'd hacked off those peoples' limbs. "Look, I get what you're saying. Maryana is insane. She could start throwing people off *New Haven* and raining them down on us. Or maybe she'll keep sending little groups to attack until we've killed every badge on *New Haven*. That's my point. That's why we can't wait for some ideal moment to strike. Every hour is another sixty minutes she has control over everyone in my city. We have to stop her now."

Jaden looked into her eyes, as if searching for something. She didn't know what he was looking for. Perhaps resolve. Perhaps something else. "My mind... it isn't right at the moment. My mental capacity, my decision making, even my control of my emotions... they're slipping, and I can't trust them. And I don't know how long it will take until I get them back. But the one thing that I do trust is my body. I've trained it for over a thousand years, and it will react as it needs to. I'm a living weapon, Alex. Your job is to point me to the target."

"That I can do." Alex couldn't help but smile. Jaden might not be in top mental form, but at least he was aware of his limitations. She could deal with that.

"Good. So what's the plan?"

Her smile quickly faded. She didn't much like what she was about to say, but she agreed with Brian's assessment. This was the only surefire way to get to Maryana. "We're going to bring *New Haven* out of the sky."

7

The clouds looked like a soft white blanket hiding the earth below it. Maryana stood in the flight control room staring out across the horizon. She didn't believe in any god, but she thought she might be standing in heaven—a man-made heaven just for her. This city-ship carried all the humans she could ever eat, and they were trapped like rats. Best of all, they were rats that she could play with for as long as she wanted. There was no one with the strength to challenge her on the ship, and the people who might dare to were trapped in a hole in a mountain. *New Haven* was paradise.

She stood with her hands crossed behind her back, completely relaxed. She'd transformed every person on the flight deck to a Twisted, just as she'd done to everyone who operated any essential system on the ship. It was a wonderful feeling—she truly controlled *New Haven*, stern to stem.

The flight control room's door opened and a Twisted marched in. He stood before Maryana, staring down at her with powder-blue eyes that looked out of place in his monstrous face.

"Hey, Mikey," she said, her voice cheerful. "Do you have an update for me?"

Mike—who hated to be called Mikey—tried not to tremble. He hated Maryana with every fiber of his deformed body. "The Twisted who attacked Agartha are dead."

She raised an eyebrow, annoyed. "So that's how it is? Straight to business? You can't open with 'you look great, Maryana,' or 'hey, how's the family'?" She shook her head sadly.

Mike waited in silence, not sure what to say.

"It's called small talk, Mikey." Maryana's voice sounded sweet and concerned. "I'll start. How are you doing today?"

Mike didn't want to speak, but his mouth responded to his mistress's question immediately. "Bad. I'm afraid of you, and I just found out that fifteen badges were killed in the attack on Agartha. They were my friends, and—"

Maryana slapped him across the face. He staggered backward, barely keeping his balance. "Shut up, Mike. I don't want to hear your whining."

Mike put a hand to his jaw, checking to see if it was broken.

Maryana burst into a fit of laughter. She squeezed out the words between giggles. "I'm just messing with you. I can't believe that you actually thought I cared how you were doing." The laughter stopped. "Seriously, I want to know how things went on the surface."

"All fifteen of them are dead."

"So you mentioned. Did they destroy some of the defenses?"

"The eyes on the ground reported several defensive

turrets were destroyed in the attack. The GMT and Jaden came out of the city to engage our troops."

Maryana perked up a bit. "Did we kill any of them?"

"No, but the report noted Jaden acting..." Mike paused, searching for the right word. "...unusual during the battle."

"Unusual how? What was he doing?"

"He didn't go for quick kills. He dismembered the badges, like he wanted them to suffer before they died."

"Huh. That's great news." Maryana threw an arm around Mike's shoulders and stood next to him. "I'm willing to bet dollars to doughnuts that all of Jaden's buddies are dead. He's never taken the deaths of his precious vampires lightly. I bet watching all of them die from the virus really got under his skin. What do you think?"

"I think you're crazy." As soon as the words were out of his mouth, he flinched, readying himself to be hit again.

Instead, she just squeezed his shoulder gently. "I appreciate the honesty, Mikey. Come on. Let's go get some new recruits to fill up the ranks. We're going to need them for what's next."

THE LOBBY of the badge headquarters was not meant to hold a crowd. Now, there were two hundred men and women standing shoulder to shoulder, terrified expressions on their faces. Twisted stood around the perimeter, rifles at the ready if anyone stepped out of line.

Maryana sauntered through the door, and muted cries of fear came from the crowd. She ignored them, marching past and jumping up on the reception desk, so that everyone in the room could see her. She glanced down at the woman directly in front of her who was nearly pressed against the desk by the pressure of the people behind her. The woman let out a soft whimper. Maryana reached down and tousled her hair. Then she turned to the crowd.

"Thank you all for coming in today." She paused, flashing a smile that exposed the pointed teeth in her deformed mouth. "Really, all of you should be thanking me. This very day, some of you will be chosen to ascend! You will become immortal, super strong, with heightened senses. Basically, better in every way. I had to fight for years for the chance I'm about to hand you, and when I did it, vampires couldn't even go into sunlight. How lucky are all of you?"

Maryana stopped and listened for a moment; the room was silent except for the sounds of their breathing and the beating of their hearts.

"Anyone who wants to volunteer, please raise your hand. There are only twenty open spots, so don't hesitate." She reached down to Mike who stood at the edge of the desk and pulled him up. "Mikey, here, can tell you how great it is to be part of the team."

Mike's eyes widened as the words began to pour out of his mouth. "The transformation that Maryana blessed me with is the greatest gift I have ever received. I am better in every way than I was as a human. Serving her gives me purpose and fulfillment. Before she blessed me, my life had no meaning. Now, I help her bring order to the world."

Maryana clapped a hand on Mike's back "Well said. Now, I need twenty volunteers. Raise your hands and receive the gift of a lifetime."

Every eye was on the floor. No one moved. After a few moments, a woman toward the back of the crowd began to cry softly.

Maryana smiled and hopped down off the desk. The

crowd pressed tighter against each other to avoid any contact with Maryana. She reached the crying woman, but the woman refused to meet Maryana's eyes. Maryana put a hand under the soft chin and raised her face.

"Aren't you a pretty little thing?" Maryana said. The woman was in her early twenties and had long blond hair and radiated a youthful beauty. "I know you're scared, but you'll feel much better soon." She nodded to one of the Twisted and they grabbed the woman under the arms.

When the Twisted's hands touched her, the woman came to life. She screamed and grabbed at the other people in the room, but it was no use. The Twisted dragged her toward the holding area in the back of the building.

The crowd pressed back even further as Maryana began strolling through the crowd again. Over the next five minutes, she chose nineteen more, seemingly at random. Some accepted their fate, but others tried to fight against the Twisted. The results were the same for all of them.

Maryana beamed at the remaining humans. "Thanks for coming in, everyone. Sorry I wasn't able to help you all, but we will do this again." She waved to the Twisted by the exit, and he opened the doors. The people filed out as quickly as possible.

After she'd watched them leave, Maryana strolled back to the holding cells. The selected humans were locked together in a large cell. The first woman she'd taken was crouched on the floor of the cell, screaming hysterically. Maryana skipped down the hall, stopping in front of the door. One of the Twisted opened it. Maryana walked toward the screaming girl, and everyone else cowered, pressing their bodies against the bars and the walls.

"Please let me go!" the woman screamed. "I shouldn't be

here! I'll do whatever you want. Just don't make me a monster!"

"A monster?" Maryana clucked her tongue in disapproval. "Are you calling me a monster? I'll tell you what, missy. I was quite the looker back in my day. But a pretty face is a small price to pay for power and immortality. What's your name?"

The woman raised her tear-streaked face. "I'm sorry. I didn't mean that you're a monster. Please, just let me go."

Maryana grabbed the girl by the neck and hauled her into the air, lifting her high enough that her feet dangled a few inches off the floor. The woman struggled for breath, her arms pinwheeling in the air. "Not to get all Miss Manners on you, but I did ask you a question. It's rude to ignore people. What's your name?"

The girl answer in a barely audible whisper. "Ashley."

Maryana let go and Ashely collapsed to her knees. "Nice to meet you, Ashley. I hope that you took a good long look in the mirror this morning because this is the last time you will have that beautiful face. Shall we get started?"

For everyone but Maryana, the next three hours were the stuff of nightmares. The mental games that she played with her victims were as bad as the physical torture. She broke each person down to the point where they begged to be turned. Once her work was done, twenty new Twisted stood before her, and the walls and floor were covered in blood.

She clapped her hands together. "This has been so much fun. I hope you all enjoyed it as much as I did. Now, there are some buckets and mops in the storage room. I want you to make this cell shine. If we leave it like this, people might think something bad happened here. Once you are finished, Mikey will give you some new uniforms. If anyone asks you about becoming a Twisted, tell them that it was the greatest experience of your life and you would do it again in a heartbeat." She walked up and down the row of Twisted and stopped in front of Ashley. "I need you to help me out with something. Get changed and meet me in the communications room."

Thirty minutes later Maryana and Ashley stood in the City Council chambers, a camera in front of them. Ashley's hair was brushed and pulled back in a ponytail, and she wore a freshly-pressed uniform. Her features were still recognizable beneath the twisted form of her new face. The camera operator counted down from three, a red light turned on, and the city-wide broadcast began.

"People of *New Haven*, I hope you are all having a wonderful day," Maryana began. "I know some of you still don't trust me, but I think you will all come to realize that I am the leader you all deserve. I will help you reclaim and repopulate the world. But first, there's something we have to do. We need to kill Jaden. If you thought he was one of the good guys, you were very wrong. He tricks people into doing his bidding. Putting an end to him is priority number one!"

She paused, and her monstrous face softened.

"I wanted to make this announcement so I could share my plans with you, but I also wanted to let you know that I'm going to need your help to make the world a better place. Just today, Ashley, here, volunteered to join the forces of *New Haven*. She might look a little different, but she's still the same dedicated individual. Only better." Maryana turned to Ashley. "Tell the people what you think of your new transformation."

Ashley's eyes flashed with the briefest moment of terror, but then she smiled. "The transformation that Maryana blessed me with is the greatest gift I have ever received. I am better in every way than I was as a human. Serving her gives me purpose and fulfillment. Before she blessed me, my life had no meaning. Now, I help her bring order to the world."

"Thanks, Ashley. I can't offer you all this gift, but I'm sure some of you will get a chance. Be good. We'll talk soon." Maryana winked at the camera and the red light turned off. She smiled, wondering once again if this place might be heaven.

Mike ran into the room, disturbing her bliss. "A ship just took off from Agartha. What do you want us to do?"

8

Brian watched on the monitor as the experimental ship headed north. It was nearly sunset, and the light glinted off the aircraft as it disappeared into the distance. Brian hoped it would be up to the difficult challenge they were about to give it. George wasn't one hundred percent confident in the ship's reliability. It seemed to be performing well so far, but its only flights had been a quick trip to *New Haven* and an equally quick trip back to Agartha. Today's flight would require a bit more from the aircraft.

"So, what happens now?" Stephanie asked. She leaned forward, her chin in her hand as she stared intently at the screen. All of the senior lab personnel had been reassigned to the control center for this mission, and space was tight. Brian and Stephanie had been forced to share a desk.

"We wait," Brian said. Now that the experimental ship was out of sight, he'd turned his attention to the radar display that showed *New Haven* far overhead.

"Did *New Haven* see it?" Stephanie asked.

Brian hesitated before answering. That was the real question. Technically, of course the small ship would show up on their radar, but it was a question of whether or not the person manning the radar was paying close enough attention to catch it going by. He and Alex had discussed the matter, and they'd decided they couldn't risk going slow. It wouldn't look as real. "I'm betting they did. But I guess we'll find out very shortly."

"If not, I guess we'll just wait down here for more Twisted to attack." She sighed and rested her chin on her hand again.

"I'm sorry that you got roped into this," Brian said. "I'm sure when you signed up to be a lab tech, you weren't expecting to be tracking enemy vampires who could attack the city at any moment. This is probably a little more than you'd bargained for."

She gave him a look that make him feel like the dumbest man on Earth. "Are you kidding me? This is awesome!"

He blinked hard, staring at her in surprise. "Really?"

"Of course." She paused. "I mean, not the vampire deaths. That sucks. Some of those guys were weirdos, but Toby was a real sweetheart. And they did right by everyone in Agartha, keeping us safe and fed for all these years. But the other parts? Helping Jaden and a ragtag group of humans from some city in the sky battle the evil vampire queen who caused all of this? As much as I enjoyed studying water samples to verify the purity, this is just a tad bit cooler."

Brian grinned. He'd been working closely with Stephanie for the past few days, and she'd managed to impress him. That was no easy task. She was efficient in the lab, innovative in her ideas, and whip-smart. He had to admit that she was pretty good looking, too. Granted he'd dated more than his share of nice-looking women on *New Haven* over the past couple of years, but most of those relationships had been fleeting. Something about Stephanie spoke to him. Her mind. Her body. Her personality. He didn't know her well, but he was beginning to think she might be the total package. "I'm glad you feel that way. I was worried this whole thing might be freaking you out."

She shrugged. "Honestly, I work better under pressure. It's just that I never got much of a chance at it down here." She paused, thinking. "There was one time when I got to shine. There was a problem with the water purification system, and the parts needed to fix it proved tough to find. It actually got pretty dire for a couple days. People were forced to ration water. Jaden and Robert finally brought back the parts, and George got them installed. All that was needed was our say so. My boss tested the water and gave it the thumbs up. Thing is, he missed something. I double checked his work and caught some bacteria. Turns out, the parts Jaden brought back were defective. I caught it and the vampires had to go back out scavenging. My boss was pissed about the whole thing, seeing as it made him look like an idiot, but Jaden thanked me. That was the only time I've ever spoken to him. Not counting when he was yelling at us in the lab a couple of days ago."

"Wow, that's pretty badass. You saved the city."

Stephanie smirked at him. "Don't be dramatic. I saved them from a bad case of diarrhea, maybe. Still, it seemed like a big deal at the time. Before all of this." She paused again, giving him a look he couldn't quite read. "People around here think I'm too intense. They say I take the work too seriously. Even the other lab techs. But what we do is important. We're dealing with life and death stuff. It's nice to work with someone else who understands that."

Brian smiled back at her. "I can relate to being called too

intense. I'd rather work with someone who took the job too seriously, rather than not seriously enough."

"You mean that?"

"Of course," he said.

"Good. Because I have some thoughts on the GMT's weapons. You're missing some key areas where you could improve the designs. Now that they're facing the Twisted, you're going to have to move beyond silver mail and daylights."

He tilted his head, surprised that this lab tech would be so bold as to tell him his business. But he had to admit, he liked it. "I look forward to hearing your thoughts."

"Heads up!" someone at another desk shouted. "We've got movement."

Brian's gaze shifted back to the radar display. Sure enough, *New Haven* was in motion, and it was heading west, following the experimental ship. Just as they'd planned. He grabbed the radio off the desk and held it to his mouth. "Alex, you read me?"

The reply came almost immediately. "I hear you, Brian."

"*New Haven* is in motion. Maryana took the bait."

"You're going to laugh if I tell you," Ed muttered, as they walked down the corridor to the transport vehicle.

"Why would I laugh?" Chuck said. "I told you mine. The thing I miss most about *New Haven* is the slop from Tankards. What could be more embarrassing than that?"

"Trust me," Ed replied. "I have you beat." He glanced toward Felix. "Why don't you go, new guy?"

Felix didn't hesitate before answering. "Oh, that's easy. The 2004 baseball season."

"Oh," Ed said. Then he stopped walking. "Wait, what?"

"Baseball. We've got an archive of every major league game since 1950. I was working my way through the seasons. I just finished the two-thousand-four season and my team lost a heartbreaker. If I never get to see them win the Series because of Maryana, I'm going to be pissed."

Frank sidled up beside him. "No kidding? I was a bit of a baseball fan myself back in the day. Who's your team?"

"The Chicago Cubs."

Frank let out a chuckle. "You're kidding. I was a Cardinals fan." He paused. "Wait, 2003 was the year they made the playoffs, right?"

Felix's shoulders slumped. "I had high hopes. But that foul ball..."

Alex walked up beside them. "You realize you don't have to watch all the games to know what happened, right? You can look up the scores, find out how they did each year."

Felix looked at her in horror. "You can also flip to the last page in a book to see how things turn out, but I don't recommend it."

"I'm with my man, Felix," Frank said. "Even if he does have terrible taste in teams. Baseball is drama. The beauty is in watching it play out." He glanced at Jaden. "How about you, Jaden? Were you a baseball guy?"

"No," Jaden replied, his voice distant. "Sports were never my thing. Though, I did get into watching boxing for a few years."

"The sweet science. Why am I not surprised?"

"Is anyone else who wasn't alive in the twenty-first century thoroughly bored by this conversation?" Chuck asked.

Alex chuckled. "Agreed. Let's focus up, people."

The team remained silent until they reached the transport vehicle, a large truck designed to hold far more than their six bodies. Alex climbed into the passenger seat while Jaden slid behind the wheel.

"You sure you want to drive?" Alex asked. "If you're not ready…"

He tossed her an annoyed glare. "I told you, my body is one hundred percent, even if my mind isn't. I'm fully prepared to carry out the mission."

She gave him a long look. Jaden wasn't the type to admit weakness. If he was posturing now, the whole team might die. But she saw resolve in his eyes. She trusted his warrior instincts to pick up any slack created by his unstable emotions. "Good enough for me. And you remember how to get there?"

Jaden scowled, his eyes on the blast door between them and the road beyond. "This is one place I'll never forget."

Alex touched the radio on her chest. "Brian, how we looking?"

There was a moment of silence before he answered. "*New Haven*'s just over a hundred miles out, headed in a direct line toward our aircraft. You should be clear."

"Roger that." She turned to Jaden. "It's time."

Jaden stuck a hand out the window, signaling to a man near the blast door who pressed a button. The door smoothly opened.

Alex took a look around the tunnel as Jaden eased the transport vehicle forward. A few days ago, this tunnel had been a battlefield. Now, it was a launchpad for a mission that just might take Maryana down once and for all. She'd taken the bait. Now, the hard part of the mission began.

"Here we go," Jaden said, and he stepped on the gas.

9

The transport thumped over a dislodged chunk of pavement, and the seatbelt bit into Alex's shoulder.

"What the hell!" Ed shouted from the back of the transport. "Watch where you're going."

"I am watching," Jaden said evenly. "The road isn't exactly smooth after more than a century's exposure to the elements. I thought the fierce GMT would be able to handle some bumps."

"We can handle bumps, but I would like to get there in one piece."

"I assure you that we will not crash on the journey. Living through the rest of the mission is less certain." Jaden kept the vehicle at an even fifty miles per hour, staying in the middle of the road, except when he needed to drift to avoid the husk of an old car. They were traveling north along an old highway the faded signs marked as I-25.

Ed grimaced. "Great pep talk. You're making Frank nervous."

Jaden turned to Alex. "Pay attention to the route. We're

taking I-25 to I-80. If anything happens to me, you'll need to know how to get back to Agartha."

Alex watched the road and the landscape go by. "I'm paying attention. You make sure to hold your shit together so we can make it back."

Jaden was silent for a moment, then he spoke again. "I used to tell my vampires that nothing is certain. I now realize that I didn't believe what I was saying. Even in the worst times I truly thought that we would always be part of the world. I didn't think it was possible for us to lose. Now, I wonder if my arrogance is the reason they're all dead." He kept his eyes on the road ahead and his voice was distant, as if the words weren't meant for anyone but himself.

"You had a thousand years of experience backing up your assumption. That's a pretty good run."

"Yes, but the run is over now. The world will move on. I need to accept my place, or the lack of one."

Alex hated the way he sounded. It was such a stark contrast to the confident leader she'd met a couple of years ago. "You still have a place in the world. It involves taking out the cause of this whole mess. Killing Maryana saves the human race. Protecting us has always been your mission, and the mission isn't over. You're not finished."

"Don't worry, I will fight until I either have revenge on Maryana, or I join my fellow vampires in the true death."

Alex didn't know how to react to that. She wasn't sure how she felt about fighting alongside a guy who seemed to have already accepted his fate. She tried to pay attention to the road, just in case the worst really did happen. The immediate landscape was mostly open plains, but mountains stuck their heads over the horizon to the west, which made it easy to keep track of the direction. Sections of the road were missing, but enough of it remained that it wouldn't be difficult to follow.

They'd been on the road for about two hours when they came to a collapsed bridge. Jaden slowed the transport and eased it off the road to go around the wreckage. The embankment was steep enough to make Alex grip the armrest tightly as they descended. When they reached the bottom, Alex spotted an old building just off the highway. The glass was gone from the windows, and a dirt hill had formed on one side of the brick structure.

"I wonder what that building was," she said. "It seems so lonely out here."

"It was a gas station. They were on every exit so people could refuel their cars." Jaden drove up the next embankment slowly to get the truck back to the highway. The truck's large, knobby tires made it with little effort. Jaden got the truck back up to speed and closed his eyes for a moment.

"Hey, keep your eyes on the road!" Alex said, alarmed.

Jaden's eyes popped open. "We are being followed."

Alex snapped her head around to see the mirror on the side of the truck. All it showed was empty roads. "Are you sure?"

"Yes. I sensed a group of Twisted when we slowed down. They are staying out of sight, but they are tracking us. As soon as I felt their presence, they backed off."

"How could that be? We left Agartha after *New Haven* was already gone."

"They must have come down with the Twisted that we fought. Maryana had a force on the ground keeping tabs on us."

"Can you tell how many there are?"

"No. More than one, certainly. I don't feel them anymore."

Alex thought for a moment. "How far away can you sense? How far back are they?"

"Not far. Less than a mile. They were probably staying farther back and didn't realize that we slowed down."

"Not exactly encouraging. How fast can you Twisted run?"

"When I was a vampire, I could keep a pace of about fifty miles per hour all night. I haven't tested myself since I've become Twisted. I'm guessing I could go for a few days, since daylight no longer has an effect."

"Keep us moving as fast as you can. We'll need a plan to deal with them, once we arrive."

Alex turned back to the passenger area. The bed of the truck was long, with benches on both sides for the passengers to sit. Small windows, each three inches high and six inches wide, lined the walls and the back doors. They'd been designed to fire through with as little exposure as possible. The team seemed relaxed when Alex stepped back into their area.

"We have a problem," she said. "A group of Twisted is following us. I'm not sure why they haven't attacked yet, but we need to be ready."

"Man, can't we even take a drive without something trying to kill us?" Felix sounded genuinely offended that he had to be on guard. "I figured we could relax a little before we had to worry about fighting for our lives."

"Welcome to the GMT," Chuck said as he grabbed his rifle and checked the magazine.

Alex turned to Owl. "Since you and Frank can see the farthest, I want you two scanning the area behind and around the transport. Everyone else, make sure your weapons are locked and loaded. We are going to keep moving as fast as we can, so the ride might get even tougher."

"What's the ETA to our target?" Ed asked.

"We should be there in less than two hours. That's assuming there are no major obstacles along the way."

The team grabbed their weapons. Alex went back to the cab. She and Jaden sat in silence as the transport headed north. For the next hour, the road was smooth enough to keep a good pace. Then Alex saw the remains of a town on the horizon. There were no skyscrapers, just small homes and remains of old commercial warehouses.

Jaden glanced over at her. "This is where we will turn east. The road is called I-80, if any signs remain."

The road did intersect another major highway a few minutes later. Alex couldn't make out the letters on the old faded signs, but she had no doubt that this was I-80.

Shortly after turning onto the new road, they reached the top of a small hill, and Alex spotted a barricade up ahead. An overpass lay crumbled, its debris blocking the road. Two rusted tanks sat near the wreckage. Some sort of battle had gone down here a long time ago.

"Any chance we can drive over that?" Alex asked.

"No," Jaden said. "We'll have to find another way around. I'll try to take us through the neighborhoods to the north, but we will have to go slowly. The Twisted might take the opportunity to attack."

"Keep us moving as fast as you can. I'll be right back." She went to the back of the truck and addressed the team. "We have to leave the main road. Jaden's going to maneuver us through some side streets, but we will be moving slow. Owl and Frank, I want you running alongside us on foot. Be ready to engage. You should have no problem keeping up with us. Everyone else, cover them and stay sharp."

"What kind of gun should I use?" Frank asked.

"Take your side arm and a sword. You're going to be on the move, so if you get in a fight, it will likely end in close combat. We will cover you with long range shots. If they get too close, you go to work." Alex handed Frank an extra clip as she spoke. "Use your strength and speed and try to keep your head on top of your body."

The cargo area bucked as the truck drove off of the highway and over the curbs. The vehicle slowed as it entered the residential area.

Alex looked at the two Twisted. "That's our sign. Let's move."

Owl and Frank went out the back. Ed and Chuck opened the side window slats and stuck the muzzles of their rifles through. Felix did the same at one of the back windows. Alex joined Jaden in the cab.

The small streets were filled with obstacles. Trees had grown through where the pavement had cracked, and the remains of cars lined the roads. On either side of them, Alex saw homes that had been torn apart by decades of storms.

Jaden eased the large transport through the streets. He slowed to a crawl as he used the front of the truck to push aside the husk of a car. "They are close. I can feel them."

Alex yelled back, "Look alive! They are close."

She scanned the roof tops of the remaining homes and check the gaps between the houses. Her finger hovered on the side of the trigger guards, ready to spring into action. She saw Frank on her side of the truck. He had his pistol in hand and moved from one piece of cover to the next. She checked the mirror on Jaden's side and saw Owl moving in the same manner, using the surroundings to hide from potential snipers.

Alex knew how fast the Twisted could move, and that

the ambush might come from any direction. "You boys see anything yet?"

"Nothing so far," Ed's voice boomed from the back.

The truck continued lurching forward as the wheels crushed an old mailbox. Jaden glanced out his side window. "I'm going right, to get us back to the main road."

The truck turned sharply, throwing the occupants in the back off balance. Felix held onto the side and kept his eyes focused out the small window. "I saw one!" he shouted. "Straight back, on a rooftop!"

"Take him out!" Ed yelled.

"He was only there for a second. I didn't have a chance."

Alex glanced out the windows, checking that Owl and Frank were still by their side.

Jaden maneuvered around another car and angled for a path to the highway. "Hold on." He gave the transport some gas, and it rumbled over a fallen motorcycle. He kept his foot on the gas, picking up speed, and plowed through a guard rail and back onto the highway.

Owl and Frank started to run, keeping pace with the transport while continuously looking back for enemy snipers. Once the transport was up to full speed, Alex signaled Felix to open the rear door. As soon as he did, Owl and Frank jumped in and slammed the door behind them. Felix let out a breath and slid the back window shut.

"Why didn't they attack?" Chuck asked.

"I think they want to see where we're headed." Alex answered. "I doubt things will go quite so smooth when we arrive."

10

"That's it, up ahead," Jaden said.

Alex squinted toward the handful of squat, concrete buildings just north of them. "I thought it would be bigger."

"Most of it is underground." Jaden turned to Ed. "Ready to do this?"

Ed nodded, but there was a look of hesitation in his eyes. "You're sure it's in there?"

"I'm sure it was there a hundred and fifty years ago. I remember the layout. I'll get us in and out, if Alex can keep Maryana's Twisted off our backs."

"I'll do my best." Alex turn to Chuck, who was now driving the vehicle. "Don't slow down too much when you get to the buildings. We don't want to tip our hand."

"In fact, don't slow down at all," Jaden said. "Ed and I will hop out."

Ed raised an eyebrow. "Um, speak for yourself. It takes me more than twenty minutes to heal from a broken bone." He lifted his right arm, showing off the cast that still encased his forearm. "You sure you don't want someone less gimpy as your wingman?"

Jaden slapped him on the back. "I'll get you there safely." He hurried to the back doors of the transport and rested a hand on the handle. Ed reluctantly followed.

"We'll swing around and pick you up in ten minutes," Alex said.

"Roger that." Jaden stared out the window, watching intently, waiting for his moment.

As they passed the concrete buildings, he threw open the doors with one hand and grabbed Ed with the other, pulling him close. Then he leaped out of the transport.

Alex watched as Jaden landed on the road behind them, his legs in motion even before they touched the pavement. He hit the ground running, carrying Ed. After slowing, he set Ed down, and the two of them ran toward the buildings. Within a few moments, they'd disappeared through a busted doorway in the farthest building.

True to his word, Chuck kept the transport moving at full speed the entire time. As soon as Jaden and Ed were clear, Felix and Owl pulled the doors shut. As they sped away, Alex felt her gaze drawn to the concrete buildings. It was incredible to think that a weapon capable of so much death and destruction lay buried beneath the unassuming exterior. And, if everything went according to plan, it was a weapon that would help them take down Maryana.

There was a certain poetry to using this particular weapon. Jaden had told Alex the story of this place not long ago. A nuclear silo that Jaden and his vampires had spent the entire night preparing to defend. Instead of going for the weapon, Maryana had killed an entire town just to mess with him. Now, assuming that the weapon was still there, they'd use it against her.

"How we doing?" Alex asked, after they'd been driving away from the silo for nearly two minutes.

Owl closed her eyes and took a deep breath. After a silent moment, she opened them and looked at Alex. "It didn't work. The Twisted... I can still feel them, but they're getting further away."

"Damn it," Alex muttered. The plan had been to lure the Twisted away from the nuclear silo so that Jaden and Ed could retrieve their target in peace, but the Twisted hadn't taken the bait. "Chuck, turn around. We're going back."

Frank sighed. "We're going to have to fight them, aren't we?"

Owl shook her head. "Frank, my man, you're one weird vampire."

"Typical Cardinals fan," Felix said with a grin.

Chuck pulled a sharp U-turn, and the weight of the truck shifted dangerously in response. Thankfully, all four wheels stayed connected to the asphalt.

"I can feel them more strongly now," Owl said when they got a bit closer to the silo.

"Any idea how many?" Alex asked.

Owl closed her eyes again, but quickly shook her head. "Sorry, I'm not that good at this yet. I have a tough time distinguishing a group, let alone a specific number."

"Eh, who needs to know the number of enemies they're about to fight?" Chuck said. "Kills the suspense, you know?"

When they were a quarter mile from the silo, Frank pointed down the road. "There! Five of them, headed for the buildings."

Alex squinted and could almost make out the forms. "Let's stop them before they get there. Chuck?"

"On it!" He stepped on the gas and the transport lurched forward at top speed, racing down the uneven road.

Despite their speed, four of the Twisted turned off the road and headed for the building before the transport reached them. The fifth crouched down, preparing to jump at the vehicle. But Chuck had other plans. As he reached the Twisted, he swerved toward him. The creature leaped, but the right side of the front bumper caught him in midair, slamming into him.

The Twisted let out a shout of pain and surprise as he careened backward, and he hit the concrete wall of the nearest building hard. Alex could hear the sound of bones snapping even over the rumble of the transport's engine. The creature fell to the ground and immediately tried to stand, though its broken legs were making that no easy task.

"I got this one." Felix threw the door open and leaned out, his rifle at the ready. He fired three shots into the Twisted's heart, then climbed back inside.

Chuck hadn't stopped the transport, he'd just turned it, going up what must once have been the silo's wide driveway. Up ahead, the other four Twisted were charging toward the busted doorway where Jaden and Ed had entered the farthest building.

Alex glanced back at the fallen Twisted. Something about the creature looked off, and it took her a moment to identify what was bothering her about him. Then she saw it. He was wearing a mask with eye holes. It made no sense. Why would the Twisted be wearing masks?

She didn't have long to consider that. The four Twisted had reached the doorway, but they'd stopped, and were clawing at something. Apparently, Jaden and Ed had set up some kind of barrier.

Owl spun toward Frank. "We have to get out there." She didn't wait for a response before jumping out of the transport's still-open back doors and racing toward the enemies.

Frank, on the other hand, hesitated.

"What are you doing?" Chuck shouted. "Don't leave Owl to fight those guys four on one!"

Alex reached back and grabbed his arm. "Listen to me, I know fighting isn't your favorite thing, but you can do this. You might not be a fighter, but you know what it means to be Feral, more than anyone. Part of that Feral is still inside you. You have to let it out."

Frank looked at her blankly for a moment, and she thought she hadn't gotten through to him. But something sparked in his eyes and he nodded, turned, and jumped out of the transport.

Up ahead, Owl had already reached the Twisted, catching them unaware as they focused on the door. She slammed into one of them, knocking him away from the others. The two of them tumbled to the ground and into the nearby brush. Alex caught a glimpse of the Twisted's face as he fell, and this one was wearing a mask, too.

Frank let out a fierce shout, drawing his sword as he ran. The Twisted were ready now, and one turned to meet him. Frank jammed the tip of his sword into the creature's neck and, instead of removing the head as Jaden would have, he yanked the blade downward vertically, cutting through muscle, bone, and organs in one long slice until he reached the heart.

"Guess you got through to Frank," Chuck said.

"Bring us around so we can shoot those other two," Alex replied, her eyes fixed on her targets.

"Mind if I try something else?" Chuck asked.

"Go for it."

Chuck stomped on the gas pedal again, sending them speeding toward the doorway. At the last moment, he slammed on the brakes. One of the remaining Twisted leaped out of the way, but the other still had his focus on the metal barricade and failed to react in time. The full weight of the transport hit him in the midsection, pinning him against the concrete wall. Black blood oozed from his mouth, but he wasn't dead yet. He glared through the windshield at Chuck, his furious eyes all that could be seen of his masked face. He put both hands against the transport and pushed with all his might.

The transport began to slide backward, but Alex was already leaning out the passenger window, taking aim with her pistol. She put a bullet between his eyes, and he went down.

Felix aimed at the last Twisted, but just before he fired, Owl leaped out of the brush behind him, put her pistol to his head, and pulled the trigger.

Alex turned back to the doorway and saw bent and dented metal still covering it. The Twisted had come close to breaking through but hadn't succeeded. She turned back to the dead Twisted on the ground. "I don't understand. Why would Maryana have them wear masks? Wouldn't she want us to see who we're killing? It makes no sense."

"It makes perfect sense," Felix growled, anger in his voice. "We know these are *New Haven* citizens. If they're masked, they could be anyone. Each time we pull a trigger, she wants us wondering if we're killing our friends, our lovers, even our own mothers."

Owl closed her eyes for a moment, then looked up at Alex sharply. "We've got more incoming. Like I said, I'm bad with numbers, but... it's a lot more than five."

As she finished speaking, they heard the whine of bending metal, and then Ed came running through the doorway. Jaden followed close behind, holding a cone-shaped object the size of his torso.

"Is that it?" Alex asked as he reached the transport.

"Yes. This is a nuclear warhead." He climbed into the passenger seat and grabbed the radio. "We've got it. Time to rendezvous."

"Sounds good, Jaden," George answered through the radio. "I'll see you soon."

"Jaden..." Owl said.

"I feel them, too," he answered. "Lots of them. Let's get the hell out of here."

11

BRIAN SLOWLY OPENED HIS EYES. His mind tried to snap back to reality but a dream was still holding on. He had been walking the streets of *New Haven* with Alex and Fleming. The three of them joked about losing the city to vampires. He woke to a hand on his back, shaking him, and the dream faded quickly. He blinked hard and realized where he was. This was Agartha, not *New Haven,* and he had fallen asleep at his desk in the lab.

He wiped the drool off his face and looked up, seeing Stephanie, a cup of coffee in her hand. He glanced back at the desk and saw a small puddle of drool. He quickly put an arm over it to try and hide the mess.

"When you can't stay awake long enough for me to grab you a cup of coffee, I think that's a good sign you need some sleep," she said, with a soft smile.

"Oh, I'm OK, I just rested my head for a second." He wiped the corner of his mouth again to make sure he didn't miss anything.

"The bags under your eyes are telling me a different story. I need a little break too. Come with me." She reached down and grabbed his hand, giving him a gentle pull.

"Wait. I need to save my work and I want to finish the equation." He let go of her hand and turned back to the screens at his desk.

"Save the work, but there is no such thing as finishing an equation. Each one leads to another."

"But I think this one really is important. It is the beginning of a new line of experiments that could lead to—"

"That's my point. They all lead to something else. Take some time to rest and we can come back fresh." The look on Brian's face said that he still wasn't convinced. "I'm not taking no for an answer. I promised an elite killer that I would look after you. Do you want to see Alex snap my neck, or something?"

That made Brian smile. "All right."

"I'll walk you to your room. What part of the city are you in?"

Brian thought about it for a moment "It's the big room next to the mechanical section. The one with all the bunks in it."

Stephanie stopped walking and looked at him with a surprised expression. "You mean the on-call bunks?"

"I don't know. If you say it's the on-call bunks, I'm sure that's what they are. I just found that place and grabbed a bed."

"You're telling me you never got a room?"

Brian's face turned red. "When we got here, I was trying to save the vampires before they died. I didn't do anything else. How could I? I just wish I hadn't failed." Brian looked down at the desk. He couldn't make eye contact when he thought about the creatures whom he'd failed to save.

There was a moment of silence. She grabbed his hand

again and pulled him down the hallway. "Come with me. We are going to get some food and rest. Then we will get you a proper room."

The two made their way to the cafeteria and grabbed some fruit and salad. After the first bite of food, Brian realized how hungry he was. He tried to remember the last time he'd taken a break for a meal, but it had just been a series of snacks since he had been here. "Thanks for making me take a break. I'll have to buy you a drink, sometime."

"What do you mean? Like, alcohol?"

"Yeah. We have a great bar on *New Haven* called Tankards. They make the beer from the leftover bread grains. Is there a place like that here?"

"All we have here are cafeterias. Some people make wine. Others make a nasty, hard alcohol that they use as a cleaner, but you can mix it with juice and drink it. Why do you ask?"

"I just wanted to take you to a place we could hang out and relax. I never really thought about how limited space is here. You would like *New Haven*. It is really open and full of light. If we live long enough, I'll take you there."

"I'd like to see it. Agartha never seemed like it had limited space to me, but I've never known anything different. I've dreamt about walking around outside. It must be wonderful to look up at the sun and sky without risking your life." She closed her eyes, imagining the world as she spoke.

Brian looked at the smooth skin of her face and ached to reach out and touch it. He hadn't had a genuine conversation with a woman in a long while, and he knew he wanted to have many more with Stephanie.

The two finished their food, and Stephanie led them to the residential section of the city. It was really just a series of hallways lined with small rooms on either side. She stopped in front of one of the doors and used her keycard to open it.

Brian had a moment of disorientation as he stepped inside. The room was so different than the sterile hallways of Agartha that he felt like he'd walked into another world. The walls were lined with photographs. The ceiling of the eight foot by ten-foot room was covered with prints that formed one large picture. Brian recognized it as an image of earth from space. A spectacular blue sphere with oceans and continents partially masked by clouds. He had seen the image on his tablet in school. Looking at an eight-foot version overhead gave it a whole new life.

The walls were covered with various images, many of which Brian had never seen. There were pictures of waterfalls, deserts, creatures underwater in the ocean, mountains that touched the sky, herds of animals on the plains. One wall contained only pictures of people. One image showed dozens of people walking along a city street filled with cars and lights. Another was of a small girl standing in front of a vast canyon. The pictures took up every inch of space on the walls.

The only other things in the room were a bed, a sink with a mirror, and a chest for belongings. Brian stood in awe of the room.

"Sorry, I know that I'm a bit weird. I just started with one image and then it built up from there." There was a slight flush in Stephanie's cheeks that gave away her embarrassment at the room.

"Don't be sorry. It's amazing. I've never seen anything like this." He stepped further into the room and gazed at the pictures on the walls. "Where did you get all these?"

"We have some pretty extensive archives of data from before the war. I love looking through the images from the time before. Sometimes I print them out and add them to the collection. I know it's really weird, but it reminds me of what possibilities are out there." She walked over to the chest of drawers. "Would you mind turning around for a moment?"

Brian did as she asked and when he turned back she was wearing pajamas that consisted of light pants and a loose shirt.

"I don't want you to get the wrong idea," she said. "I brought you here to sleep. Can I count on you to be a gentleman?"

Brian turned a dark shade of red. "Oh, yeah. I never thought this was going anywhere else. I mean, it's not like I would be opposed to it going there sometime, but... That came out creepy." He gathered himself. "Yes, I will be a gentleman. No funny business, here."

Stephanie laughed. "I feel pretty safe with that answer. She tossed him a shirt from the chest. "You can sleep in that. It might be a little small, but it's a step up from the clothes you've been wearing for the last week."

Brian changed into the shirt and slid into the bed. Stephanie turned off the lights, and by the time she got into bed, Brian was asleep.

THE TWO AWOKE to a loud banging on the door. A voice yelled, "Stephanie are you in there? We need you in the lab, now!"

Stephanie sprang to her feet and turned on the light. Brian jumped out of bed and started to change back into his clothes.

"I'm on my way," she shouted. "Let me get dressed and I'll be there in a minute."

"Do you know where Brian is? I can't find him."

"I'll grab him and meet you in the lab."

Five minutes later the two entered the lab, still wiping the sleep from their eyes. Brian checked the clock; they had only been asleep for three hours. He didn't know what this was about, but it had better be big. He had been woken from the best sleep he'd had in weeks, and he'd really wanted to wake up peacefully next to Stephanie.

"What's going on?" Brian asked.

The closest tech simply pointed to the window to the examination room. It was the same room in which Frank had been tested a few days ago. Now, a different Twisted sat on the examination table. Brian just stared in shock for a moment. His first thought was that they had captured one of Maryana's soldiers, but this Twisted was not restrained in any way.

"Holy shit!" Stephanie said. "Is that Chad? What the hell is going on?" She looked as confused as Brian felt.

"Yep, that's Chad." the tech replied. "I'll let him tell you about it himself."

"Who's Chad?" Brian asked.

"One of the security staff. He's like one of your badges," Stephanie said, as they stepped into the exam room. She turned to the creature on the table. "What happened?"

"Hey Stephanie," the Twisted said, his voice a bit slurred by his oversized teeth. "I'm sorry, but this needed to be done. Jaden left us defenseless. We just don't have the strength to protect ourselves."

"Jaden is out there protecting us right now. How did you become Twisted?" Stephanie could not take her eyes off of the deformed guard.

"He injected himself with one of our blood samples," Brian said, as the realization hit him. "I need to know, which one did you use?"

Chad didn't meet his eyes. "Look, I just wanted to give us a chance, if there is an attack while Jaden is gone. Hell, he may never come back. Someone had to step up." He seemed to be trying to convince himself as much as Brian and Stephanie.

"What sample did you use?" Brian repeated.

He pointed to a now-empty vial on the table next to him. "I didn't inject myself. I just cut my arm and poured the blood over the cut. The change was much worse than I thought it would be."

Brian looked at the label on the vial. The blood had come from Owl.

12

The transport truck rumbled and bounced along the broken road as the GMT sped north, away from the nuclear silo and the Twisted chasing after them.

Alex glanced back through her side view mirror. The Twisted were gaining on them as they drove along this nearly ruined road. While the broken asphalt slowed their truck, the Twisted were able to run across it at top speed. Three of them were now close enough that even her human eyes could easily make them out.

"Can't this thing go any faster?" she shouted.

Chuck grimaced as he pressed the pedal down a bit harder, increasing their speed a couple of miles per hour. "Should we be concerned about the nuclear warhead? I assume jostling it around like this isn't exactly safe."

Jaden clutched the warhead to his chest. "Don't worry about the unlikely possibility of the warhead exploding. Worry about the very real possibility that the Twisted are going to catch us and rip out our throats."

Alex got out of her seat and turned toward the back of the truck. "The rest of you, get ready. It's almost time to engage. Felix and Ed, your job is to pick off as many of them as you can before they get to us. Jaden, Frank, and Owl, get ready, you'll have to take out any that get close. Questions?" She paused long enough to ensure there were none. "Good. Let's light these bastards up."

She moved toward the back of the truck with Ed and Felix. The small, slotted window wasn't big enough. In order to give all three of them access to shoot, they had to throw one of the doors open. It banged and rattled against the side of the transport. Alex raised her rifle and looked through the scope at one of the charging Twisted. For a moment, she wondered whose face might be hiding under that mask. She was familiar with enough of the badges that there was a good chance she knew the Twisted's name. But she quickly pushed the thought away. These were the enemy, acting under Maryana's complete control. If they wanted a chance at stopping *New Haven*, there was no time for sentimentality. Alex took aim again, trying to account for the jostling of the truck, and fired. The Twisted was knocked backward, a bullet through his head.

She lowered her rifle and took stock of the situation. Ed had dropped a Twisted, but Felix had missed his shot, hitting his target in the stomach. The creature still sprinted forward, a hand over its wound. Alex raised her rifle and finished him off.

"Guys, we've got some rough road ahead!" Chuck shouted. "I have to slow down a little."

"Wonderful," Ed muttered.

Alex grimaced. She could see a dozen Twisted. They were moving in quickly, taking advantage of the truck's loss of speed. This time it was Alex who missed her mark. The truck hit an unlucky bump, jarring her just as she fired, and her shot went wide. As if in response, the Twisted surged forward with an insane burst of speed. Alex raised her weapon, but Jaden touched her shoulder.

"I got him," he said.

As the Twisted approached the back of the truck, Jaden slid toward it, the warhead held in one hand and his sword in the other. He swung the blade with blinding speed, neatly removing the Twisted's head from its body.

"Nice," Alex said, as Jaden stepped back, giving Felix room to reclaim his position. "Now we just need to—"

Out of nowhere, a Twisted leaped at the back of the transport. Somehow, it must have gotten alongside them. Its leap appeared to be short, but at the last moment, it snaked out one deformed hand and caught Felix's ankle.

Felix let out a grunt of surprise as he fell, dragged from the truck by the Twisted. Frank surged forward, grabbing Felix's hand and holding tight. Felix dangled from the back of the truck, careening wildly from side to side, the Twisted hanging onto his ankle.

Alex dropped her rifle and drew a pistol off of her belt, aiming it with a two-handed grip, but it was no use. Felix was bouncing around too much; there was no way she could hit the Twisted without risking putting a bullet in her teammate. As she watched, the Twisted held fast to Felix's ankle with his right hand and reached up with his left, sinking his talons into Felix's thigh. He pulled himself up a bit, let go of the ankle and sank the claws of his right hand into Felix's stomach.

Felix cried out as the Twisted clawed his way up, digging into his body and using it for leverage. Alex still couldn't get a clean shot, and she cursed in frustration. Her guy was being torn to shreds, and there wasn't anything she could do for him.

Suddenly, something brushed past her, and Owl was

crouched next to Frank, who still clung to Felix's hand. She leaned down at an angle that would have been impossible for Alex and jammed her pistol against the Twisted's head. Then she pulled the trigger. The creature let out a yelp as it fell away from Felix, and its body bounced twice when it hit the broken pavement.

Frank hauled Felix inside, and Alex ran her eyes up and down him, trying to gauge the extent of his injuries. His leg was bleeding badly, but she was more concerned about the lacerations in his stomach.

No sooner had Frank set Felix down than another Twisted leaped at them. This one's jump was not short, and he landed soundly in the truck, shoving Owl roughly aside as he charged at his target.

The warhead, Alex quickly realized. He was going after the warhead in Jaden's hand. Unwilling to fire her pistol in the transport, she started to draw her sword, but the Twisted spun and slammed his hand down on hers, shoving her half-drawn sword back into its scabbard.

Ed charged, wrapping his arms around the Twisted's midsection and knocking it backward, against the side of the truck. The Twisted hissed and delivered a mean backhand, sending Ed onto his ass.

Alex was about to make another attempt at drawing her sword when Frank let out a fierce growl. He lunged forward, hands outstretched, and dug his claws into the Twisted's chest. He pulled them back and struck again, digging at the creature's rib cage with a ferocity Alex had never seen, until he finally sank his claws into the Twisted's heart. Then he tossed the body out the back of the transport.

"Damn, Frank!" Ed said as he got to his feet. "You sure go berserk a lot for a guy who doesn't like to fight."

Frank looked down at his blood-covered talons, an

expression of horror on his face. "That's not me," he said. "Not the real me."

Owl shook her head in awe. "Whoever it was, I hope he sticks around. That wasn't the last of them."

Alex couldn't disagree. She could see more of them in the distance, chasing after the truck, trying to close the gap. "They're getting smart. Attacking from the flanks instead of from the back."

The radio came to life with a burst of static, and then a familiar voice came through it. "I'm almost to your location," George said. "I see you on the road."

Alex marched to the front of the truck and looked through the windshield, scanning the open sky. She spotted the ship a bit to the north. To her relief, it was still pretty high. She snatched the radio off the dash. "George, we've got a lot of Twisted down here. Don't risk getting below five hundred feet until we give you the all clear."

"Listen, we don't have a lot of time," he replied.

"What do you mean?" Alex asked.

"Everything went according to plan, at first," George said. "I led *New Haven* a hundred miles away and landed in the mountains, so they lost track of me. I kept them on the hook as long as I could, cat-and-mousing them, but thirty minutes ago, they started heading south again."

"They're going back to Agartha," Jaden growled.

Alex's mind raced. If *New Haven* made it back to Agartha, the plan wouldn't work. "We have to do this fast. We'll make the hand off. Then you have to cut them off before they get to the city, George." She turned back to the others. "I'm going to stay up here for the moment to see if I can get eyes on any Twisted trying to attack our flanks. Ed, make damn sure no more Twisted get through that door."

"You can count on me, Captain." From the determination in his voice, Alex had no doubt.

Owl pulled the first aid kit from the compartment mounted on the wall of the transport. "I'm going to see what I can do about patching up Felix. Shout if you see any Twisted, and I'll get back in the fight."

For a few minutes, the truck was silent. Up ahead, George's ship was slowing to keep pace with the transport and descending to five hundred feet. From what Alex could see, the road on either side of them was empty. The sound of her own breathing filled her ears as she watched, waiting, knowing the next attack could come at any moment. She felt something wet on her forearm and looked down to see a cut she had no memory of receiving. It could have come from the Twisted in the transport, the fight at the nuclear silo, or even something earlier. She had no idea.

"You holding it together?" Alex asked Chuck.

"So far," he said. "Keeping her as steady as I can."

"You're doing a damn fine job."

He nodded up ahead. "The pavement looks pretty intact up there. If we can make it a bit farther, we should be able to put some distance between—"

Movement on both sides of the road cut him off. Two Twisted on each side of them burst out of the brush, leaping at the transport. There was a loud thump, quickly followed by another as two Twisted landed on the roof.

"They're on top of us!" Ed shouted.

Jaden didn't waste a moment, shoving the warhead into Ed's hands. "Hold this. Owl, come with me."

Ed staggered backward under the sudden weight of the three-hundred-pound weapon. Jaden jumped out of the back, hauling himself onto the roof of the transport with one hand. Owl quickly followed.

From the cab of the truck, all Alex heard was a series of grunts. A Twisted fell off either side of the vehicle.

Alex glanced in the side view mirror and saw that three more Twisted had emerged from the side of the road and were racing toward them. She knew Jaden and Owl could handle them if they tried to go for the roof, but the back door was uncovered at the moment with Ed holding the warhead and Felix injured. She scooped her rifle off the floor of the truck and rolled down the passenger window. Then she slipped her torso through, sitting on the window, her legs still inside the vehicle. The Twisted were far enough away and the pavement was smooth enough that see was able to take careful aim, dropping all three in quick succession. She slipped back inside.

Chuck glanced at her. "We're not going to get a better shot than this, Alex. The road is smooth and clear."

"Roger that," she said, and grabbed the radio. "Come on down, George. It's time to make the transfer."

"On my way," he answered, a somber tone in his voice.

The ship above them quickly dropped down. As it reached thirty feet and matched their speed, the cargo door opened.

Jaden's head appeared, hanging down from the roof at the back of the transport. "Ed, hand me the warhead."

"Gladly," Ed grunted as he struggled to hoist the weapon into Jaden's outstretched hands.

"Alex..." Chuck said, his voice thick with concern.

"I see it." Up ahead, the road was in even worse condition than most of what they'd encountered so far. She leaned her head out of the still-open window. "Jaden, we have to do this now."

"Got it," Jaden shouted back. He shot into the air with a

mighty leap and disappeared into the open cargo door of the ship.

For a long moment, the ship kept pace with them.

"Hold it steady, Chuck," Alex muttered.

The truck hit the rough part of the pavement, and Chuck was forced to slow down. Just as the ship above them started to pull ahead, Jaden jumped out, his arms and legs pinwheeling as he fell through the air. He landed on the roof with a thump.

Alex grabbed the radio. "You're clear, George. Get out of here!"

Ed let out a laugh. "Holy shit, I don't believe it! We did it. The plan worked!"

Jaden's voice was laced with sadness as he climbed back into the vehicle. "We completed the first step. But the hard part still lies ahead."

13

Tankards never struggled to find patrons, but today there was standing room only. The simple bar had always given men and women a place to meet after a hard day's work, a place to laugh and bond with each other. Some looked for love, at least for a night; others drowned their sorrows. Today, however, the bar was filled with somber tension and the low rumble of hushed voices.

Billy, the owner of Tankards, stepped out from the back room. He scanned the bar with his eyes and nodded to the bouncer by the door. "We all clear?" The bouncer opened the door, looked around outside for a moment, and nodded back at Billy. The owner disappeared into his office for a moment and came back with Jessica by his side. The crowd went silent when they saw her.

"Thanks for coming," she said, addressing the crowd. "I know that we're all risking our lives with these meetings. The fact that we're here means that *New Haven*'s will is not broken. As long as we are still willing to fight, we have a chance." She hoped she sounded confident. She felt like her knees were about to buckle.

A voice came from the back. "Do you have a plan?"

This sent a murmur through the crowd.

"Yes, unfortunately I can't share all of the details yet. If any of you are turned, Maryana will get all the information you have. For now, you'll have to trust that we are planning to make our move soon. We are going to kill her; we just have to pick our moment."

"Is she really that bad?" asked a woman near the front. "Ashley seemed okay after she was turned."

Jessica looked the woman in the eyes. "That, I can answer. Maryana is pure evil. Her goal is death and torture. She will try to manipulate us, and she is very good at it. I need you all to see past her lies and make sure that everyone else does, too." She looked at Louie, the bartender. "Is it ready to go?" He gave her a thumbs-up. "I'm going to show you something that isn't going to be easy to watch, but you all need to see it. I tapped into the city video circuit and took this footage from Maryana's last recruitment session."

The monitor over the bar clicked on and footage from the Badges' holding cell began to play. The footage was bad enough, but the audio pumping through the bar's powerful sound system made it even worse. There were plenty of screams and lots of crying, but the most horrific sound was Maryana's laughter as she worked on the citizens she'd captured. Jessica watched the crowd; most averted their eyes from the screen. Some of them appeared to be frozen, unable to look away, despite the expressions of horror on their faces. After two minutes of footage, one of the men in the room ran over to a garbage can and vomited. Jessica gave Louie a signal to cut the video.

The room fell silent. The men and women stared into space, shaky and pale.

Jessica let the silence hang in the air for a few moments

before speaking. "That tape is three hours long. I apologize that you had to see even a few minutes. When Maryana speaks to you, she may seem fun and charming, but that is just part of the torture. She is a monster all the way through. I need you all to see that. I need all of you to make your friends and family see it. The only way we can beat her is together, and the only way we can be united is to see through her lies."

"What can we do?" The question came from a small woman standing off to the side of the bar.

"For now, keep your eyes open and tell everyone you know about the danger we are in. If you see any weakness in Maryana's security, let Louie know. Pass along anything you think may help. Other than that, stay safe and stay hidden. Once Maryana realizes that there is a resistance, things will get ugly, fast." She looked at the crowd and tried to make eye contact with each one of them. "Louie will serve you some drinks. Once you are composed, I want you to leave in small groups, like it's just a normal day at Tankards. I'll call another meeting when I have more information."

Jessica turned and walked to the back room with Billy. The people in the bar tried their best to act normal as they discussed what they had just seen.

"You did great out there." Billy said. "CB would be proud."

He opened a drawer to his desk and pulled out a bottle of brown liquid. He put a glass in front of Jessica.

"No, thanks, I'd better keep a clear head," she said.

Billy pulled the glass back in front of himself and began to pour. "I'm fine with anything that will erase what I just saw." He took a large sip and let out a sigh. "What is the plan? How do we take her out?"

Before she could answer, there was a knock at the door.

Billy frowned as he walked over and opened it a crack. His expression changed to a smile. "Look who's here. Sick of domestic life already?"

He pulled the door open the rest of the way, and Wesley stepped through.

"Not at all, but I'll be damned if I let a vampire rule this city." Wesley glanced at Jessica. "Especially after what she did to CB."

Jessica felt a rush of mixed emotions at the sight of Wesley. On the one hand, having an experienced soldier would make things much easier. On the other, she did not want someone else she cared about to put himself in harm's way. "Are you sure about this, Wesley? Your family…"

"I'm sure," he said quickly. "They're with Vanessa's mom. They're as safe as anyone can be, with Maryana in charge."

Billy shrugged. "I'm not going to turn down your help. Not at a time like this. Jessica here was just about to tell us the plan."

Jessica considered trying to convince Wesley not to help, but Billy was right. They were in no position to turn him down. "We need to get a strong explosive close to Maryana. If we can rig up something small, we can get in range without drawing suspicion, I can handle the rest."

Wesley thought a moment. "Can we get some charges from the GMT's storage?"

"I don't think so. The Twisted are always swarming that area. They don't allow any humans in there, so it would be hard to sneak in. I think I can rig something up with the supplies from other departments, but it won't be easy. I'll need parts from electrical, farming, and communications."

"Assuming we can do all that, how will you get the device past her guards?" Billy asked.

"I'll turn myself in. I can't risk them finding the bomb so

I will need to hide it well. I'm thinking, a small incision in the stomach cavity. I will be the delivery device, but I will need you to detonate it. They will find the detonator if I have it on me."

Billy and Wesley exchanged a surprised glance. Then Billy looked straight into Jessica's eyes. "No. There has to be a better way. I know you will do anything to save this city, but losing you is not an option. *New Haven* will need you after Maryana is gone."

Jessica's voice was hard. "Billy, I don't want to die, but it might be the only way."

"That's right. It *might* be. There may be other ways. Let's figure out how to get an explosive. Then we can work on blowing Maryana to bits. I know you are smart enough to find another way."

Billy reached for the glass on the desk, but before he touched it, it suddenly slid across the desk and shattered on the floor. Other items fell along with it as the room seemed to shift and tilt. Jessica and Wesley grabbed onto the desk to steady themselves.

"What the hell?" Billy said.

"The ship is accelerating fast." Jessica thought for a second. "It must be the GMT. Either they're coming for us, or Maryana is going for them. Either way, I've got something to do."

Jessica grabbed her tablet and pulled up a list of parts. She transferred the information to Billy's device. "I just gave you the list of things I'll need for the bomb. You two get to work. Hopefully the GMT will save us, but we can't count on it."

Before the men could respond, Jessica opened the vent to the duct in the floor of his office and climbed in headfirst. The first few feet of duct work were just wider than her shoulders. As she squeezed through, her body blocked almost all of the light coming from the office. Her heart raced as she squirmed through the dark space. She came to a tee junction and things opened up. After that, it was still tight, but she had enough room to crawl on her hands and knees.

She traveled as quickly as she could without making much noise. The image of a Twisted claw tearing through the ductwork and grasping her neck flashed in her mind. She tried to stay focused on the task. If the Twisted did find her, she knew that she couldn't fight them off, so she decided not to worry about it.

After a few minutes of crawling, she checked the ship's map on her tablet. She crawled to the next junction in the duct and went right. Then she opened a grate and lowered herself into an electrical room.

The hum of the fans cooling the equipment filled the air as she surveyed the large breakers and levers protruding from metal cabinets. She connected her tablet to the control computer and looked up the information that she needed. Standing in front of the circuit breakers, she checked the numbers one more time. She removed two of the breakers and smashed them. Then she climbed back into the ductwork.

The movement of the ship felt more pronounced as she crawled through the ducts. It was moving erratically, nothing like the steady path and gradual changes in speed she was used to. She guessed that they were chasing something.

She crawled through the ductwork as fast as she could, but it was slow going. She worried that the ship would catch up to the craft it was chasing and blow it out of the sky. The backup circuit for the defensive systems was still operational, and if she didn't get to it in time, it might mean the death of her friends.

She came to the next vent covering and checked her tablet. She was a long way from the other electrical room, and she needed to move faster. She listened for a few seconds and when she didn't hear anyone in the hallway beneath her, she opened the vent and dropped to the floor. Thankfully, the hall was empty.

Jessica ran down the corridor and turned left at the first junction, nearly careening into two coverall-clad men standing in the middle of the hall. Both men brought their hands up in a defensive position, clearly startled. The three stood motionless for a moment. Then one of the workers said, "Jessica? What are you doing here?"

She recognized his face but couldn't remember the man's name. "I'm in a rush. You know, life and death stuff."

He stepped aside and nodded at her. "Don't let me slow you down."

Jessica breathed a sigh of relief and continued on her way. As long as she didn't run into Twisted, she should be able to shut down the ship's defenses in time.

MARYANA LEANED BACK against the flight control room's bulkhead, her arms crossed, contemplating what Jaden and his pet humans were attempting to accomplish. Five hours ago, a ship had left Agartha, heading north, and *New Haven* had followed. The ship had led them deep into the Canadian Rockies before suddenly disappearing among the mountains. Maryana had held position, wondering what Jaden wanted to find in such a remote location. The ship had appeared back on radar a half hour later, and they'd given chase until it once again disappeared. The cycle repeated itself three times before Maryana realized the truth.

She'd been duped, and Maryana hated being duped. The little ship that had led her away from Agartha had been a distraction, and she'd fallen for it. Worse yet, she was out of radio range with her Twisted on the ground, so she had no idea what Jaden had been distracting her from.

She'd immediately changed course and headed back toward Agartha.

And now, a few hundred miles from the city under the mountain, the small, speedy ship had once again appeared on radar. Whatever its game, Maryana was done playing. She wanted that ship out of her sky.

"How long until we can fire?" she asked the room.

Councilman Horace squinted his strange, Twisted eyes at a monitor. "Less than two minutes."

"You have ninety seconds to fire or I'm pulling off your left ear." Maryana had to admit, Horace was proving to be quite competent. Since the City Council wasn't doing too much actual counseling since her takeover, she'd sent Horace back to his former role as head pilot. She wanted the best man behind the yoke, and he was it.

Yet, despite the competence of her pilot and the smoothness with which her plan was operating thus far, the spark she'd felt a few days ago was already starting to fade. It was fun to torture the people, but even that joy was fleeting. She'd hoped the people of *New Haven* would prove to be a unique challenge. After all, weren't these the hardened descendants of the last survivors of her infestation? They'd spent a century-and-a-half living in the sky, surviving against all odds. But they'd disappointed her, proving to be just as weak and easily cowed as the people of the twenty-first century. It was a shame.

Still, she was trying to look on the sunny side. She ruled over a flying city. That wasn't all bad. And there was the hint of an intriguing possibility on the horizon. In every torture session, every meeting about possible threats with her Twisted, there was one name that kept coming up. The light of hope sparked in the citizen's eyes when they said the name, even in the direst circumstances.

Captain Alexandria Goddard of the Ground Mission Team.

The people believed that Alex would save them.

Maryana had met Alex Goddard. She'd even driven a knife into her shoulder. The woman had seemed spirited, but she hadn't struck Maryana as extraordinary. Perhaps the people just needed a hero, and in this de-populated future, this woman was the closest thing to it. Or maybe there was more to Goddard than Maryana had seen in their brief encounter. Either way, she looked forward to facing the woman again. She looked forward to breaking her spirit, to forcing her to beg for her life. Preferably in front of the entire city. There was something truly wonderful about forcing a large group of people to see the fallibility of their heroes. It killed a tiny little piece of their souls.

The sound of a beep from the radarman's station roused her from her thoughts.

Horace turned to her. "We're ready to fire."

She frowned at him. "Then why are we talking about it? The clock is still running on the ear thing."

Horace turned to the young woman at the weapons station. "Fire! Now!"

She hit a quick sequence of keys. Maryana stared out the large window at the tiny ship to the south. It was far enough away that she couldn't see any details, but close enough that she could watch it explode. She waited for a long moment, but nothing happened.

"Councilman Horace, please don't tell me we missed," she said, her eyes still fixed on the black speck in the distance.

"No, ma'am. I mean, the weapons didn't fire." He turned back toward the young woman. "Try again!"

The woman pressed the keys, then shook her head. "I don't understand. The weapons aren't responding.

All eyes on the bridge were fixed on Maryana now, watching her in terrified silence.

To her own surprise, she didn't feel any anger. In fact, she was intrigued. She tilted her head. Was it possible there'd been some sort of sabotage? Were the people of *New Haven* showing some backbone after all? "Isn't that interesting." She crossed the distance between herself and Horace in an instant. "I am going to take that ear, though. Can't go around breaking promises in front of the crew."

She grabbed his left ear and tugged it hard, ripping it off in one clean piece. He cried out in pain and surprise, his hand going to the wound.

"Oh, my God!" he shouted. "Oh, my God!"

"Shut up!" Maryana snapped. He instantly fell silent. "Can someone get Engineering on the radio, please?"

She waited in silence as Engineering looked into the problem. Horace crouched in the corner, his hand over his ruined ear, clearly in pain, but unable to scream due to his master's order. Idly, she wondered if the ear would grow back. There was still so much she didn't know about these Twisted bodies.

Finally, the man at the radio turned to her. "Engineering says some circuits were destroyed. Whoever did it knew what they were doing. They destroyed specific circuits that powered the primary and backup weapons, but none that powered any essential systems."

"Uh-huh." In the distance, she saw that speck of a ship, still floating there, taunting her. "How long to get it repaired?"

There was a long pause as the radioman checked with engineering. "It's going to take a couple of hours, minimum. It will take time to get replacement parts, and they need to work around some delicate systems to fix it."

At that news, Maryana felt her first twinge of real anger. She didn't mind competence from her enemies. In fact, she sort of liked it. A worthy challenge was a rare and beautiful thing. But incompetence from her underlings? That, she could not and would not abide.

She took another look at the ship mocking her in the distance. "Councilman Horace, would you please head down to the Engineering? Oversee their progress and rip out one of their throats every ten minutes until the task is complete."

Horace immediately stood up and headed for the door.

"Wait," she said, and he halted in his tracks. "Tell me, who would have the knowledge, the skills, and the sheer balls to deactivate the weapons, knowing the consequences they'd face when I caught them? Who do you think did this?"

Horace didn't hesitate before answering. "Jessica Bowen."

Maryana didn't know the name, but the fact that he'd given it so quickly meant that this woman was worth talking to, and perhaps turning. It would be nice to have a slave with some intelligence, for once. She missed Stephen a little, and it saddened her that she'd had to sacrifice him at the battle of Agartha, but no one was ever going to accuse

Stephen of being a Brainiac. "Fine. Send some badges to get Jessica Bowen. Have her brought to me at once."

"Yes, ma'am," Councilman Horace answered.

As he left, Maryana scowled. Whatever Jaden was planning, he now had a brief window to pull it off. Maryana glared at the ship in the distance and willed Engineering to hurry.

14

"THE CITY'S OVER THE PLAINS," George said through the radio.

The sky was a perfect powder blue over Montana. Alex squinted toward the horizon, trying in vain to spot *New Haven*. She hoped Brian's plan was sound. If it wasn't, eighty percent of humanity was about to die.

George's voice trembled when he spoke again. "I don't think I can do this."

Alex and Jaden exchange a glance.

"I know you can do this, George," Jaden said into the radio. "You helped make Agartha the city it is. Not because of your talents but because of your love for the people. I have seen you care for those around you and watched you sacrifice for them. I know that we are asking everything of you, but you have the strength to help save us all. Your love is what will give you the strength."

The people in the transport truck waited, the rumble of the engine and the tires along the road the only sounds.

A voice came through the radio a little stronger than before. "I always thought I would die an old man, in my bed in Agartha. Ever since you opened the door for Alex, my life has been pretty messed up. But I'm really glad you saved her, Jaden. I've lived in ways that I never would have under that city. Right now, I'm looking down at the Earth and the view is incredible. It is where we belong. Out here in the open, under the sun. I really wish I could be around when everyone gets to enjoy it."

"Your sacrifice will not be forgotten," Jaden said. "Every person on earth will owe you a great debt."

"Just make sure you finish this. I want you all to promise me that this will mean something."

"I swear it. We will honor you by making the world safe for humans again."

Alex grabbed the handset from Jaden. "You have our word. The GMT will not let you down. I always knew that you were a badass. Today, you are officially part of the GMT."

George gave a small laugh. "I know you're only giving me a spot on the team because I'm about to die, but I'll take it. It's been an honor working by your side." He paused. "*New Haven* is gaining on me. I guess it's now or never. Maybe I'll see you on the other side. Over and out." There was a click as George shut down the radio.

Guilt washed over Jaden. He had caused so much death in his lifetime. Men that he had sent into battle. Men that he had killed. George was just another in a long chain. The death of his vampires had woken something in him. He could no longer think of death as just another part of a necessary equation. George would cease to exist today, and that mattered.

THE DOOR CLOSED with a small thud when Councilman Horace left the room. Maryana looked at the ear she was still holding in her right hand. There was a certain beauty to its pointed tip and its elongated curves. She gently placed the ear on a shelf along the bulkhead, leaning it against one the manuals that stood there. She truly hoped that the Councilman's ear would grow back. If it did, she could make a game out of ripping it off. She envisioned the shelf lined with left ears and smiled.

"The ship is accelerating," the Twisted manning the radar called out. "Should we go after it?"

Maryana suddenly wished that she hadn't sent Horace out of the room. "Yes, we are chasing that ship. If it goes faster, keep up. If you lose the ship, yours will be the next ear on that shelf."

Maryana went back to the window and could just make out a small speck on the horizon. She felt *New Haven* accelerate and marveled at the engineering of the ship. "You know they built this ship because of me. I always bring out the best in people."

She glanced at the monitor and saw that they were keeping pace with the small ship. "How fast can we go in this thing?"

The Twisted at the main controls answered. "The ship can reach eleven-hundred fifty knots. I don't think we have ever tried going that fast before."

"Let's try it now." Maryana could feel the ship continuing to accelerate as the Twisted responded to her order. The speck on the horizon started to grow. She hoped that they would be able to ram into it. A red light turned on in the room and several monitors flashed warning signs. "What's all that about?"

"The ship is diverting power from other systems in order

to accelerate at this rate. Everything except essential systems are going offline to divert power to the engines. Should we slow down?"

"Will it do permanent damage to the ship?"

"No, the systems should come back when we stop the power draw."

"Then keep going." Maryana could now make out some of the details of the distant ship with her vampire eyes.

Suddenly, the small ship slowed down and made a wide half circle, until it was facing *New Haven*. The ship accelerated and gained altitude rapidly. A second later, it shot over the top of *New Haven*, still gaining altitude.

"Do not lose that ship! Get us turned around." Maryana knew that the mass of New Haven would never turn fast enough to catch it. She moved over to a monitor and watched the radar, steadying herself against a desk as the ship strained to turn. The dot on the radar was quickly moving miles away from them.

New Haven was still decelerating hard as it started to turn. She looked around the room and wanted to kill every person there. She restrained herself, since that would help the ship to escape.

Suddenly, the monitor went blank. Maryana looked around the room and saw that *every monitor* was blank, and she felt a brief moment of free fall. The others in the room let out panicked screams. Then the ship stabilized. Two red lights turned on in the room, but everything else stayed dark.

"What is happening? You said we would not do permanent damage." She moved in a flash to the Twisted who was working the controls. She grabbed him by the throat and lifted him off the ground.

"I don't know," he said, in a choked voice. "We lost power."

Maryana tossed him to the ground. "Get the bridge working again. Now." In the distance, she heard a familiar sound. It was screaming.

She grabbed her radio. "What's going on out there?" She let go of the button and waited, but no response came. She pushed the button down again but realized that the channel display was dark. She stared at the dead radio in her hand and then looked around the room at the blank monitors.

Maryana threw the radio across the room and it shattered into a thousand pieces. Her muscles were tensed and her sharp teeth stood out as she snarled. She suddenly understood what Jaden had been up to and what that small ship had done.

She walked over to the window and saw the ground slowly getting closer. "What happens if there is a catastrophic power failure on the ship?"

"I have no idea," the tech said, "but we're losing altitude.

"Thank you for that brilliant observation." Maryana thought for a moment. Yes, they were going down, but they weren't in freefall. She heard the whir of engines. If it had been an EMP, as she suspected, there must be some sort of mechanical backup system providing enough lift to slow their decent.

One of the techs cleared his throat. "Maryana, what do we do?"

Anger flashed inside her at the question, and she sprang forward. She turned her body as she swung her right arm, connecting with the Twisted's head. A loud crack echoed through the room as his jaw imploded and he fell to the floor. She straddled his torso and punched him in the face again and again, her arms moving so fast that they appeared as twin blurs of motion. After a few moments, hits became dull, wet thuds. Nothing remained of his head.

"You're supposed to give me answers, not more question." Maryana stood up, covered in blood and bits of tissue. She pointed to another Twisted. "Take me to Horace. Maybe he has some answers."

The two walked through the building on the way to Engineering. All around them, people were panicking. A man kept pressing the communication button on a blank panel. He yelled out, "Engineering, do you copy? We have total power failure. Engineering, do you copy? We have total power failure." He continued to repeat himself into the dead panel as they walked by.

Outside the building, the electric carts that moved through the city had all stopped. Some drivers still sat in them, trying to figure out what was wrong with the vehicles. People were coming out of buildings to see if power and devices were working in other parts of the city. Some people were crying, others were screaming. The city was in chaos.

Maryana stopped and focused her will. She mentally commanded the Twisted to come to her. She needed her army in one place in order to contain this mess.

15

Alex watched in shocked amazement as *New Haven* fell. They were far enough away—nearly a hundred miles by Jaden's estimation—that the details of the ship weren't clear. It was just a speck in the distant sky. But even that was incredible to see.

After the distant explosion to the north, the flash of light faded and the tiny dot that was *New Haven* began to fall, losing what had to be a thousand feet or more in a few seconds. Then, as the emergency backup systems activated, the ship slowed from freefall to a controlled descent. By the time it disappeared from view, it seemed to be floating.

The team stared in silence for a long while after the city-ship was no longer visible. Every one of them knew they were watching history. The world had changed forever. For Alex, it felt like the ground under her feet had become unstable. All her life, there had been two constants—the surface was dangerous, and *New Haven* glided safely through the clouds. Now, both of those truths had been flipped upside down. The Ferals no longer ruled the surface, and *New Haven*'s hull was now resting on the dirt.

Though she'd helped conceive the plan, her mind struggled to accept the new reality. It was as if the oceans had suddenly dried up, or the clouds had suddenly begun sprouting trees. The world had once again shifted, in her mind perhaps even more than when she'd released the virus. Humans walking around on the surface was going to be the new normal.

But the surface wasn't safe yet, was it? It had been their plan to force *New Haven* down and take away Maryana's permanent high-ground advantage, but now she would be on the surface, and likely angry. She'd come at humanity hard now; at least, that was Jaden's prediction. They'd have to stop her quickly, but the plan for how to do that was still a bit shaky.

"I can feel the Twisted leaving," Jaden said. "They're heading in the direction of where the ship went down. I imagine they're drawn by the instinct to protect their master. We're safe, for the moment."

"Well, that's something," Ed said, his voice distant.

Jaden looked the team over, realizing for the first time how this was hitting them. "I know it must seem unnatural to have *New Haven* on the ground, but it is not. Believe me, there were plenty who doubted a ship could stay in the air perpetually, without landing to refuel. The woman who proposed the idea almost got laughed out of the room."

Alex turned to him, surprised. "You were there when they came up with the idea for *New Haven*?"

"Oh, yes," he replied. He smiled thinly. "Remember what I told you about *New Haven* when we met?"

Of course, she remembered. It had blown her mind and provided her with her first real insight into Jaden's age and the scope of his knowledge. "You told me that you helped build it. I asked you if that meant you were physically holding a wrench. You refused to answer, saying you didn't trust me enough yet."

He chuckled. "Now that you've obliterated my kind, I suppose I trust you enough. I didn't physically build the ship, but I was heavily involved in the planning. The project probably never would have gotten off the ground, had humanity not been so desperate, but it was becoming more and more clear that the infestation was not going to be easily stopped. Perhaps I'll tell you the full tale someday as we sit beside a fireplace, toasting our victory as Maryana's ashes scatter on the wind."

"I'd like that," Alex said. Her eyes were still fixed on the distant horizon where *New Haven* had disappeared.

"For now, I'll just say the woman who came up with the idea for *New Haven* and oversaw its development was brilliant. And ultimately flawed."

"Just like the rest of us, then," Owl said. "Minus the brilliant part."

Ed slapped Chuck on the arm. "Remember our first mission? You and Patrick were so scared, leaving *New Haven* for the first time and heading for the surface."

Chuck took a step back. "Me and Patrick, huh?"

Ed's face reddened. "The point is, I felt like I was headed to an alien planet. I had no idea what to expect. Sure, I'd seen the pictures and the video snippets, but I didn't know how the earth would feel under my feet. How it would smell. Every citizen of *New Haven* is going through that right now."

"They'll adapt," Frank said, in a soft voice. "Just like my friends and I did. When it first took off. A life in the sky seemed as impossible and unnatural as a life on the surface does to them now."

Alex tilted her head in surprise. Somehow, she'd

forgotten that Frank had been there from the start. He'd been one of the original passengers of *New Haven*. "What was it like that first day?"

He stared off into the distance for a long moment before answering. "Terrifying. Keep in mind that we were refugees at that point. We'd watched our homes be torn apart, and we'd fled our cities as the infestation spread. Every person aboard that ship had lost almost everyone they knew to vampires."

The scene came alive in Alex's mind as she imagined a crowd of forty-thousand people herding aboard this giant ship, trusting their fates to a technology they did not understand. She suddenly couldn't believe she'd never asked Frank more questions about that time. "How'd they decide who got to go?"

"It was merit-based. They selected those with the skills necessary to maintain and fly the ship, and those with expertise to keep fighting the vampires. They also brought the families of those people." He paused, remembering. "Keep in mind, this was the end of the war. It's not like there were millions of people roaming around. Nearly everyone was dead. Still, decisions had to be made. There wasn't room for everyone."

Ed's eyes narrowed. "How'd you make the cut?"

Alex shot him a look.

"What? The guy said he was a janitor. Why'd they take you along?"

Frank's eyes were fixed on some distant point in the sky. His voice was so dry when he spoke that he could only be hiding a deeply buried emotion, one he didn't dare risking letting loose. "My wife. She was a nuclear engineer, and a damn good one. She secured our place on the ship. Only, it didn't turn out that way. The infestation reached us two days before we were scheduled to leave for the launch site. The vampires poured over our small city like a living wave of destruction. By some miracle, I made it out. She did not. Retreating and leaving her body behind was the toughest thing I've ever done."

"That's why you volunteered," Owl said softly. "That's why you let them inject you with vampire blood."

Frank nodded. "They let me keep my place on *New Haven*, even though I didn't really deserve it. So, I made the only contribution I could think to make. My wife died in the service of humanity. I was honored to do the same." He glared toward the area where *New Haven* had fallen. "But now, the woman who caused all if it is there. I can wrap my fingers around her neck and make her pay. I didn't let myself believe it would be possible until now. Maryana is on the ground. We can kill her."

A gentle breeze blew from the west, caressing Alex's face and drying the tears that had gathered in her eyes. "Then that's what we do."

"Hell, yeah," Ed said. "Enough running. Let's get surgical, and remove that tumor once and for all."

So far, their desperate plan was working perfectly. George had led Maryana away from *New Haven* long enough for them to get the warhead. He'd retrieved the warhead and flown high into the atmosphere to detonate the nuclear weapon. The resulting EMP had brought *New Haven* down. Agartha had been built to withstand nuclear war, and was therefore shielded. While all the electronics aboard the transport were fried, the vehicle itself was running perfectly.

There was only one thing that they hadn't foreseen—the Twisted pursuing and attacking them.

Felix leaned forward out of the shadows in the back of

the transport where he'd been resting, and a groan escaped his lips. Owl had attempted to bandage his injuries, but the blood was already seeping through.

Alex leaned toward Owl. "How bad is it?"

"He needs medical attention," she replied. "I don't think he'll die, but I might be wrong. He definitely needs a proper doctor."

Felix grunted again as he tried to sit up. "I'm good. I can play hurt."

Ed put a hand on Felix's shoulder "I knew you were true GMT material."

Alex bit her lip. It was an impossible choice. Continue with the admittedly shaky plan to charge into *New Haven* and attempt to take out Maryana, or head back to Agartha and get help for Felix. She turned to Jaden. "What do you think?"

Jaden started off toward the north. "She's going to be expecting an attack right now. I believe rushing in would be a mistake. The only way we're going to take her out is to be methodical. We have to keep her guessing." He nodded toward the transport. "I say we get him home and regroup."

Alex frowned. It wasn't what she wanted to hear, but Jaden was right. To attack now would be a suicide run. *New Haven* was on the ground, and that wasn't going to change. They would likely only get one shot at attacking *New Haven*, so they needed to plan it carefully and execute it with precision. This was too important to rush. She had the skeleton of a plan in her mind, but there was no flesh on it, yet.

"Okay, we're going with Jaden's approach on this," she said to her team. "Let's load up and get back to Agartha. But don't get comfortable, because we'll be back soon. I intend to keep my promise."

16

Maryana looked up and cursed the clouds overhead. She much preferred standing over them in her flying city; now it felt like they were looking down at her. The clouds strolled across the sky leaving her behind, stuck on the Earth.

An army of Twisted surrounded Maryana at the base of the Hub. If Jaden and his friends tried anything, she'd be ready. She knew that time was essential when a city went into panic mode. She felt strange, trying to control the chaos, instead of causing it.

She pointed to the Twisted to her left. "All of you, go around the city and tell everyone to return to their quarters. Let them know the power will be back on soon. Do not let them gather in numbers. We wouldn't want to have to battle an army of humans and lose our food supply. I'm sure these scared little rats will not try to leave the ship, but make sure they know the penalty for stepping outside the city is death"

The Twisted stood and waited for her next command. "Don't just stand there like a bunch of idiots. Go get the citizens into their homes."

Half of the Twisted army scattered throughout the city

to obey her orders. Maryana cocked a thumb toward the City Council building. "The rest of you need to guard this building. I want five of you standing guard on every floor. Everyone else can set up a perimeter defense outside. Let me know as soon as you see enemy forces. Horace, you come with me, and bring me the head engineer."

Councilman Horace walked into the building by her side. They went up the stairs to the old Council room. Maryana turned to Horace. "Something looks different about you. Did you get a haircut?"

He turned his head, revealing the dried blood flaked on the side of his jaw and neck. "You ripped my ear off."

Maryana laughed. "I sure did. You're a good kid and I really want to keep you around, but proper discipline is important."

Horace looked at her with cold eyes. "The GMT did this. They are coming for you, and they will kill you."

She threw an arm around his shoulder. "You're just saying that because you're mad about the ear thing. I promise that death will come, but it will not be mine. The GMT might try to kill me, but they will just go on top of the mountain of bodies that have tried before. For now, I would like to get my city back up in the air. I'm not done playing with this toy yet. How do I get this thing flying again?"

"I don't know that it is possible. The EMP wiped out all of our computer systems. Rebuilding them will require parts that we don't have. I don't know if we have the knowledge to fix the systems without the information on them."

"The ship flew down to the ground safely. There must be a way to keep it flying."

"The emergency landing system is a series of old mechanical switches. The system is incredibly basic. It drew off the power reserves from the batteries and turned the motors enough to get us to the ground in one piece. Flying the ship requires power regulation computers, navigation computers, the nuclear power plant, and a hundred other systems running in tandem. I don't think we have the materials or knowledge to fix it."

"I'm losing faith in you, Horace. What about that girl you mentioned, Jessica? Can she fix this?"

"She is the best we have. If anyone can fix the system, it's her." Horace looked down as he spoke.

Two Twisted entered the room, each hauling a human behind them. One of the humans was an older woman with silver streaks through her hair. The other was a balding man in his forties. The man flinched and turned away from Maryana when he spotted her.

Maryana turned to them. "Who are these two?"

One of the Twisted answered. "They run the mechanical and electrical divisions."

"Great. We are going to start small. I want you to get the basic systems working again. Let's start with some communications. I want to be able to tell all of these people what to do. I need you to work really hard on this, so those fragile human bodies are going to have to go."

Maryana charged forward and grabbed the man before he could react. She gripped one arm and pushed his head to the side with her other hand. He tried to scream but with his head pulled back and the pressure on his neck, only a whimper escaped his throat. The woman tried to break free from the Twisted that held her, but she was no match for the strength of her captor. Maryana drank deeply from them both.

Jessica raced back toward Tankards. She ran through the mechanical level, hoping that she wouldn't bump into a Twisted. She heard the chaos in the city above and figured that they were busy with other problems. When she reached the area under Tankards, she climbed back into the ductwork.

She opened the vent and entered the office. Billy watched her climb up and he locked the door to the room. He held a small flashlight that cast shadows across the room. "What the hell is going on? Did you do this?"

Jessica brushed old dust from the ducts off her arms and legs. "No. I think the GMT did something that killed our power. I just shut down our defensive systems. That shouldn't have caused any of this. Where's Wesley"

"He went to check on his family." Billy pointed the light in Jessica's direction. He tried to hide the tremble in his gruff voice as he spoke. "What is happening to the ship? Something feels very strange."

Jessica realized how foreign the concept of being still was new to everyone on *New Haven*. "We're on the ground. *New Haven* made an emergency landing."

Billy sat down slowly in his chair. "Holy shit." The words came out in a whisper. "What do we do now?"

"I'm sure that the GMT will be coming for Maryana. We need to get as many people as we can out of the city. I have a feeling that this place is about to become a war zone."

Billy still had the bottle of liquor open on his desk. He slowly filled a glass. Then he emptied it in one long gulp. "You know if we get caught leaving the city, we will all be killed. Or worse."

"Yeah. But if we can get enough people to leave, it will spread her forces thin and make it harder to defend the city.

I think we need to work quickly, before any systems are restored."

"Okay, the bar is still full. We can start to organize everyone here."

Jessica walked toward the door to the bar area, and Billy followed.

"Wait a sec," Billy said. Jessica paused with her hand on the door knob as Billy went back to his desk and took one more quick drink, this time straight from the bottle. "Okay, let's do this."

The two entered the crowded bar. When the people saw Jessica, an explosion of questions came from the group.

Jessica raised her hand and everyone went silent. "I know this is scary, but the GMT is on their way. We all need to pull together and help them."

MARYANA STARED out the window of the Council chambers. The Twisted were doing a good job of shepherding the people back to their quarters. She wondered how the human race had ever lasted this long. She was unorganized and off balance from the unexpected loss of all systems on the ship. If the forty thousand people aboard *New Haven* attacked right now, they would probably kill her and her Twisted. Instead, they cowered and did as they were told.

Not all the humans were so soft. She really wanted to get her hands on the group that had taken down her ship. She doubted that they would put up much of a fight, but Jaden was with them. He was the real danger. After he was gone, humanity would fall in line. She wanted to check with her team in the field, but there were no working radios. She hoped that they had already killed the GMT and were bringing Jaden's head to her.

Then she saw her field team marching through the streets of the city toward her building, their hands empty of even a single head. Their numbers were considerably less than when they'd left. The leader of the team entered the council room a few moments later.

Maryana smiled. "You can put Jaden's head on the table now, please."

"I don't have his head. We followed him to a nuclear silo and he was able to get a warhead. We were still engaging him when we saw *New Haven* descending. I brought the team back to defend you."

Maryana lost control of the rage inside. She moved across the room and put her hands around the leader's neck, squeezing hard enough to hear the bones in his neck grind together. "I won't need you to defend me if you kill Jaden. Are they coming here now?"

He tried to answer, but nothing came through his windpipe. She released her grip enough to allow him to answer. "No. I believe that they're going back to Agartha."

"How fast are they moving? Can we catch up to them?"

The Twisted didn't want to answer the question, but his mouth moved and the words came. "If we hurry, we should be able to catch them."

"Excellent." She released her hold. "Gather your men. I intend to finish this."

17

Brian stood up from the chair where he'd been sitting for the past four hours and stretched. His back let out a loud crack, and he nearly groaned with pleasure. He really needed to set an alarm to remind himself to move once in a while.

While Agartha itself was protected from EMPs, the outside equipment was another matter. Since they'd known the EMP was coming, they'd had time to blanket a good portion of the turrets with Faraday netting, protecting it from the pulse. It hadn't been feasible to cover everything though. They'd lost most of their exterior cameras and a few turrets. There was plenty of work to be done, and Cynthia wanted everything back on line as quickly as possible.

Still, four hours was probably long enough to spend sitting at a desk. He walked over to a nearby station where a lab tech was furiously typing. Brian bent down and squinted at the screen.

"Working on the defense turrets?" Brian asked.

"Uh-huh," the tech replied. "We have to recalibrate the sensors for a shorter proximity. That way we can keep them activated until Jaden and the GMT get close. Their radios won't be working because of the EMP, but we should be able to spot them on the cameras as they approach on the road. Then we can deactivate the turrets."

Brian nodded. "The turrets really are a brilliant design. The automation is impressive. Even if it did shoot my away ship out of the sky a couple of years back."

"Thanks," Stephanie said, popping up over the cubicle wall. Her hair was pulled back in a ponytail, and a single curl had fallen loose. It hung over her right cheek, bouncing as she moved.

Brian raised an eyebrow. "You created the automation?"

"Uh-huh," she answered. "Well, I designed it. George's team built it. So, I guess I owe you an away ship."

Brian thought of the experimental ship George had flown out of Agartha to lure Maryana away. Both George and his ship would be destroyed by now. "Actually, I think you've paid us back for that one."

"Right. The experimental ship." She paused a moment. "It seemed like you were thinking about something, just now. Are you bummed that you didn't get to go on the mission with your friends?"

He let out a laugh and walked over to her cubicle, leaving the other lab tech to his work. "No. I have a long history of waiting for the GMT. It's kind of in my job description. At first, I used to get anxious, wondering if they were okay. Hoping all my equipment worked properly. Stuff like that. But I got used to it over the years. I guess by now, I've accepted that my worrying isn't going to help anyone, so why do it?"

"Wow, that's a mature attitude."

"Like I said, it didn't come naturally," he replied, with a shrug. "Besides, I've seen enough missions to last a lifetime.

Trust me when I tell you, staying back in the safety of the city beats the pressure of a GMT mission any day."

Stephanie tilted her head in surprise. "You went on missions?"

"A few," he said. "Well, one really, but it was a doozy."

"Yeah? Tell me about it." She leaned back against her desk and crossed her arms, a slight smile on her face.

Brian hesitated. Normally, he'd say it wasn't that big of a deal and try to move on from the conversation as quickly as possible, but he liked this woman. She was smart, cute, and seemed to like him back. If she was interested in a story, he was going to tell it. "I was part of the GMT mission to the island of Puerto Rico. The one that recovered the virus. It was intense. There were so many Ferals, not to mention Jaden and his team of scouts. We slept on oil rigs off the coast, terrified that we'd get overrun by Ferals at any moment. When we finally found the records and raw materials, I was able to produce the virus while the GMT held off Jaden and his vamps..."

He trailed off when he noticed her face. Somewhere during the course of his story, her smile had faded. Of course it had. He'd just confessed to creating the virus that killed the heroic vampires of Agartha.

"Huh," she said. "I guess I should have figured it was you. I just never put two and two together."

He swallowed hard. "I'm sorry, I shouldn't have... I mean, we had good reasons, so I'm not sorry I did it, but... talking about it like it was some big, heroic deed..." He silently cursed himself for sounding like such an idiot. He was back to the same old stammering nerd he'd been for most of his life.

"No, I understand that you had reasons. You killed the

Ferals. But the vampires here were different, and it sucks that they had to die. Especially like that."

"It does suck," Brian agreed. "I hope you don't think less of me. If you want to talk about it—"

"No," she quickly answered. "I want to talk to you. Just not about that. Not now. I'm the kind of person who needs time to process before I'm sure exactly how I feel about things."

Brian was the exact same way, though he'd never put it into words. "I get it. I'll lay off. If you decide you want to talk about it, or if you have questions..."

"Yeah. For now, how about we stick to talking about work."

"Okay." Brian tried hard not to feel deflated, but it seemed like a door between them had just closed. It felt so stupid, being worried about something like that now, when all of *New Haven* was under the control of a tyrant. There were far more important things on which he should be focusing. But he couldn't help it. He'd dated dozens of women over the past couple of years, but he'd never clicked with someone as naturally as he had with Stephanie. He just hoped that she could look past the part he'd played in the annihilation of a species. "So, let's talk about work."

She stared at him for a long moment, wanting to say something. Then she looked away, toward her monitor. "The downside of working in a city where vampires have kept everything running smoothly for a century and a half is that sometimes, you have to do a little digging to figure out what problems need solving."

"I might have one." Brian felt himself relaxing a bit as he spoke. He was far more comfortable talking about work than his own feelings. "I wonder if there's a way to extend how far our radio communications reach. If the GMT starts going out on missions from here, it would be nice to stay in touch when they're farther away. We'd likely need to set up a physical relay to boost the signal."

Stephanie thought for a long moment before answering. Then she looked up, a sparkle in her eyes. "There are copper connects to all the defense turrets outside the city. Theoretically, we could use each one of them as receivers. It would take some doing, but…"

Brian's face broke out in a wide smile. "What are we waiting for? Let's give it a try!"

18

Screws and small parts littered the desk in Billy's office. The small wires inside of the radio handsets made Jessica feel comfortable. She knew how the components would respond to her adjustments. She needed something predictable after so much time dealing with people. The last meeting had not gone as she'd planned. Most of the people wanted to hunker down and wait for the GMT to come in and save them. Some thought leaving was a good idea, but they wanted to gather supplies and make plans. She could tell that those people were really just afraid to act. There were some that were willing to risk their lives to draw Twisted away from the city.

The radios did exactly what Jessica wanted. She removed the processor that connected them to *New Haven's* network. She didn't have a soldering iron, but without power, it would not have worked, anyway. Instead, she used copper wires taken from a clock in the office and glued them in place. She hoped that the connection would hold. Once the fried components were bypassed, she reassembled the handsets. She held her breath as she pressed down the button and said the word testing. An echo of her voice came from the three other sets. She couldn't help but smile. Thanks to the EMP, she was probably the only person in *New Haven* with working radios. Finally, they had a small leg up on Maryana.

"You sure are handy to have around." Billy said.

"Thanks. This is a rush job, so these may break if you drop them or shake them too hard. They're also stuck on one channel, so if we are compromised, we'll have to stop using them."

"I'd say that is still pretty good, for a quick job in a dark office." He grabbed three of the radios. "I'll get these to the other guys."

"Good. Tell them not to use the radio until they have their group ready. I don't want to risk the Twisted picking up our signal or realizing that we have working radios."

"Got it."

Jessica grabbed her radio and opened the vent to the duct.

"You are all business," Billy said. He crossed the room and gave Jessica a quick hug. "Be safe out there."

The physical contact caught her off guard. She stopped planning for a moment and looked at him. She could tell that he was afraid. She didn't know whether it was for her safety or his own, but his eyes looked like those of a lost child trying not to panic. "You stay safe, too. This is dangerous, but I'm going to give every breath I have to make sure the people of this city survive. I know you have a big heart; I need you to use it. Help me get as many people out of the city as you can." With that, she climbed into the duct.

As she crawled down to the level below the street, she thought about how much simpler mechanical systems were than people. Then she thought about the little hug Billy gave her, and the deep embraces she'd had with CB, and the time she'd spent with Alex and the GMT. Maybe the messy, complex people that made her life harder were also what made it worth living.

THE HOUSING COMPLEX that Jessica called home held over one thousand people. After rushing through the hallways knocking on doors, she had gathered forty people who were willing to leave the city. She'd instructed them to gather any food they had and fill the rest of their packs with extra clothes. She knew that they would not be able to survive long on the surface. None of them had any idea how to live outside of the city they had known their entire lives. She just wanted to distract Maryana's forces long enough to give the GMT a fighting chance.

The group gathered on the lowest level of the building. Jessica looked them over. They were all young men and women, mostly people in their twenties, who still had a sense of immortality that older people lacked. Jessica was glad that there were no families with children in the group. It would slow them down, and she didn't like the idea of risking the life of a child.

The group stood in nervous silence. They had makeshift weapons that ranged from wrenches to kitchen knives. Jessica knew that none of that would matter if the Twisted caught up to them, but it gave the group a sense of security.

She spoke into her radio. "Group one, ready."

The replies came a few moments apart.

"Group two, ready."

"Group three, ready."

"Group four, ready."

"Move quickly and quietly. Stay safe." Jessica clipped the radio to her belt and grabbed a flashlight that was attached to her pack.

She led the group out of the building through the mechanical room in the basement. They went through the corridors under the streets of the city, following the beam of Jessica's flashlight, and holding their breath as they rounded every corner. Jessica knew that if they ran into Twisted in the small spaces of the mechanical corridors, they stood no chance.

After they'd been walking for ten minutes, they found the door they were looking for. A large warning sign read —*Pressure lock will not release if outer door is not engaged.* Jessica took a deep breath and grabbed the large lever on the door. She tried to push it down, but it didn't budge. Finally, with the help of three of the larger men, she pushed the level down, and the latch released with a hiss.

The room beyond the first door was just large enough for all forty people to squeeze inside. Benches lined the walls along with oxygen tanks, masks, and emergency parachutes hanging above them. Once everyone was inside the room, they shut the interior door and turned to the airlock's exterior door.

The door had a small window just above the warning sign. Jessica peered through and saw that they were about thirty feet above the ground. An image flashed through her mind of someone trying to use a parachute at this height and a small smile creased her lips. She enlisted some help again, and a moment later the door to the outside world swung open.

A soft wind blew into the silent room. The air was different than anything the people in the room had ever experienced. It was not the clean and sterile air of a filtered duct system. It was sweet and soft, carrying the dust and pollen of the Wyoming plains. The temperature outside was warmer than it had been in the city, and soft sunlight painted the room.

Jessica opened a compartment next to the door and pulled out a rolled up, fifty-foot rope ladder. She inserted the red eyelets on the end into red clips on the floor. Then she tossed the ladder through the door and watched it unroll. The ladder hit the ground, sending a small cloud of dust into the air.

"Here we go," Jessica muttered. She took hold of the ladder and began to climb. Each step down felt like a dream. When she finally touched her foot to the dirt, she felt the world change.

Jessica knew that they needed to move fast, but it was hard not to be overcome by the moment. As the final member of the group climbed off the ladder, she turned to face them. "We are the first settlers of a new world."

There were a few murmurs as people tried to express their disbelief at what was happening. Jessica had been on the surface before, but for everyone else, this was uncharted territory.

"We need to focus," she continued. "We are going to head east and keep moving until the sun goes down. Let's get as many miles as we can between us and the Twisted. Stay low until we get over that ridge." She pointed to a hill in the distance and started to move.

They had gone about a half mile when one of the women in the middle of the pack screamed. Jessica turned, pulling a knife from her belt. She expected to see a group of Twisted; instead, she spotted a prairie dog sticking its head out from a hole in the ground. Several of the men raised their weapons, ready to fight the small beast.

Jessica couldn't help but chuckle. "The animals that live on the surface are not dangerous, for the most part. If you see a creature smaller than you, don't worry about it. And stay quiet." She turned and continued toward the hill.

They stayed low and moved quickly, but there was little cover on the plain. Small shrubs and grass came up to their knees, but there were few trees. Jessica hoped that they would find better cover once they made it over the ridge. As they reached the top of the hill, she looked back at *New Haven*. The shiny, metal city seemed so out of place on the Earth. She saw a person jump from the side of the ship. She stared for a moment and another person dropped to the ground. No, not people, she realized. Twisted. She counted five of them. Once their feet hit the ground, they started sprinting toward the group.

"Run!" Jessica yelled.

The group immediately took off, running as fast as they could. They started to fan out, hoping that their numbers would keep some of them safe. They never stood a chance. The Twisted were on them before they crested the hill. A few of the humans used their weapons. A woman stabbed a Twisted in the shoulder, but the Twisted barely seemed to notice. He pulled out the blade and grabbed the woman.

One of the Twisted shouted loud enough for everyone to hear. "Stop running, or we will kill you! Surrender, and you live!"

Jessica stopped and turned toward the Twisted. She held her knife out, ready to fight. The rest of the group followed her lead.

"Our orders from Maryana are clear. We are to bring back anyone who tries to escape. But if anyone resists, we are to remove every one of your heads. Please don't make us do that. None of us wants to hurt you, but we can't disobey."

The Twisted grabbed the nearest woman and wrapped an arm around her throat. "Please, I don't want to take her head off."

The veins in the woman's face pulsed. Her head would be torn from her body in a moment. Jessica's heart sank. She'd thought that they would make it farther. She thought that the Twisted would spend days searching for them. She'd even secretly hoped that they would never be found. Instead, they'd made it just over a mile from the ship.

She slowly bent down and placed her knife in the dirt.

19

Alex watched the terrain roll by outside her window. It was odd. In her time with the GMT, she'd seen so much of the world. Jungles. Mountains. Oceans. Deserts. And now, she was stuck in this one area. Was this her existence now? A few hundred miles in any direction, and that was it? Were her days of exploring the strange corners of far-flung continents passed? She hoped they weren't, but she couldn't see how she'd be able to travel again any time soon. They'd just blown up one of the last two ships in a successful attempt to ground the other. It made her wish she'd paid more attention to the facts Owl had shared on every mission. Alex had visited so many places, and she couldn't even remember most of their names.

She sighed and pushed the thoughts away. She wasn't annoyed at her inability to travel. Not really. It was Maryana who was bringing her down. The evil vampire was on the ground, practically within striking distance, and they were driving away from her. And why? To go back to Agartha? To huddle and hide, trying to come up with some perfect plan, while Maryana launched an assault of her own?

The GMT was oddly quiet as they drove, except for the occasional groan of pain from Felix. Alex wondered if they were all experiencing thoughts similar to her own, or if they were all battling unique demons.

The grassy plains continued to roll by for another fifteen minutes before the scenery started to change. The gaps between man-made structures lessened, until she saw the tell-tale signs of a city up ahead. She remembered remains of a sign they'd seen when passing through here the first time. There'd been just enough of it left to make out a single word printed in large letters—Cheyenne.

Alex sat up a bit straighter. She remembered a spot near the downtown of Cheyenne. An overpass with a ten-story building next to it. She'd thought at the time it would be the perfect place to defend, assuming you had control of the building and the high ground.

She waited until they'd reached the spot she'd been thinking of, then she tapped Chuck on the arm. "Stop the truck."

Chuck shot her a surprised look, but he did as she ordered. The passengers in the back of the transport heard the order, too, and they quickly moved to the windows, weapons in hand, looking for the source of the danger.

"Relax," she told them. "We're not under attack. We're going to be the ones doing the attacking." She climbed out the passenger door, walked to the back of the transport, and pulled the doors open. "Come on. Everybody out."

The GMT quickly loaded out, but Jaden stayed in the transport, a frown on his face. "What are you talking about? Who are we supposed to be attacking?"

Alex set her pack on the ground and began digging through it. "Maryana. Or at least her Twisted. I'm not positive she'll come, herself. Hey Chuck, let's catalog the explosives you have on hand. We're going to need a lot of them."

Jaden grimaced, displeased to have been dismissed so quickly. He jumped out of the transport and marched toward Alex. "Do you still not get it? If you think you can predict what Maryana is going to do, you've already lost. She's not like other opponents."

Alex closed her pack and stood up, her hands on her hips. She gave Jaden a long, appraising look. "You keep saying that, and maybe it's partly true. But you want to know what I think? I think Maryana has gotten into your head. She's psyched you out."

Jaden's eyes widened and he took a small step back. "Are you kidding me right now? This woman brought down civilization, and you're saying I'm overestimating her?"

"No, that's not what I mean." She paused, choosing her words carefully before speaking again. She knew that Jaden prided himself on his mental toughness, and rightly so. But he seemed to have a blind spot when it came to Maryana. "Look, I get that she's crazy. I've seen her handiwork myself, not to mention the stories you told me. But I've also seen something else. When she has a goal, she goes after it hard. If we know what she wants, we can predict at least some of her moves."

"Like we did during the fight in Agartha?" Jaden countered. "We fought and nearly died, and it was just a big distraction."

"That's exactly what I mean. Attacking Agartha to keep us busy while she took *New Haven* wasn't an insane move. It was a brilliant one. She wanted to enslave humanity, right? And in taking *New Haven*, she enslaved the vast majority of them."

Jaden glared at her, nonplussed, but not disagreeing.

"All we have to do," Alex continued, "is figure out what she wants now. She has one more goal. One mountain left to climb."

"Agartha," Jaden said, with a growl. "She wants to take Agartha."

Alex shook her head slowly. "As far as she's concerned, Agartha is easy pickings. She can take it anytime she wants, and she will, eventually. But it's not urgent."

"Then what's her goal?"

"You."

He stared at her for a long moment, his eyes filled with doubt.

Alex took a step toward him. "Think about it. You said she was obsessed with you. She chased you around the globe for a decade, trying to get you to change her into a vampire. And I've heard the way she talks about you. She's still just as obsessed. You're her last real enemy left. Taking you out would be like finishing what she started so many years ago."

He scratched at his chin. "Okay, say you're right. That doesn't mean she's going to attack us now. *New Haven* just went down. She has bigger things to worry about."

"There is nothing bigger. Not to her. You're isolated, with just a few soldiers on an abandoned road. How could she possibly resist taking a shot at you now, rather than letting you go back to your well-fortified city under the mountain?" She paused, gauging his reaction. "Jaden, I'm right on this. Trust me."

"And what about Felix?"

"I'm good," Felix groaned.

Owl rolled her eyes. "He's not exactly good. He needs medical attention. But the bleeding has slowed. I think he's out of danger, for the moment.

"What do you say, Jaden?" Alex asked.

Jaden looked into her eyes, taking her measure. He nodded. "What's the plan?"

They went to work immediately. Felix and Frank drove the transport and parked it out of sight, a block away. Far enough that the enemy wouldn't see it immediately, but close enough that they could make a hasty retreat, if needed. They'd decided that Frank would stay with Felix, to defend him if needed. Chuck, Alex, and Ed went to work planting explosives. They rigged the pillars holding up the overpass first, carefully placing the explosives at stress points. Then they headed for the nearby ten-story building, planting enough explosives to collapse the structure.

When they'd finished, Chuck brushed the dust off his hands and smiled at Alex. "Not bad. Now all we have to do is lure them inside."

Alex chuckled. "Baiting a bunch of vampires into a fight? That, I can do."

Jaden appeared in the doorway, his approaching footsteps making no sound on the ancient, creaky floor. "I found us a way out."

"Do tell," Alex said.

"Empty elevator shaft. If we have some ropes ready, we can drop down to the basement level and exit through the drainage system."

"Ah, moving through the drainage system under a city with Jaden, and fighting for our lives," Ed said wistfully. "Just like old times. If only Firefly were here."

"Indeed," Alex said, a hint of sadness in her voice. Of all the friends and brothers-in-arms she'd lost, she found herself thinking about Firefly the most. Partly because his death was the most recent, and partly because of the bond they'd shared. She admired the way he'd taken ownership of his mistakes and fought so damn hard to make things right.

With everything set up, the team headed upstairs. Owl would wait on the rooftop, acting as a lookout. Even Jaden admitted that Owl had the best eyesight among them. The rest of the team would wait on the top floor, sniper rifles at the ready. When the Twisted showed up, they would go to work.

They'd only been on the top level for a few minutes when Jaden's eyes grew distant for a moment. He turned to Alex. "You were right. They're coming. Quite a lot of them."

Alex just nodded and hunched back over her sniper rifle, ready to take aim as soon as the enemy appeared.

They waited ten more minutes in uneasy silence. Then Owl spoke into Alex's earpiece.

"I see them, Alex. They're here."

20

THE SHADOW of the building stretched long across the ground. It was still a few hours before nightfall, and the sun was at the GMT's backs. Alex hoped that its position would make it harder for the Twisted to pinpoint where the attack was coming from. This fight could get ugly fast, and she needed any advantage that she could get.

Chuck waited in a small room on the far right corner of the building. Alex crouched in the left corner, watching through her scope as ten Twisted sprinted down the road at full speed. She waited for Chuck to take the first shot. He fired, and one of the Twisted was knocked back off his feet. The group stopped for a moment, looking in Chuck's direction. The injured Twisted stood back up, blood pouring from his abdomen. His head exploded as another report from Chuck's rifle echoed through the abandoned city.

The remaining Twisted pinpointed Chuck's location and took cover. Alex smiled; the plan was working. They'd protected themselves against Chuck's position, but Alex could still see them from her vantage point. She looked through her scope and quickly checked for Maryana. The vampire woman was nowhere to be found, but Alex made note of the position of the Twisted. One of them fired a shot in Chuck's direction. He didn't get a chance to fire again.

Alex had experienced enough battles to control the adrenaline coursing through her body. Time slowed down so much that it almost seemed to stop. She let out a breath and squeezed the trigger, the crosshairs resting on the Twisted who'd fired at Chuck. She didn't wait to see the spray of mist come from the back of his head before moving her barrel to her next target. She watched as another Twisted flinched from the report of her first shot as she squeezed the trigger again. Without hesitation, she moved the barrel to another Twisted. This one was behind a chunk of concrete. She spotted Alex and raised a rifle. Before she could get off a shot, Alex put her third round through her chest.

The remaining Twisted opened fire. Some shot in Alex's direction; others shot at Chuck. They reacted faster than any human would have, but they were not battle tested. They were badges, not soldiers. Their shots were wild and without focus. Alex stayed low and backed away from the window. She heard a report echo from the top of the building as she moved. Owl must have taken a shot. Alex stayed low as she raced to the room adjacent to the corner. She crawled on her stomach through an inch of dust until she could see the Twisted. A few stray bullets punched holes in the floor-to-ceiling windows, but the fire was concentrated at her prior location.

Through her scope she could see that the five remaining Twisted had taken cover under the overpass. "Now, Chuck!"

A moment later, the charges exploded and the bridge collapsed in a cloud of fire and dust.

Alex hit the button on her radio as she watched the rubble through her scope. "Report in."

"I'm still in one piece, no injuries," Chuck responded.

"I'm good," Owl said.

"I've got movement on my side of the building," Ed said. He was positioned on the opposite side of the building to guard from a rear attack.

"Copy that. What can you see, Owl?"

After a brief pause Owl responded. "They are everywhere. I'd guess fifty, plus or minus a few."

"Give them hell, and then meet us at the shaft," Alex said. "Do you have our backs, Jaden?"

"No one will reach the top floor." A chill ran down Alex's spine at the hard tone of his voice.

Alex heard Ed fire from the other side of the building. She counted two shots from him before gunfire erupted from the ground. Alex moved closer to the window to get a better vantage point. She saw flashes of movement. The Twisted were sprinting from one area of cover to another, trying to get closer to the building. The movement was fast enough that she couldn't get a shot off before they were gone. She heard more shots coming from the roof. She flinched in surprise as a Twisted jumped through the air, heading toward a window on a floor below her. She moved fast and shot at center mass. The bullet from her rifle stopped his momentum mid-air. It looked like the Twisted had hit an invisible wall, and he fell to the ground as blood poured from his body.

Suddenly, a window to Alex's left exploded. She rolled backward toward the door, while a stream of bullets flowed past her. Most of the bullets hit the ceiling of the room, due to the angle of the shots. Alex was sure that they had the attention of the Twisted now.

"Get to the shaft!" Alex said, as she crawled out of the room toward the hallway on the tenth floor.

She stayed in a crouch as she went down the hall. The gunfire inside the building stopped, but the Twisted continued firing, the sound getting closer with each passing moment. She heard glass break on a lower floor, and the sound of more shattered glass quickly followed.

Alex moved toward the center of the building, where the elevator shafts waited. She heard high-pitched screams, and gunfire echoed in the building.

Ed and Chuck were already at the elevator by the time she got there. Chuck was already clipped into the rope hanging in the shaft. She gave him a quick nod and he descended. Ed clipped on as Owl ran toward them.

"They are coming in fast," she said.

"Make sure Chuck is ready to blow this thing the moment we are all down," Alex told Ed.

"Roger that." There was a high-pitched squeal from the rope as Ed quickly descended.

Another scream came from below. The agony in the voice made it impossible to tell if it was a man or a woman, but the words were clear. "My legs!"

Alex clipped onto the rope just as a Twisted charged around the corner. Owl was ready and took aim. At that moment, two more Twisted rounded the corner on the other end of the hallway. Alex had both hands on the rope. There was no way she'd get to her weapon before they fired. She heard a gunshot, followed by a blur of motion. Twisteds' hair rustled as the phantom went by them. A small red necklace formed around each of their throats, and they went limp, falling to the ground. The smell of blood was thick in Alex's nose as she watched the heads slide off their bodies.

She kicked off and descended through the shaft in a controlled freefall. Owl and Jaden shot past her in the tight space. Neither needed a rope or to slow their descent. Alex reached the basement a step behind her immortal allies.

The grate to the drain had already been removed and Ed was climbing down. Owl aimed her rifle up the shaft, watching for anything that tried to follow them. Alex took her clip off the rope and hustled to the drainage opening. She hurried down the ladder, almost landing on Ed.

"Owl, time to go!" Alex shouted.

Jaden and Owl landed in the tunnel, one after the other. As their feet hit the water, Chuck pressed the second button. The tunnel shook around them and a wave of concussive force hit Owl, knocking her back against the wall. Dust and rubble came through the shaft just after the wall of energy.

The living members of the team coughed and covered their mouths as dust filled the air. Alex heard a loud thud come from above them. She wondered if something was trying to smash its way into the tunnel, but she quickly realized that it was chunks of the building, raining down from the explosion.

The dust dissipated as it drifted through the tunnel. Alex could see the team again as it cleared, and she did a quick check to make sure everyone was standing. Her ears rang from the blast. For a moment, she wasn't sure that she could hear at all, but then she kicked at the water under her boot. The sound was there; it was just muffled by the ringing.

Ed patted Chuck on the back. "Goddamn, buddy, you know how to bring down the house."

"What?" Chuck shook his head and rubbed at his ear.

Ed yelled, "Good job blowing the place up!"

Chuck smiled and gave a thumbs up. "I may not be the

best shot, but you can't miss when you blow up the battlefield."

"Is anyone injured?" Alex asked.

"I feel like I just got punched in the brain," Owl muttered. "That concussion wave feels extra intense with vampire senses. Other than the headache, I'm fine."

"Don't worry, Ed's proof that you can still be a great warrior with almost no working brain cells." Chuck smiled and gave Ed a light punch in the arm.

"Thanks, I always thought of myself as a great warrior." Ed smiled back.

Alex turned to Jaden, who'd been silent during the battle. "Do you think we got all of them?"

He answered as he wiped blood from his blades. "I can still feel the Twisted. It may just be survivors buried in the rubble."

"Thanks for saving my ass up there. I owe you one."

"I've lost track of the amount you owe me. I might have to turn you, just so you live long enough to repay me."

Alex paused. "Are you razzing me?"

"I'm part of the GMT, aren't I?" he asked. "That's kind of in the job description." He paused and looked her in the eyes. "That was a good plan."

"Thanks. Now let's get back to the transport and get the hell out of here."

Owl led the way through the dusty haze of the tunnel as the team sloshed through the water behind her. Alex felt a sense of pride that the five of them had just killed a small army. There was a change in the way they carried themselves, even Jaden. All of a sudden, they had hope. It was disappointing that Maryana hadn't been among the Twisted, but they would regroup and find her. When they faced her, they would be ready.

Owl turned the corner and jumped back as a gunshot rang out. Her hand went to her suddenly bloody shoulder. The bullet had missed her heart by inches.

The rest of the team drew their weapons and hugged the wall.

A voice echoed down the tunnel. "I hope you aren't all tuckered out. I'm really looking forward to playing with you." Maryana let out a laugh that sent chills down Alex's spine.

21

For a moment, the only sound was the sloshing of water as the Twisted moved through the tunnel up ahead. One positive about the three inches of water in the tunnel—even vampires couldn't keep their footsteps silent.

Alex scanned her surroundings, bathing the walls of the tunnel with the light from her headlamp. They had a decent position. Maryana's voice had come from around a corner twenty yards ahead. If they camped here, they could pick off whatever Twisted she sent at them. Even with the Twisted's unnatural speed, the GMT would have time to take them out, unless Maryana had many more of the creatures than it sounded like she did. Alex breathed in deep through her nose, ignoring the musty stench of the tunnel, and slowly let the air out through her mouth. Her heart was racing, and she needed absolute calm, absolute clarity.

Maryana was here in this tunnel. They could end it, free *New Haven*, break her mastery over the Twisted, if Alex and the GMT executed perfectly for the next few minutes. What happened in this tunnel could change the world.

Alex signaled to her teammates, letting them know to

stay quiet and hold position. She locked eyes with Jaden last. He hesitated before nodding, and even in the sickly glow of her headlamp, she saw the concern in his eyes. Alex had been right; Maryana had gotten into his head. He was worried, when he should be preparing for the most important battle of his long life.

"I'm sort of impressed with you," Maryana called out from the protection of the blocked corridor. "Jaden, I thought you were much too proud to work with humans in any real way. Usually, you just make them think you consider them equals, until they are no longer useful. And then you disappear into the night and leave them to their fates. Assuming that you don't rip them to shreds like you did with Project White Horse. But this time, you seem to be serious about working with these people. What's different?"

She paused to let him answer. Jaden gritted his teeth and said nothing, so she continued.

"Maybe it's because they're the only allies you have left. All the rest of your buddies came down with something, didn't they?" She paused again, letting that hang in the air. "And then, we have the Ground Mission Team. My Twisted have blabbed quite a bit about you. They genuinely respect you. I figured it was only because they hadn't seen what real warriors could do, but I have to say, I'm impressed with this little ambush you set up. I wouldn't have expected that of you. Luckily, I didn't have to. I've got somebody on my side who's very familiar with GMT tactics." Her voice lowered, as if she was no longer talking to them. "Get out there."

A Twisted stepped around the corner. As one, the GMT prepared to fire, but something about this Twisted gave them pause. His arms were outstretched, and he held no weapons. He stood as still as a statue.

Alex stared at the Twisted. The shape of his face under

the mask was the same as that of any other Twisted, but something about the way he held himself felt uncannily familiar.

"Alex," Jaden said, his voice urgent. "Don't let her bait you. Remember what's at stake."

Alex heard, but she wasn't listening. Her eyes were fixed on the Twisted.

Maryana called out from around the corner. "Take it off."

The Twisted reached up with a mangled hand and grabbed his mask. He tugged on it, removing it slowly, revealing the face underneath inch by inch, as if everything within him was fighting the order he'd been given. Alex's eyes widened in horror as the mask slid upward. Then it reached the top of his head and slipped off, leaving his entire face exposed. Even with the elongated jaw, the long teeth, and the misshapen ears, there was no mistaking that face. Not for Alex.

"CB," she said, her voice hoarse.

"Alex," he answered, weakly. Though his massive teeth affected his pronunciation, his voice sounded the same as it always had, and it rolled through Alex's body like an electrical current. Joy and anger twisted together in a double-helix in her guts. CB was alive, but he belonged to Maryana.

"I guess you know Colonel Brickman," Maryana said. "He commands my Twisted for me. Pretty easy to anticipate your moves when my commander is the guy who taught you everything you know."

"I'm sorry, Alex," CB said, his eyes filled with despair.

Alex saw movement out of the corner of her eye and whipped her head around just in time to see Jaden raising his rifle. "No!" she shouted, her body already in motion. She grabbed the barrel of his rifle and slammed it against the side of the tunnel.

"This is getting interesting," Maryana said, with a laugh.

Jaden pulled his rifle free of Alex's grasp. "You think he wants to live like this? We were agreed. Any Twisted under her control is the enemy."

"Not him." Tears stood in her eyes. Jaden was right; they had agreed that Maryana's Twisted had to be killed. And CB, even more than most. He was a master tactician, and he knew the GMT better than anyone alive. Alex's mind understood those things, but her heart was another matter. "I can't lose him, too."

"Fine," Maryana said. "If you're not going to shoot him, CB will do it himself. Colonel, put your gun to your temple."

CB's hand went to his holster and he drew a pistol. Though his eyes were wide with fear, he obeyed with no hesitation, pressing the barrel to his head.

"No!" Alex screamed again. Before she knew what she was doing, she was running down the tunnel, racing toward CB. She drew her sword, ready to remove CB's arm rather than allowing him to kill himself. Her sword was half-drawn when something grabbed the back of her vest, yanking her to a sudden halt.

"Sorry, but I'm not letting you die just yet," Jaden growled. He reached into his pack and pulled out a grenade. Letting go of Alex, he pulled the pin and threw it hard. The grenade ricocheted off the wall behind CB and bounced into the tunnel where Maryana and the other Twisted were waiting. "Let's go, GMT!"

He turned and ran back the way they'd come, and the GMT followed. As Alex turned, the grenade exploded, and she heard shouts coming from the tunnel behind them.

"I'm starting to remember why I hate that guy," Maryana said. "Play time's over. Go after them. That's an order, CB."

Alex ran hard, trying and failing to push aside the

emotions swirling inside of her. She knew just enough to understand that she was in no state to lead the team at the moment, so she just followed Jaden.

"Here!" Jaden shouted, stopping suddenly and pointing upward. It took Alex a moment to figure out what he was pointing at. Then she realized that there was a manhole overhead. "Owl, we'll hold off the Twisted. The rest of you, get topside, now!"

Chuck raced up the ladder in just a few seconds. When he reached the top, he stopped, and it took him a moment to lift the ancient cover off the manhole. As the first sliver of light came down through the opening, Owl hissed.

Alex turned, realizing the Twisted were upon them.

Owl dove forward, hands outstretched, sinking the claws of her left hand into the first Twisted's chest. She hurled him to the ground, drew her pistol with her other hand, and shot him in the head. Jaden's twin swords flashed as he went to work, quickly dropping two more of the enemies.

Alex glanced up and saw Chuck disappear into the daylight. She drew her pistol and took aim at another Twisted. His eyes were wide, and she saw terror in them. Was it any wonder? Not only was he going up against the legendary GMT, but he'd just seen three of his comrades torn apart by Owl and Jaden in mere moments. Alex steeled herself and fired, putting an end to the Twisted's fear and his life.

Ed was at the top of the ladder now. "Come on, Alex! Your turn."

She put a hand on the ladder, ready to start upward, but glanced down the tunnel. Strangely, there were no more Twisted coming. She didn't have a clue how many Twisted Maryana had with her, but it was certainly more than three. "Where's the rest of them?"

"Don't know," Jaden said. "We need room to maneuver. Head up."

Alex considered overriding his order for a moment, but decided she didn't want to be stuck down in this tunnel with a bunch of Twisted anyway, and began to climb.

When she pulled herself through the manhole, she saw Ed and Chuck standing on either side of her, weapons raised. She quickly got to her feet and drew her own weapon. Less than half a block east lay the remains of the building they'd destroyed. At least ten Twisted had already pulled themselves from the rubble, and more were emerging by the moment. To the west, a Twisted leaped up through a manhole, joining a group already waiting. Including Maryana and CB.

"Looks like they've got us flanked, Captain," Ed muttered.

"Thanks for that astute observation," she replied. Owl climbed through the manhole, followed by Jaden.

The Twisted on either side stood watching, waiting for the kill order that they knew was coming. Maryana looked at the GMT with something bordering on pity.

"You could give up, you know," she said. "I might let a couple of you live. Not Jaden, of course. But Alex, maybe. I could make you and CB fight to the death. That'd be interesting." She paused. "On the other hand, I guess I can already do that."

There were twenty Twisted near the rubble to the east, now. The GMT was cornered, and from what Alex could see, there was no escape route.

"What do you think, CB?" Maryana said. "Answer honestly. Are they going to surrender?"

"No," CB said.

Maryana gave him an amused smile. "What do you think is going to happen?"

His voice was cold. "I think Alex is going to kill you."

The smile melted off Maryana's face, and anger flickered in her eyes. "And here, I thought you were smart." She raised her voice, addressing all the Twisted. "Listen up! It's time to—"

The sound of a gunshot split the air, and Maryana staggered forward. Behind her, Felix stood, bandaged and bloody, smoke curling skyward from the barrel of his rifle.

22

THREE POINT nine grams of lead might not seem like much, but sometimes the smallest things can make the biggest difference. There was nothing small about the hole the bullet put in Maryana's chest. Blood and bone tore through her shirt, and the Twisted standing next to her were covered in the spray. Alex watched her fall to the ground and for one glorious moment, she believed the war was over. Maybe Maryana was dead and CB was free. But unfortunately, in his weakened state, Felix's shot was a little off. The bullet missed her heart by half an inch. The smallest things can make the biggest difference.

Maryana screamed and tried to get up, but her legs didn't function. The shot might have missed her heart, but it tore her spine in half. She clawed at the ground around her, desperately trying to rise, but stuck on her back. Alex intended to make sure she never got up. She leveled her pistol and squeezed a round off. One of the Twisted jumped in the way and covered Maryana with his body.

"Protect me! Kill them! Kill them all!" The words came

out muffled through the blood leaking from Maryana's mouth.

The Twisted closest to Maryana circled around their mistress, while the ones near the rubble charged the GMT. Alex fired one shot into the group surrounding Maryana before she focused attention on the group running at them. The GMT was completely exposed on the street. Alex knew that they would not survive long without cover.

"Move!" Alex shouted, as a bullet flew by her ear.

The team rushed toward an alley between two buildings. Only Jaden did not follow Alex's order. He raced toward Maryana with a sword in each hand.

Most of the Twisted coming from the rubble were moving slowly. They were broken and mangled, injured by the building that had fallen on them. Alex could see the pain in their eyes as they ran toward her with gaping wounds and bones protruding from the skin. Ed's rifle crackled to life and one of the Twisted flipped onto her back. The team continued firing at the approaching Twisted, while they moved for cover.

Jaden raced toward the Twisted guarding Maryana. He covered the distance to them in an instant, watching gun barrels, trying to avoid their fire. The number of enemies and the open space made it impossible. He spun and stumbled when a bullet tore into his left shoulder and another pierced through his right calf. His momentum carried him into the tight group of Twisted.

Alex and the team reached the alley and darted between the two brick buildings. Each building rose four stories into the air and the alley between them was wide enough to drive a large truck through. Alex crouched against the building on one side of the alley and Ed was against the other, both of them in a position to defend the entrance.

They didn't have to wait long for the enemy. A Twisted dashed into the alley, and Alex shot him in the chest. As he fell, Alex recognized him as a badge with whom she'd occasionally played cards. But there was no time to mourn him; more Twisted were dashing toward the alley.

"Chuck, we need a sniper!" Alex shouted, while she and Ed fired at incoming Twisted.

Chuck scanned the windows twenty feet up on either side of them. "Roger that. It will take time to get up there."

"I've got you." Owl wrapped an arm around Chuck's waist. She jumped halfway up the building, landing on the wall to her right and pushing off with her legs. The push was enough to get them on top of the second building.

"Holy shit, thanks," Chuck said as he orientated himself to the sudden change in location. He settled on the edge of the roof with his rifle in hand. Owl jumped down, landing next to Alex and Ed.

Up ahead, Alex saw Jaden smash into the line of Twisted who were protecting Maryana. He knocked them off balance, pushing Twisted into each other. An ancient sword went through one Twisted's heart as he crashed into the group. The chaos of the close fight worked against the inexperienced soldiers. Several tried to grab Jaden, but he slashed off hands as they shot toward him. One of the Twisted raised his rifle a foot from Jaden's head. Jaden moved to the side and pulled in one of the others who had grabbed him, moving his captive's face in front of the barrel. The Twisted shot his comrade in the face at point blank range.

Twisted charged into the alley. Ed's rifle blasted in rapid bursts. He shot four Twisted in center mass, stopping their forward movement. He missed two of their hearts, but Alex finished each of them with a shot to the head. She edged forward toward the end of the alley, and spotted a group of ten Twisted headed for Jaden.

"Chuck, they are trying to protect Maryana. Don't let them get away." As she finished speaking, a clawed hand reached around the corner of the building and grabbed her, pulling her out of the alley and tossing her into the street. She flew twenty feet and rolled as she hit the asphalt. Shaking her head to clear it, she struggled to her feet and raised her pistol. The Twisted who had grabbed her was still crouched at the alley's opening. It was CB.

Alex gritted her teeth, and forced herself to fire, but he was already in motion, diving to his right.

She cursed softly, unable to believe the absolute chaos of the fight. A strategic ambush had turned into a street brawl. She saw Jaden struggling in a group of Twisted to her left. He looked badly injured. Chuck fired from the roof above, while Ed and Owl defended the alley below.

Alex tried to focus on CB, but before she re-engaged, something else caught her attention. A group of Twisted was pulling Maryana away from the battle. Two of them carried her, while the rest formed a tight, protective circle around them. One of them dropped, a victim of Chuck's elevated position, but there were so many that he wouldn't be able to take out all of them.

Still, she knew she had to finish CB while she had the chance. He was back on his feet now, angling toward her. She focused on the task at hand, pushing her knowledge that this was CB to the back of her mind, and began to fire. He moved fast enough to stay ahead of Alex's shots and dove behind the remains of a bus. Bullets sparked against the metal as he took cover.

Alex dropped her clip and slammed a new one into her pistol. She was ready to fire at the first sign of motion. CB came around the front of the vehicle and threw an old tire at Alex. His strength sent the object flying with enough speed to kill her. The side of the tire brushed against Alex's arm as she ducked out of the way. She crouched, her pistol ready, but CB was already on top of her. He hit her hand hard enough to send the pistol flying across the street. She sprang to her feet as he drew back a clawed fist. Before he could land the deadly punch, Owl crashed into him at full speed.

Owl clawed at CB's face while they tumbled away from Alex. CB grabbed Owl's arm and controlled his fall as they tumbled to the pavement. By the time they stopped rolling, he was on top of her. He held her arm pinned behind her back while she lay on her stomach, face against the street. Owl struggled as CB began to pull the arm from the body. Despair crossed her face. In all their sparring matches, she'd never beaten CB.

But she wasn't alone in this fight. Alex sprang toward CB, her sword raised. She swung at his neck, but he saw the blade in time to bring up an arm and deflect the blade. Owl used the opportunity to push up off of the ground and flip CB onto his back. Blood dripped from his arm as Alex pressed the attack.

Alex swung her sword, but CB moved with vampire speed. The blade made the air sing as he ducked below it. She knew his fighting style and moved her head back to avoid an uppercut that would have removed her head. She spun while dropping low. The blade became an extension of her body. It moved with her, slashing toward CB's knees. He jumped back in time to avoid the strike.

Owl punched him in the side as he landed. He moved with the force of the blow and grabbed Owl's arm, pulling down hard and bringing his knee up into her forearm. The crack was loud, and Owl's arm bent where there was no joint. She screamed and slashed wildly with her other arm.

The crack of Chuck's rifle rippled through the air and a scream came from Maryana's direction. Another burst of fire came from her group in the distance.

Alex saw Jaden slice his sword into the last Twisted from the crowd that he had been fighting. She hoped he would help to subdue CB, but he only took a single step before falling to one knee among the pile of dead Twisted.

Ed stood at the opening of the alley now, rifle raised as he tried to get a clear shot at CB. CB was still focused on Owl; he gave her a side kick that sent her flying into the bus. The old, rusted shell crumpled when she slammed against it.

Alex moved to the side, giving Ed his opening. Alex's eyes darted to his position and CB spotted the glance. It was all the warning he needed. He sprinted across the street a step ahead of the trail of Ed's bullets. From above them, Chuck's rifle cracked again.

CB sprinted three steps and lunged into the air. His leap carried him impossibly high, and he managed to snag the edge of the roof with his hand. He quickly pulled himself up. In a moment, his hand was around Chuck's throat.

Alex watched in horror as CB raised Chuck into the air, over the edge of the building. Even from the ground, she could see CB was shaking.

"I'm sorry," CB said. Then he squeezed, and Chuck's neck bent at an impossible angle. Then he let go, and Chuck's body fell to the ground.

23

ALEX WATCHED in horror as Chuck's body tumbled from the rooftop to the pavement below.

How the hell had things gotten so terrible so quickly? She remembered the beginning of the fight, when she'd first heard Maryana's voice in the drainage tunnel. She'd thought then that this fight was going to change the world. And for Alex, it *had* changed the world, but not in the way she'd expected.

Chuck was dead, and CB had killed him.

Jaden was right. Everyone under Maryana's control was the enemy, including CB. She couldn't afford to hold back against him. Not only for her sake, but for his. Being forced to kill his teammates? Alex could imagine no worse fate.

She raised her pistol, hoping to get off a shot, but CB had disappeared. Her head swiveled as she searched for some sign of him, but she saw nothing. He must have retreated, along with the others.

Alex heard the slightest sound behind her, so soft, that she couldn't even be certain it hadn't been her imagination.

She spun toward it, raising her weapon, and as soon as she saw CB's distinct form, she fired.

Of course CB hadn't retreated. She knew him better than that. Maryana had ordered him to protect her, and CB knew that the best way to do that was to kill Alex.

The round from Alex's pistol hit him in the chest, knocking him back a step, but he kept his feet. The pain, emotional and physical, stood out in his eyes.

Alex steadied her weapon, preparing to fire again. This time she would hit his heart. She took careful aim, wanting this shot to count. Or perhaps, a little voice in the back of her head suggested, she was stalling. For all of her bluster, she wasn't sure she could kill CB.

"Twisted, to me!" Maryana shouted.

CB's head swiveled toward the sound, and he immediately took off toward it. Frustration and relief flooded Alex. She'd failed to kill CB, and now she'd have to face him again. But at least she wouldn't have to kill him today. As CB sprinted off, Alex snapped out of her shocked state. Her team needed her. "Owl, get Chuck!"

Owl paused, knowing just as well as Alex did that Chuck was beyond help, but then she nodded and ran to where he'd fallen.

"The rest of you, let's thin the herd!"

All around, Twisted were retreating, pulling back at Maryana's orders. The GMT fired at their fleeing enemies. Ed got in a shot, taking down one of them, but the rest managed to limp off, each sporting a few new bullet holes. Alex considered giving chase, but she knew there were still too many Twisted left. They might be running now, but if the GMT attacked their master, they'd turn around mighty quickly.

"Team, let's regroup," she said. She turned back toward the building where Chuck had fallen. "Owl—"

What she saw made her stop talking. Owl stood in the road behind them, Chuck's corpse in her arms.

ALEX DIDN'T like the morgue. It was all cold steel and overly bright lighting. The chilly air prickled her skin, and goosebumps sprang out on her arms and neck. She didn't move. Her eyes remained fixed on Chuck's body.

Agartha's coroner had yet to go to work, so Chuck looked exactly as he had when Owl had lain him in the back of the transport. He still wore his GMT uniform, complete with black vest and a holstered pistol at his belt. His boots were dusty from the rubble where they'd battled the Twisted, and the bottoms were caked with mud. From the chest down, he looked normal. Battle-ready, even.

But look a bit higher, and there was no mistaking that the man was dead. It wasn't just his slack face or his bluish lips. It was the angle of his head. No matter how many times they'd tried to straighten it, they couldn't quite get it to look natural. CB had so demolished Chuck's neck that his head refused to stay upright. It lolled to the side every time.

"I figured I'd find you here."

Alex bristled with annoyance at being disturbed here of all places, but then she recognized the voice. She turned and hugged Brian. "It's all fucked up. Every bit of it."

Brian tried futility to keep the disturbed expression off his face as he caught his first glimpse of Chuck's body. "I'm so sorry, Alex."

She let go of Brian and turned back to her fallen friend.

"There's been too much death. Is it ever going to end? And now it's not just our enemies. CB did this."

Brian put his hand on her shoulder. "Just remember, he's not himself. It wasn't really him who did this."

Alex tilted her head in surprise. "It was, though. He has to follow Maryana's orders, but he's still CB. That's what makes this all so terrible. Without his skills, his battle savvy, they never would have survived our ambush. He's going to be one step ahead of us, just like he's always been. Only, Maryana gets to take advantage of that now."

"Until you kill her," Brian said with a weak smile.

"Yeah." All of a sudden, the weight of it hit Alex. They were counting on her. Brian. The GMT. Agartha. Probably *New Haven*, too. They were all counting on her to come save them. She felt like she might break under the weight of it all.

Brian nodded toward Chuck. "He was a good man. GMT through and through."

Alex couldn't help but chuckle. "You know, he almost shot Hope in the face on his first mission?"

"No kidding?"

"Yep. He was a freaking mess at the beginning. If it hadn't been for the GMT being stranded down here, he never would have gotten the call." She paused, and melancholy entered her voice. "But he worked at it. Harder than any of them. He was always the first man to step up and volunteer, whether it was filling in for Owl as pilot or taking over as demolitions man when Wesley retired."

Brian nodded. "He asked more questions than any GMT member I've ever worked with. Most of you just want to know which way to point the new weapons. He was actually curious about how they worked."

"I failed him, Brian." There was a hitch in her voice as she said the words.

"You didn't—"

"I'm not asking for absolution. I'm just stating a fact. I saw a spark in him. He could have been a great leader. But I didn't develop him like I should have. I got busy with other things, and I was content to keep him as a rock-solid team member."

"To be fair, you did have some stuff going on."

They stood in silence for a long while, standing vigil over their fallen friend. They were interrupted by Jaden's voice coming through Alex's radio.

"Alex, I'm going to see that idiot who injected himself with Owl's blood. Meet me in the vampire quarters if you want to be part of the discussion."

Alex swallowed hard. Brian had told them about the man injecting himself just after they'd arrived, and Jaden had acted sullen ever since.

She took one last look at Chuck and sighed. Duty, it seemed, infringed even here. "I'm on my way."

As she walked through the corridors of the city, Alex tried to get her mind right. As much as she would have liked to work through her grief about Chuck, she knew from painful experience that the GMT rarely got that luxury. Instead, she thought of the person she was going to see. As much as she disapproved of what he'd done, she did sort of admire his initiative. It wasn't like she was instantly going to offer him a spot on the GMT, but she was anxious to take his measure. If he had his head on straight and could take orders, it wasn't out of the question. They could certainly use another Twisted on their side, especially with Chuck gone.

Jaden was waiting for her in the common area of the

vampire quarters. The place was oddly quiet. The few times Alex had been in this room, it had been bustling with activity. Now, with Jaden and Frank as its only occupants (Owl preferred the human quarters), it was nearly empty.

"Let's get this over with," Jaden growled.

He led her down a long corridor, past the sleeping quarters and to an isolated room. When Jaden swiped his keycard and opened the door, Alex realized it was a holding cell.

A young man with shaggy blond hair and piercing green eyes sat behind a metal table. He must have been handsome when he was human, but his Twisted features made it impossible to tell for sure. He wore his nervousness openly on his face.

He rose from his chair when Jaden entered. "Jaden, I'm so glad you're here. I know I broke the rules, but I'd like to explain why I did what I did. For so long, you've been our protector, and I felt it was time that we—"

In a flash, Jaden drew his sword and swung it. It whooshed through the air, not even slowing as it passed through the young man's neck. His mouth still hung open, mid-sentence, as his head slipped off his shoulders and fell to the floor.

Jaden sheathed his blade and marched out of the room.

24

THE BLOOD from the young Twisted man ran out of his neck, pooling around him on the stone floor. Alex stood frozen, watching it spread slowly toward her feet. Her world had cracked today. The death of Chuck and the knowledge that CB was now her enemy had shaken her. Watching Jaden kill this young man with the demeanor of a person swatting a fly pushed her over the edge. She felt like she was floating out of her body. She watched the pool of blood grow until it reached the head that lay next to the body. The two were connected again in a way.

Alex reached down and touched the butt of her pistol. She wondered why she hadn't pulled it and shot Jaden. He had just killed an unarmed citizen of his own city. She knew the answer to her question before she asked it. She still needed him. Her team was dwindling, and Jaden was an amazing warrior. He was also becoming a monster. Or maybe Alex was just seeing the monster he'd always been.

The dream state began to fade and Alex decided the pistol was still an option. She turned and went after Jaden.

Night had fallen and the city was quiet. She found Jaden

sitting on a bench in front of the empty school facility, his face calm. Alex approached with her hand on her weapon.

"I wanted you to see that, Alex." Jaden said without turning to look at her. "I am well aware of the issue you have with secrets."

Alex moved slowly around to face him. Her muscles were tense and she was ready for an attack. "I think you're also aware that I'm really against killing innocent people."

"I am. And I hope you are aware that I am always fighting for the greater good, no matter the cost. I haven't lost my mind and I am not your enemy. Relax and have a seat, or stand with your weapon drawn. Whatever makes you more comfortable."

Alex stayed standing, with her hand on the butt of her gun. "I didn't see any good in what you just did. You didn't even listen to what he had to say."

"I knew what I needed to do as soon as I heard that he existed. Telling you what was happening and fighting over what could not change would have been a waste of time."

"Why, Jaden? Why couldn't that change?"

"I believe that my actions just saved thousands of lives." He paused, noting Alex's confused expression. "When Maryana became a threat and we started to realize how many vampires she'd created, the council met to discuss ways to stop her. She already had thousands of vampires spread across the globe. Even with our resources, we could not hope to make a dent in her army with only 100. It was decided that we would increase our numbers to combat her forces. That decision is one of the reasons why we are under this mountain."

"This isn't the old world. No one turned that kid. He did it to himself."

"The story isn't over; be patient. When Maryana engaged

the group of vampires that we'd sent after her, she reacted in a way that we hadn't predicted. They were volunteers with military training. She had a strong hold in Moscow. We had made twenty vampires to help their forces attack her. Once she realized what we had done, she had her followers create twenty *thousand* new vampires in the city. We never considered she would expose herself to the world like that. We never dreamt that a move like that was on the table. That decision was one of many that changed the world forever."

Alex tried to imagine that number. The wave of Twisted that attacked Agartha the first time had seemed massive. She had never even seen twenty thousand people in one place at one time. An army like that was unimaginable.

"If Maryana sees us create one new Twisted warrior, she may turn all forty thousand humans into her deformed slaves. She might do it anyway after today's battle. The last thing she wants is a fair fight."

Alex moved her hand away from her gun and took a seat on the bench. "Why didn't you tell me this before? There were other options. We could have kept him here. He would still have been an asset in the city."

Jaden rubbed his head. "The risk of Maryana finding out about him was too great. He also could have set a dangerous precedent for others who wanted to be turned. This decision was obvious. I have centuries of death in my shadow. I have seen the entire population of the Earth come and go hundreds of times. I hope to see future generations. Every moment that Twisted existed put all of you at risk." He pointed to the school in front of them. "One life is a small price to pay to give the rest of humanity a chance. It is why I need to protect you. It is why you need me."

Alex wanted to punch him in his arrogant deformed face as those words hung in the air. Instead, she just stood up and sighed. "You might think that I'm just another stupid person passing through time, but if you really think we should continue as a species, you need to realize that each one of us matters. We aren't just some abstract question for you to debate. That kid was a fighter. He was willing to sacrifice himself and think outside the box. His life was worth more than just a conversation or a swing of your sword. If you knew every damn thing and were so much wiser than us, we wouldn't be in this stupid mess."

Jaden sat without any change in his expression.

"You need us as much as we need you, probably even more. You need to adapt to the world we are in. You need to deal with the loss of your vampires. I see how out of control you are right now, even if you don't. Get your head out of your ass and realize that you're not some savior sent to protect us. You're part of a team." Alex was almost shouting now. "Why don't you go clean up the mess in the holding cell? Maybe you will realize that it is a person that you are picking up off that floor."

Alex turned and stormed off. She was exhausted, but she knew some hard training was in her future. She didn't know if she could sweat out the events of the day, but she was going to try.

THE CAFETERIA WAS BUZZING with people getting their morning meal. Plates clattered as people moved from the food lines to the tables. Ed stood with a tray in his hand, watching the motion around him. He hated everyone at that moment. He saw them smile and talk with each other while enjoying their first meal of the day. They didn't care that Chuck was dead. Not one of them had visited Felix in the med center. His hands shook as he tried to keep himself from throwing his food at the wall and punching every one of their ungrateful faces.

"Ed! Hey, Ed!"

Ed turned to see Brian waving a hand in the air. He took a breath to calm down and walked over to Brian's table. Brian was sitting next to a pretty woman, and Ed took a seat across from them.

"Did you get any sleep?" Brian asked. "I was calling your name for, like, two minutes before you heard me."

"A little. I stayed with Felix in the med center. I just crashed in a chair next to his bed."

"How's he doing?"

"He's okay. He got scratched up pretty good, but the kid has heart. He'll be back on his feet for the next mission." He turned to the woman next to Brian. "Who's this chick?"

Brian blushed a little. "This is Stephanie. She works with me in the lab. She's Agartha's version of me."

Stephanie gave a little laugh. "I'm sure you know that Brian is one of a kind. I can't put myself in the same class as him." She reached a hand across the table and Ed shook it. "It's nice to meet you, Ed. Sorry for your loss."

She looked Ed right in the eye when she spoke, and he could tell that her condolences were more than just empty words. Her eyes were deep and her voice was gentle and true.

"Thanks. It's been a rough time for the GMT, lately." He suddenly thought of Patrick and the smell of the fire that burnt his body seemed to fill the room. Tears sprang to Ed's eyes, but he managed to blink them back. "Sorry about that chick comment. I can be a little rough around the edges."

"No problem, I can handle a rough edge or two. I'll let you tough guys catch up." She stood up and picked up her empty tray with one hand. With the other, she touched Brian's shoulder. "See you back at the lab. It was nice meeting you, Ed."

"Same here." Ed poked at his food with his fork.

"You okay, Ed?" Brian asked.

Ed sighed. "Honestly, I'm pretty messed up. How about you?"

"The same. I'm just burying myself in work to hide from it." Brian gave a little smile.

"You sure you're not burying yourself in Stephanie?" Ed asked, with a smirk.

"Hey, don't be a dick. She is a great woman."

"Sorry. That came out way creepier than I wanted it to. I just meant, is there a thing between you two? It seemed like there might be."

Brian's face relaxed. "Maybe. I mean, nothing has happened yet, but I think we have a real connection. It's different than I've had with any other girl."

Ed set down his fork and leaned forward. "Listen, I feel stupid giving you any advice, seeing how you're a genius and I'm about as smart as a rock. I know everything is messed up right now, but everything is always messed up. I thought Patrick would be giving me crap about how ugly my grandkids were some day. Instead, I had to watch his body burn. Chuck had our backs yesterday. I think he was one moment away from ending this whole thing. Now, he's cold in the morgue. All I know is that this moment is all we have. It might not feel like the right time, but that time may never come. If you think she is something special, go for it. Don't wait." Ed turned his eyes down and took another bite of food.

"I think that is considerably better advice than a rock could give. Thanks."

Ed laughed. "Well, that's a pretty low bar, but I'll take it. Now, go get that girl. If you've got a little extra time, make me some crazy laser gun that can shoot through walls and only kills Twisted."

Brian gave him a sideways smile. "You've got it. One laser gun that shoots through walls and ..." Brian stopped talking. His eyes stayed open, but he didn't move at all for a few seconds.

The pause was long enough to make Ed think he was having a seizure, or something. "Hey, are you still with me?"

Brian snapped out of it. He stood up and pushed his tray back, leaving it and his food on the table. "I've got an idea. I'll see you later." He ran out of the cafeteria before Ed could say another word.

25

Jessica rubbed her arms, trying to combat the shivers that threatened to overtake her body. She didn't have control of much in her current situation, but she'd be damned if she'd give her own body up to her involuntary functions.

She and the other nearly two hundred attempted escapees huddled together in a large, metal structure that had once been a warehouse. Now it was the biggest holding cell that Jessica had ever seen. She sighed, and she noticed she could see her breath. Though it was no consolation, it wasn't just the holding area that was cold that night; the temperature regulation systems were knocked out along with everything else by the EMP. Jessica wondered how the citizens were dealing with it. Their first night on the surface, and they had neither light nor heat.

Not that the lack of either was bothering their guards. The dozen Twisted had vampire vision on their side, and they were no longer concerned with frivolities like body temperature. They stood with their backs to the metal walls, keeping careful watch over their prisoners, just as they'd been ordered to do.

The warehouse wasn't completely dark. Their captors had acquired some headlamps and set them on the ground shining upward. Thin beams of light shot up from the ground in five places in the warehouse, providing just enough light to allow the humans to move around safely, without bumping into each other. That was what was so difficult to understand about their guards. They were still the same people they'd always been. None of them relished what they were doing; indeed, before the sun went down, Jessica had clearly seen expressions of disgust and revulsion on some of their faces as they forced weeping, desperate people to remain in this metal box rather than allowing them to go home to spend the night with their families. They'd gladly provide any comfort their orders allowed them to provide.

For all the good it did. These Twisted would not hesitate to murder any of them who ever attempted to leave. It was as if they were the humans Jessica had always known, but trapped inside killing machines. Machines with controls that Maryana, alone, held.

Jessica tried to push those thoughts away. Thinking about the Twisted meant thinking about CB. And that, she wouldn't—couldn't—let herself do. Not now. Her husband was alive, sort of, but she had only seen him once across a crowd since he'd been turned. He belonged to Maryana now, mind and body. Who knew what terrible things she had him doing? In truth, Jessica didn't care what he was forced to do, as long as he survived. As long as he weathered the storm and eventually returned to her. But that seemed like too much to ask now. She wouldn't stop fighting, and part of her believed she'd still succeed in helping some *New Haven* citizens escape, but killing Maryana was a possibility so remote that she didn't even allow herself to consider it. Not right now.

"Jessica," a male voice whispered. "You holding up okay?"

She turned, and in the darkness it took her a moment to identify Tony. He'd worked for her in Engineering for a couple of years. She hadn't even known he was among the escapees. "I'm doing fine. As well as I can be."

"Same here," he said with a weak smile. "Listen, I'm sorry about what happened to CB. It's a hell of a thing."

She swallowed hard. "Yes, it is. Thank you."

He touched her arm. "The GMT...what's left of it... Alex and her people will come back to save us, and when they do, CB will be free. He'll still be Twisted, but he won't be a slave."

"Let's hope so," Jessica said, weakly. She looked Tony up and down. He appeared to be unhurt, and he'd always been a bold man, not one to shirk from tough situations. Maybe he could help her. "But Tony, we can't wait around for that. Maryana's unpredictable. She could come in here and kill us all tomorrow. If we wait for the GMT, we might be dead when they arrive. We need to make a move."

Tony blinked hard. "What do you mean?"

She lowered her voice even further when she spoke again. She knew the power of vampire hearing, but she hoped the chatter of the nearly two hundred other people would drown out her words. "I don't mean now. That would be suicide. They have a huge advantage at night. But come morning? There's only a dozen of them. If we all rush one door, I'll bet a good portion of us make it out." She paused, registering the surprised look on his face. "I know it's scary, Tony, but if we want to live, we have to try."

"It's not that. I'm not scared." He looked away. "Okay, I

am scared, but that's not the main thing here. Have you looked around at these people? They're shell-shocked. They're mentally broken down. I'm sorry to put it so bluntly, but if you think these people are going to charge the doors and take on twelve Twisted, you're crazy."

Jessica flinched as if she'd been slapped. She couldn't believe what she was hearing. These were the people who'd been bold enough to try to escape. They were the brave ones. If they couldn't do this, what chance did the rest of *New Haven* have?

But was that still true? She tried to remember what signs of bravery she'd seen in them since they'd been captured. She could think of none. Instead, she saw cowed faces and hunched figures in her mind. They may have been brave when standing in Tankards, when all of this was theoretical, but now they'd faced real danger. They'd been on the battlefield, and their minds had not escaped unscathed.

She looked toward the nearest wall, and she could just make out the Twisted standing there in the pale light from the headlamp. His name was Thomas, Jessica knew. He'd been a badge, and a very good one. More than that, he'd been a candidate for the GMT, once upon a time. CB had told her that it had been between Thomas and Wesley for a spot after Simmons died. Thomas had withdrawn his application after he'd been passed over, content to live out his career with the badges.

Now he stood there, the discomfort clear on his face, even in this light. He was practically shaking. Yet, he diligently observed the prisoners, just as he'd been ordered.

Tony was right, Jessica realized. There would be no heroic charge to escape in the morning. If they were going to get out, it had to be another way. She settled in, adjusting her position on the floor. There was still a long night ahead, and she had no intention of sleeping.

CB scanned the perimeter of the main street through the city, checking for any sign of danger. It could be that the GMT had somehow doubled back and beaten them to *New Haven*. Or perhaps a citizen had gotten hold of a rifle and was waiting on a rooftop to take a shot at Maryana. He didn't want to think about these things. In fact, he wanted nothing more than to wrap his hands around Maryana's throat and squeeze.

Just like he'd done with Chuck.

He wanted to vomit when he thought about it. He'd wrung the life out of one of his own soldiers. He'd felt the small bones in Chuck's neck snap and crack until the pressure of his vampiric grip broke the man's spine. He only wished he could do the same to Maryana.

But he'd been ordered to protect her, and that was what he had to do. And not in some half-assed way. Every fiber of his being, every instinct honed by years of training and field experience, it was all dedicated to the task set before him. As much as he wanted to kill Maryana, he wanted to protect her even more so. Even if his mind and heart didn't, every other cell in his body longed to obey his master.

He'd faced many difficult realities since being turned. Not seeing Jessica. Tracking down the GMT. But the worst was the knowledge that he was the perfect weapon to help Maryana to accomplish her goals. He'd spent his life developing the mind and body of a warrior. Now, his body's purpose was to serve his master. He'd throw his life away in an instant at her whim, and it sickened him.

"You know what really bothers me?" Maryana said, her voice strained. "It wasn't Jaden who shot me. It wasn't even this Alex person you all seem to worship. It was some random dude who just happened to get the drop on us. It's an insult, really."

CB glanced back at her. Maryana still wasn't able to walk. Two Twisted carried her in a seat made of their linked arms, one set under her and the other supporting her back. Her severed spine made sitting up on her own impossible, let alone walking. Still, she didn't seem all too concerned about her injury. Her pain was clear, and she seemed almost offended that such a thing had occurred, but she seemed confident that she'd heal.

"Felix," CB said. "His name is Felix."

Maryana frowned at him. "Well, thank you, Colonel. Now that I know his name is Felix, that makes everything better."

CB ignored the comment and turned back to the road ahead of them. It was night, and the darkened streets were nearly empty. Mostly, people were huddled in their quarters, trying to adjust to this new reality of *New Haven* resting on the ground and the sky dark and painted with stars. The few people who were out scattered as they saw the grim parade of Twisted escorting their bloody queen.

"Colonel Brickman," Maryana called. "Walk with me."

CB immediately dropped back, falling into step beside the Twisted carrying her.

"We've only been working together for a short time, but I hope you've seen that I like to have fun on the job. Work hard, play hard, right? Preferably at the same time."

CB wasn't sure what to say to that, so he grunted noncommittally.

"The point is, I wanted to handle this thing with a deft

touch. Toy with Jaden for a bit. Kill everyone he cares about. Let him think he has a chance. Then crush him. In a perfect world, this could have gone on for years." She groaned and her face scrunched up in pain. "But this severed spine thing has me thinking. As much as I wanted to do this cat-and-mouse style, I may have to let out the wolf. Do you take my meaning?"

"No, I don't think I do," CB said, dryly.

She frowned at him, clearly disappointed. "Play time's over, Colonel. Prepare the Twisted for a full-scale offensive. As soon as I can walk again, we're going to Agartha. I want every person under that mountain, Twisted or human, dead. It's time to end this."

CB swallowed hard as his body responded, his muscles tensing as every fiber of his being prepared to obey his master.

26

STRENGTH CAME FROM THE MIND—THAT'S what Alex always told herself. She worked as hard as any of the guys in the gym, but she was still sixty pounds lighter than them. She was able to beat her larger foes because she kept her mind strong. She channeled her rage in battle and kept control. She anticipated movements and used good form. It was her mind that made her strong. Alex needed that strength right now as she carried Chuck's corpse toward the incinerator.

The body was on a wooden plank with a handle on each corner. Alex, Ed, Felix, and Owl carried it toward a conveyor that led to the open mouth of the incinerator. Alex knew that they should be headed back to press the attack at *New Haven*, but the leaders of Agartha wanted to honor Chuck's sacrifice. She also knew that the team needed this. The constant battles and losses were taking a toll.

The small march toward Chuck's last resting place was broadcast throughout the city. The cremation room was small and it held the former citizens of *New Haven*, along with Cynthia, the leader of Agartha, and Jaden. A cameraman and sound person were there, broadcasting the funeral. The lights were cold and the room was silent as they placed Chuck's body on the conveyor.

The four pallbearers let go, and the conveyor carried Chuck's body into the cold incinerator. The four GMT members stayed silent and hugged one another. Alex stood next to the switch that would ignite the fire. She knew that she was supposed to say something, and hoped that she would not embarrass Chuck's memory with her poor words.

"Chuck Williams was a great soldier. He faced monsters without flinching and gave his last breath protecting humanity. The members of the GMT will remember him." Alex paused. She turned from the GMT to the camera.

"I know that the GMT seems heroic and we can be placed on a pedestal. We all need to remember that Chuck was just a man. He failed at times, but he picked himself up and continued. That is what every member of the GMT does. We are not superhuman; we are just normal people who rise to face the world we live in. That ability is not something unique to Chuck or the GMT; it is an ability that lives in every man, woman, and child in Agartha.

"Chuck would not want to be remembered as being anyone special. He would want you to realize that you all have the ability to be great. You can all face monsters with the fierce, unflinching nerve of a warrior. The time may come when you need to. He did not give his life because he thought people were weak and needed protecting, but because he knew the potential that we all have. Remember him as a man. He is your friend, your neighbor, your family. That hero lives in each and every one of you."

Alex stepped back and flipped a switch on the wall. Flames shot out inside of the incinerator and Chuck turned to ash.

The Savage End

THE CRATE BANGED when Frank dropped it on top of another just like it. It was five feet long and three feet wide, painted a dull army green. The sound echoed in the transport and carried out to the rest of the hanger where the team was gearing up.

"Holy shit, Frank!" Ed shouted. "Don't just toss those. There's enough explosives in there to give this mountain a sky light."

"Sorry, I'll be more careful." Frank looked at his deformed hands as though they had caused the issue.

People bustled around the room, grabbing supplies and checking the transport. Alex stood next to Jaden, observing the organized chaos. She checked a tablet, making sure that everything they needed was on the list.

"We each have demons to face on this journey," Jaden said, as he ran a stone across one of his blades. "Are you ready?"

Alex raised her head and glared at him. "Of course, I'm ready. Can you control yourself and stick to the plan when Maryana tries to mess with you?"

He frowned thoughtfully. "I believe I can. This will be our best shot at victory. I will make sure that we succeed." He paused. "I saw you miss the kill shot during the battle. I have fought alongside you enough to know that was not lack of skill. Will you be able to kill CB this time?"

"I won't have to. I'm going to save CB when I put a bullet through Maryana's head. That is the plan," Alex said, flatly. "I'll kill him if I have to, but I'm going to do what I can to avoid it."

"I fear that plan may cause all of our deaths. CB is your greatest adversary. He taught you, and he can predict your moves. Right now, he is Maryana's puppet. If we have the chance, we need to take him out."

Thankfully, Owl walked up, interrupting before Alex said something she might regret. "We'll be ready in five minutes. There's enough ammo and explosives for a small army."

Alex clapped her friend on the back. "Good work. I'll let them know we are good to go."

"You think we can pull this off? I like the plan, but there are only six of us. A tactical strike force is great, but we are about to fight an army."

Jaden answered before Alex could respond. "The odds are against us, but I see no better option. We are the only ones who can save everyone, so that's what we will do."

"We've got this. All we need to do is get to Maryana. Once we take her out, this will all be over." Alex sounded strong. She needed to lead without fear, but she felt they were missing something. There was a resource that they weren't using. She just couldn't figure out what it was.

The image on the monitor showed the transport leaving through the outer blast door. Brian watched it drive away and then turned back to his work. Ed had sparked an idea that had consumed him since the moment it had come to him. He'd started off making progress quickly, but now, he was at a standstill. The monitor in front of him blinked, waiting for its next command just as it had for the past ten minutes.

He knew this weapon could save the GMT, but they were on their way to almost certain death. They needed every advantage they could get, and he hadn't been able to deliver before they left. Now his mind was locked with doubt, fear, and panic.

"You okay?"

"What?" Brian turned to see Stephanie staring at him. "Yeah, I'm fine. Why?"

"You're looking extra pale and not typing like a madman."

"I'm just a little stuck. I've been trying to write an algorithm to make this work. I just can't seem to concentrate."

"I can't either. My brain is mush." She let out a yawn and stretched in her chair. "I'm going to sleep for an hour or two. Can I get you anything before I go?"

Brian looked over at the sandwich next to him. He'd taken two bites and set it aside. He wasn't sure how long ago that had been, but the bread was already going stale. He was about to ask if she could grab him something to eat, but stopped.

Brian remembered what Ed had said to him about seizing the moment. Stephanie wore a lab coat which hid most of her form, but it couldn't mask her youth and beauty. A single brown curl hung in her face, contrasting nicely against her pale skin. He felt guilty that with everything that was going on, he still desired her more than anything else.

"What are you looking at?" Stephanie asked.

Brian realized that he had been staring long enough to make it awkward. "Oh, nothing. I was just lost in thought." She relaxed a little and smiled. That smile gave Brian courage. "Actually, that's not true. I was looking at you."

"Oh." She turned, trying to see her reflection in the blank monitor, "Do I have something on my face?"

"No, not like that. I meant I was noticing how good you look. You know, like, checking you out." Brian turned bright red. "Sorry, that came out all wrong."

Stephanie laughed. "No, it didn't. That was one of the best compliments that I've gotten in this lab."

"I find that hard to believe." He steadied his nerves "I don't want to come off like a creep, and I know the timing isn't great, but can I go with you to rest?"

This time, a hint of red touched her cheeks. She thought for a moment and gave him a smile. Then she stood up and pulled him out of his chair by the hand. "Okay, big guy. Let's go. Just don't make me regret this."

As they walked out of the lab hand-in-hand, Brian made a mental note to buy Ed a drink the next time he saw him.

27

CB PAUSED before entering Maryana's chamber. Even through the thin metal of the door, he could hear wet, sucking sounds. She was feeding. It was the last thing in the world he wanted to see, partly because he didn't want to watch some poor *New Haven* citizen suffer, and partly because he knew it would make him hungry. He'd only drunk from blood packets so far, and he intended to keep it that way. Unless of course his master told him to drink from a human. Then there would be nothing he'd be able to do, except obey.

Speaking of which, Maryana had told him to gather a report and return to her as quickly as possible. So even though he wanted to wait outside until she was done eating, he couldn't. His fingers found the door knob before he even told them to reach out.

When he stepped inside, he was surprised to find Maryana's usual seat empty. Odd, especially since she still couldn't walk. Then he heard the sucking noises again and he saw her on the floor, hunched over a body, her teeth buried in the poor man's neck.

CB cleared his throat loudly, announcing his presence.

Maryana released her hold on the man and looked up at CB. "Just a moment, dear. I've got to drink every drop, if I want to heal. Besides, if I don't, he's liable to get up and start walking around in a few minutes. The last thing I need is another Twisted. This city is lousy with them." She went back to feeding.

CB waited, trying not to grimace at the horrific sounds emerging from the corner.

After a few moments, Maryana let out a contented sigh. "Ah, all done. Mind helping me back to my chair?"

As if he had a choice. CB scooped her small frame up in his arms, all too aware how easy it would have been to rip her head from her body. Easy, if it hadn't been impossible. He set her down gently in her chair and stepped back a respectful distance.

"How did you get down there?" he asked.

Maryana smirked. "I had a notion when this man was brought to me. I'm injured. That means a lowly human might actually have a fighting chance of escaping me. So I ordered the guards out of the room and told the man that if he beat me to the door, he could leave.

CB glanced at the bloodless body in the corner. "How'd that go?"

"Like most things in life, it was disappointing. He wasn't fast, even for a human." She paused and chuckled. "But you should have seen his face when I flopped onto the floor and dragged myself across the room with my arms. He was freaking out."

CB could only imagine how terrifying that must have been. A crippled vampire, dragging her broken body across the floor faster than a human could run. If he'd still been human, he might have shuddered. "I can't imagine that was good for your healing body."

She shrugged. "Maybe not. Still, you've got to admit I'm healing nicely. I bet I'll be walking in a day or so. Must be my good genes."

Or the rate at which you're feeding, he didn't say. Every hour, she had another captive brought to her. Every hour, one more person died.

Maryana gave him a long look. "I appreciate your concern. Maybe you're starting to grow fond of me. Maybe you have a little crush."

He said nothing, just hoping she didn't order him to say what he really thought of her. He might not survive the string of expletives and filth that would pour out of his mouth.

"Maybe you should come over here and show me how much you care," she said, her voice suddenly soft.

"I'm a married man," he said, his face stone.

She raised an eyebrow. "You think that matters? I could order you to undress me with your teeth. I could order you to do all sorts of nasty things. I bet I could make you forget all about Mrs. Brickman."

CB gritted his teeth and said nothing.

She broke out in a laugh. "I'm kidding, you idiot. You think I'm in any shape for that? I don't even have any feeling below the waist. Besides, you're a little long in the tooth for my tastes. I mean, sure, I'm technically older, but I don't look it." She shook her head, chuckling. "All right, give me your report."

He nodded sharply and told her what he'd found. "We still have two hundred of your Twisted guarding the perimeter of the city. No one else has tried to escape, since that first group."

"Good. And how about power?"

"It's a work in progress. Engineering has some backup generators and solar cells up, but it's nowhere near what we need to power the city. Most of the major systems are still down. It's going to take time and leadership to put this place back together."

Her lips curled in a smile. "Lucky for you, we have both. I'll tell you one thing that can't wait, though. The public-address system. That's the priority."

CB couldn't hide his annoyance at that. "Are you sure, Maryana? What about Agriculture? Or lights?"

"With the PA system, I can issue all my Twisted orders at the same time. Without it, I have to hope they're listening on their radios. Besides, I like to remind my humans what I'm going to do to them every now and then." She wagged a finger at CB. "You have your orders. Get to work."

Jessica's eyes snapped open and every muscle in her body tensed. By the time she remembered where she was, the warehouse was oddly quiet. Yet, something had startled her awake. Maybe it was someone crying out, or a door slamming as they dragged yet another captive off to wherever they were taking them.

She squeezed her eyes shut at the thought. Every hour, a Twisted selected one of them, seemingly at random, and dragged them out of the warehouse. These people never returned. What were they doing with them? Interrogation? Turning them into Twisted? Letting them go free? That last option seemed pretty farfetched, but Jessica had to at least pretend it was possible in order to keep herself sane. She couldn't believe she'd managed even a moment of sleep in this stressful environment.

If only she could sit down with CB for five minutes. Yes, he was a Twisted now, but he was still CB. If she could just talk to him, touch him...

She pushed the thought away before it could go too far. She couldn't think like that, hoping for the impossible, not if she wanted to survive this and give everyone else in this warehouse the best shot at survival. Needing to distract herself, she stood up and stretched, feeling her joints crackle and pop in protest at having to move after spending hours jammed in a seated position. She looked toward the door and saw Thomas standing bolt upright, observing the people, the same as he had done all night. She wandered over and stood next to him.

"Hello, Thomas," she said as casually as possible. "How you holding up?"

He glanced at her, surprised by the question. "I'm fine. I'm a vampire now... err, a Twisted. I can stand for days on end without getting tired."

"That's not what I meant. Can't be easy, holding all these innocent people captive."

His look darkened. "I have my orders. There's nothing easier than following your master's orders."

She nodded slowly. "You know who I am?"

"Of course. You're CB's wife."

She chuckled at that. "That's sort of a reductive way of putting it. I'm the Director of Engineering, too. As well as plenty of other things. But yeah, I'm also CB's wife." She paused. "How is he?"

Thomas stood up a bit straighter. Though he wasn't happy about his situation, he was proud to be serving under

CB. "He's still the same old CB in most ways. He works hard as hell, fights his enemies with everything he has, and stands up for his people. And he doesn't talk about his feelings much, so I'm not sure I have the answers you're looking for."

"No, that's fine Thomas." She paused. "What can you tell me? Do you know what's going to happen to us?"

His face wrinkled in concern. "I don't think Maryana would like me telling—"

"Did she order you not to?" Jessica interrupted. "If she didn't order you, then you can tell me."

He thought about that before answering. Then he looked her in the eye for the first time. "No one's getting out of here alive. The lucky ones will be turned. The rest of you will just be killed."

It was no more than she expected, but still she flinched at the words. Tony had been right the previous evening. The people here were mentally worn down and battered. But it didn't matter. She had to unite them and get them to attempt an escape. CB would do it, if he was in her place. But he wasn't; it was all up to her.

Suddenly the door to the warehouse burst open and a Twisted marched inside. "Time for another one," he said to Thomas. Then he noticed her standing there. "Ah, I see you were waiting for me."

He grabbed her arm and pulled her through the doorway and out onto the streets of *New Haven*. She fought hard, for all the good it did her. If she wasn't in the warehouse, she couldn't lead the escape. The people were doomed. But all her fighting was fruitless. The Twisted barely seemed to notice.

She opened her mouth to yell at him, to convince him to

let her go back, but she didn't get the words out before being shocked into silence.

Just outside the hull of *New Haven*, something exploded.

28

The windows rattled from the shockwave of the explosion. The sound was muffled in the Hub, but even there, it was clear that something was wrong. Maryana pushed herself off of her chair and dragged her limp lower body with her arms. She looked out of the window, searching the city for the source of the blast.

A few moments later, CB marched through the door.

"Things sound exciting out there. What happened?" Maryana asked.

"I sent some men to check on the cause of the explosion. They have not reported back, yet."

She looked him over. "What do you think caused it? I'm guessing that it isn't some kind of accident. Did Jaden make an army to come for me?" She pulled herself back to her chair with her arms.

CB wanted to lie to her, or say nothing, but he answered the question. "It's the GMT. They know that you're hurt, and they will attempt to kill you with a strike force. If Jaden has created more Twisted, we haven't seen them. I'm guessing that the team will strike from two or three different points. You'll be the target."

Maryana choked back a laugh. "You think a team of less than ten is going to take on my army, in my city?"

"I know the GMT. I think they have a decent chance of succeeding."

Maryana smiled. "Maybe they would have had a chance, but you sure hurt their odds."

CB balled his fist hard enough to make blood drip from his hands. "Screw you."

"I told you, my body isn't ready for that yet, but I'll remember it for later." She smiled and winked at him. "What strategies would you suggest for killing the GMT?"

"We need to use our numbers. We know that they'll be attacking from the area of the explosion, and we know that they will be coming for you here. Send half of the Twisted after the point they are attacking and have half stay here to defend you when the strike comes. There may be other ways that would probably risk less Twisted, but that should give you the best chance at victory."

"I like having you around, CB. You are useful. I think you overestimate the skills of your team. They are annoying, but I doubt they will take out too much of my army before each and every one of them is dead. My only concern is Jaden. He is our number one priority. Make sure that we find and kill him."

"It wasn't Jaden who put that hole in your back. It wasn't even Alex. I still think there's a good chance I'll be looking down at your corpse by the end of the day." CB couldn't help himself. He wanted to hurt her in any way he could.

Maryana glared at him. "Bend down and put your face next to mine." CB did as he was told. The two were eye to eye and inches apart. Maryana stretched out her index finger and buried a sharp claw into CB's cheek. A drop of blood escaped and ran down his jawline. Then she dragged her nail across his cheek toward his eye. The path left a deep cut. Blood dripped down his face like warpaint. The nail reached the corner of CB's eye socket and he felt the claw against his bone. She stopped there.

"Remind me to take out that eye when the battle is over. That will help you remember to mind your manners around me." She pulled the nail out of his cheek and gave him a light slap.

CB straightened up. His mind raced, trying to think of ways to break the hold that she had on him. He needed to help the GMT in any way he could.

"Gather the Twisted. I want them all working on killing Jaden and the GMT."

There was another explosion. The windows rattled once more.

He stood up straight and gave her a long look. "So, killing Jaden and the GMT is our number one priority right now?"

Maryana glared at him; he was an imbecile. "Obviously. Repairing the ship can wait until we are no longer under attack. Stop wasting time and make it happen."

The first explosion gave Jessica a sliver of hope. She knew that the Twisted dragging her by the arm was taking her to die. She thought that he might put her back in the holding area when the explosion happened, but he kept marching toward the Hub. He barely reacted to the second explosion.

"Didn't you hear that explosion? Those are not accidents. We are under attack. Aren't you supposed to protect the city?" She hoped that he could choose which set of orders to obey.

"I was ordered to get a prisoner and bring her back to Maryana. I couldn't do anything else if the city was burning down around me. You don't understand. There is no option." The tone in his voice told Jessica that he had completely given up.

As they reached the base of the City Council building, Jessica realized that she was not going to get out of this. She hoped that her death would be quick. Most of all, she hoped that she would not be turned.

The door to the Council building opened and a Twisted walked out. Jessica's knees went weak and she trembled as CB stepped in front of her. His face was deformed and his back rounded, but Jessica instantly recognized her husband. She tried to speak, but the words caught in her throat. Tears began to stream down her face.

CB looked at the Twisted holding her. "We have new orders. They take priority over everything else."

The Twisted stopped and waited for instructions.

"Maryana needs the army to defend her and the city. All other tasks are on hold until we neutralize the attacking force. Help me gather the army, so that we can prepare the defenses. I need you to find all the Twisted you can and tell them to meet here."

The Twisted let go of Jessica and ran back toward the holding cell. Jessica ran over and threw her arms around CB. He gave her a quick hug, then pushed her back.

"I'm sorry. I have to follow my orders." He was already moving away from her.

She trotted along next to him. "CB, stay with me. I'm scared. I need your help." Tears continued running down her cheeks as she spoke.

He turned toward her, his eyes fierce. "Run and hide. Don't tell me where you are going. She may send me to find you, and I will not be able to disobey her. This is your chance. The Twisted will be focused on the attack."

Jessica shook her head. "CB, you can beat her. I know you can. Fight against her control."

Tears sprang to his eyes. "I wish you were right, Jessica. I love you so much. I'm sorry." He turned and ran at full speed, leaving her alone in the street.

Jessica stood for a moment, unable to move. Seeing CB like that, knowing that he was Maryana's puppet, crushed her soul. She wanted to lie down and give up. Then she thought of the people in the holding cell. There was still hope for them. CB had given her a chance to get them to safety. She started running toward the holding cells.

She tried to stay in the shadows next to the buildings, but there was no one else on the streets. Three groups of Twisted passed her on the way to the building. None of them even glanced in her direction. She reached the makeshift holding cell in time to see the Twisted file out and head toward the Hub.

Once they left, she went inside. The people were still huddling on the floor. The light from outside filled the room and glowed around Jessica. "Come on, people. This is our chance. Time to go."

She expected a mad rush of people to head for the door, but no one moved. Finally, a woman spoke in a soft voice. "They said they would track us down and kill us if we leave this room."

"They are going to kill you, no matter what. Each person that has been dragged from this room is dead. You can either run and take a chance at survival, or you can stay here and face certain death. Anyone who wants to roll over and die, stay here. Everyone else, come with me."

Tony stood up. "I'm with you Jessica." He walked over and stood by her side.

A few seconds later the entire room was standing. Jessica led them out of the building and through the streets as quickly as she could. They pried open an access hatch in the street and headed down to the mechanical level. Once they were all below street level, they heard gunfire in the distance.

"What do we do now?" Tony asked.

"That sound is the GMT putting it on the line to save us. We are going to do whatever we can to help them."

29

Five hundred yards west of *New Haven*, Owl lay prone on a small hill, sniper rifle at the ready. Her vampire eyes allowed her to see the Twisted gathered in the area where the explosion had taken place very clearly. She put her eye to the scope and dialed it in, getting a much clearer look at her enemies.

There were at least three dozen of them, and most were milling about aimlessly, their eyes occasionally scanning the distant hills. It was clear that they were nervous, and that made Owl smile. She hoped that they were whispering to each other, wondering when the GMT would attack. Maryana may not understand what the GMT could do, but her Twisted surely did. They'd grown up hearing tales of the brave exploits of the toughest men and women *New Haven* had to offer. She hoped they'd be able to use that legendary status to their advantage. It might not mean a lot, but every little bit helped when you were fighting an army of super-vampires. She was about to find out how much leeway their reputation bought them; it was time to begin.

She drew a breath and spoke softly into her whisper mic. "We're set, Felix. Fire charges one through six."

"Roger that," he replied, his voice calm and steady. "Get ready, team. Firing charges one through six in ten seconds."

Owl started the mental countdown and adjusted her position one more time, preparing for what was about to happen. She didn't love the role she'd been assigned; her larger Twisted fingers had caused her accuracy problems in the past. She'd much rather be with Alex and Jaden. It wasn't like they didn't need the help. At the same time, she understood why it had to be her at the sniper rifle. She was faster than Felix, and Frank had zero training with the sniper rifle. And Ed had another task to perform.

Owl believed she was comfortable enough with her new hands that she could do what was needed. Whether or not that was hubris remained to be seen, but one thing was certain—her mind was ready. It was time to take Maryana down.

The countdown in her head reached zero, and for a moment nothing happened. Then all hell broke loose.

Six charges went off in quick succession, each detonating near where the group of Twisted was standing. Bodies flew into the air, along with dirt and rock. As the sounds of the explosions faded, they were replaced with shouts of confusion and surprise, and more than a few cries of pain. At the edge of the dust cloud, a Twisted staggered forward, his left arm missing.

Owl resisted the urge to put a bullet through his brain. Not yet. Soon, but not yet.

As the dust began to settle, the chaos continued. The Twisted weren't exactly reacting to the attack in a disciplined fashion. Maybe this was going to be easier than she thought.

Then, as if in response to her thoughts, the Twisted fell silent. The ones she could see through the dust stood up a bit straighter. Owl knew why, but she still needed to confirm it. Then she saw him.

CB had arrived.

He marched to the front of the group, an army of at least a hundred Twisted at his back. Figuring in the areas still obscured by dust, there could easily have been a hundred of them.

"It's time, boys," Owl said, into her mic. "Get ready."

It was very likely that CB would have found her out quickly, whether by sensing her presence or noticing a glint of sunlight off her scope. But she didn't have a lot of time, and she wasn't about to leave anything to chance. She needed to draw his attention. She selected her target and looked through her scope.

The Twisted directly to CB's right suddenly collapsed, his brains lying on the dirt behind him.

CB's head whipped around. For a human, it might have been impossible to locate a sniper that far away from a single shot, but CB was no longer human. "There!" he shouted, pointing at Owl's position. "We have our orders! Get the GMT!"

In an instant, CB and his Twisted army were in motion, sprinting toward her. It wasn't exactly the elegant battle strategy CB was known for, but Alex and Jaden had predicted this would be his reaction. CB's instinct to protect his soldiers would be overridden by his all-driving need to obey his master.

How right they'd been.

CB and the Twisted ran with no formation, no order to their ranks. They charged like a herd of animals. Owl had been counting on this, too.

She selected her next target and fired. A woman near the front of the pack fell backward, as if yanked by an invisible rope. Owl took aim and fired again, dropping an older man on the north side of the horde. Then again, and a young man fell.

While her Twisted hands had taken some getting used to, she had to admit that being a Twisted marksman did have some advantages. Firing accurately at a distance required stillness. Human snipers had to account for their breath, firing only after they'd exhaled and their respiration wouldn't throw off their shots. Even their heartbeats could affect their accuracy. Owl had to worry about neither breathing, nor a heartbeat. She was the picture of stillness. As the enemies charged, loping toward her at top speed, kicking up dirt and dust in their wake, she lay unmoving, dealing out death in carefully measured doses, one squeeze of the trigger at a time.

She fired once more, dropping a woman just in front of CB. She let go of her rifle, leaving it in the dirt. It was time to go. "I'm in motion, guys!"

"Copy that," Felix answered.

Owl took one more look at the charging horde. They were less than a hundred yards away now, and she could see that she'd initially underestimated their numbers. There were at least two hundred of them. She just hoped she'd given herself enough distance to retreat.

She turned and sprinted west, directly away from the city.

Up ahead, she heard the rumble of the transport, and she charged toward it. She crested a small hill and saw it, rolling slowly westward, its back doors open.

"Come on, Owl!" Felix shouted.

"Working on it." She took long strides, half running and

half leaping, covering eight feet with each exaggerated step. As she neared the vehicle, she put all of her strength into one more leap, catapulting off the ground with a power that surprised even her. She flew fifteen feet through the air and landed hard in the back of the transport, skidding across its metal floor.

As she landed, Frank stepped into the still-open doorway, an automatic rifle in his hands. He fired on the charging Twisted, sweeping the barrel back and forth, going for maximum coverage, rather than accuracy.

"Punch it, Felix!" Owl yelled. The transport lurched forward, bouncing along the uneven road. Owl looked past Frank and saw the Twisted army still in pursuit. She spoke into her mic. "We've pulled off as many as we can, Alex. Now, it's up to you."

AT THE SOUND of Owl's voice in their ears, Jaden and Alex broke cover, exiting the brush where they'd hidden, and ran toward the city's western hull. They moved silently; both knew their mission, and they knew what they had to do to accomplish it.

When they reached the hull, Jaden lifted the cutter and went to work on gaining them access to the city. Alex watched their perimeter, hoping that Owl had been able to draw away enough Twisted that they would have the few minutes that Jaden needed to get them inside.

She knew they wouldn't have long. CB was no idiot. He'd soon realize that the GMT was trying to draw him away from the city. Jaden was less worried about that. He was convinced that CB's orders would be to kill the GMT. His only goal would be to carry out those orders, so if there were

GMT members in front of him, he'd do whatever it took to take them down, even if it meant weakening the defenses of the city. Alex just hoped he was right.

If a few random Twisted came upon them, or if they needed to abandon the mission and retreat, they had a contingency plan—Ed was hiding in the brush a few hundred yards away, sniper rifle at the ready. Alex hoped a group of Twisted didn't stumble across him... But with all of the noise Owl had been making, that seemed unlikely. Any Twisted outside the city would be focused on her.

As Jaden worked the cutter, Alex thought about the promise she'd made the last time she'd left the city. *I'm coming back for you*, she sworn. It had been a vow spoken to Maryana, the city, and herself. In the past few days, she'd fantasized about fulfilling that promise many times. She'd envisioned an aerial assault, leading a huge army toward Maryana, and so much more. The way it was playing out was different from anything she'd imagined, but somehow it felt right. Two of them, sneaking into the city to assassinate Maryana. *New Haven*'s greatest warrior and Agartha's sole protector, fighting for the future of humanity, against the woman who brought down civilization. There was something poetic about it.

Alex just hoped she'd be the one to drive the sword through Maryana's heart.

She heard a thump and turned to see a piece of the hull lying at Jaden's feet, and a hole large enough for them to pass through.

"We're in," Jaden said. "Let's go."

Alex patted herself, checking that everything was in place. She had her pistols. She had her sword. She was ready.

Alex looked Jaden in the eyes. "Whatever happens, we don't leave until she's dead."

Jaden met her gaze, his eyes stone. "Agreed. We don't leave until she's dead."

With that, Alex and Jaden entered *New Haven*.

30

THE QUICKLY LOWERING sun cast long shadows in the streets of *New Haven*. Alex had never seen the city so still and quiet. The streets were empty of humans and Twisted alike, and the monitors that usually displayed announcements and upcoming events were blank. The city looked dead, and she had pulled the trigger that had killed it.

When they were nearly to the Hub, Jaden slowed and walked beside Alex. "I feel her, which means she can feel me, too. I also feel Twisted. Lots of Twisted. We are headed in the right direction, but this is the point where we should separate. I will work to draw her out."

"I'll be ready once you do. As soon as she shows herself, I'll take her out."

"She will want to kill me herself, which means I may be in a bad spot before she reveals herself. Do not expose your location until you have her in your sights."

Alex nodded. "You just get her to an exposed location. I'll be ready." Jaden started moving again, but Alex stopped him. "I hear you're the deadliest thing on the planet. Today is the day to prove it."

"This will certainly be a test of my skills. I'm glad to have you on the battlefield with me."

Alex nodded once again, and Jaden disappeared into the shadows. She made her way two blocks farther and entered the Hub. She knew exactly in which building she wanted to set up. It was a high-end residential building across from the council building. The rooms were large and had floor-to-ceiling windows. From a corner unit, she would have a great vantage point on two sides of the council building.

Alex stayed low and glanced around a corner. The path to her target looked clear. She moved quickly across the street and went to the back entrance of the building. The door was unlocked and she headed up the stairs. Once she reached the third floor, she drew her pistol and calmed her breath. She slowly opened the door to the hallway. The glow of the evening light made it possible to see down the hall. She breathed a sigh of relief. The hall was empty. She reached the door to the corner unit and tried the handle, but it didn't budge. Kicking down the door would make too much noise. Instead, she knocked softly. After a moment, a voice came from the other side. "Who's there?"

"It's Alex Goddard. I'm here to help."

The door opened and Russell, one of the pilots of *New Haven*, stared at her in shock. "What's going on, Alex? Are you attacking Maryana?" In the living room behind him, a woman and a small boy huddled on the couch.

"I don't have time to answer. I need to use your home. Get your family out of here now. Take them to a unit on the other side of the building, lock the door and stay low."

"Why? What's going on?"

Alex swung the rifle over her shoulder to the front and chambered a round. "Sorry, but your home is about to be a war zone. Go, now!"

Russell and his family rushed out of the unit and headed back the way Alex had come. She closed the door behind them and stayed low as she moved toward the window. She crawled the last few feet on her belly, stopping when she could see the street below her and the entrance to the council building. She'd known that this was going to be a difficult mission, but seeing the enemy's sheer numbers made it seem impossible. Two rows of Twisted stood around the base of the building. They were staggered, a soldier standing every five feet.

She had hoped there would only be a skeleton crew left in the city. Instead, she estimated at least two hundred Twisted around the outside of the building. And there had to be plenty more inside, guarding Maryana.

Alex spoke into her radio. "I'm in position. I can see the front doors and the east side. There are hundreds of them, Jaden."

"Just be ready."

JADEN CROUCHED behind a small electric vehicle and peered through the window. Since he was so greatly outnumbered, he knew that speed was his only chance. The Twisted would descend on him as soon as he made a move. The way they were so spread out would allow him the opportunity to strike, but he needed to be smart about it. He needed to keep his objective in mind. *Draw out Maryana.*

To his left, he spotted a bench on the sidewalk. He grabbed it, pulled it off the ground, and threw it as high as he could, sending it in a long arc toward the City Council building.

"Incoming!" one of the Twisted shouted as he trained his gun on the projectile.

The Twisted next to him followed his line of sight. "Is that a bench?"

While the object was still in mid-flight, Jaden sprinted toward the line of Twisted. The nearest badge spotted Jaden, but it was already too late for him. Jaden's blade sang its deadly song, removing the Twisted's head before he understood what was happening.

Jaden did not pause after the kill. He weaved through the line of Twisted, killing two more before the first shot was fired. One of the badges screamed out, "Jaden is here!" The badges around him fired as fast as they could, but Jaden moved in an unpredictable path, reaching out with his blades as he came. Bullets flew through the air where he had just been, or hit the empty spaces where the Twisted had assumed he was going. In a matter of moments, eight Twisted lay dead on the ground.

Jaden let out a grunt of pain as a bullet stung him, removing the bottom of his left ear. He turned to his right and saw dozens more Twisted pouring out the door of the Council building, coming to join the fight. He'd done enough to bait them. Now, it was time to set the hook.

He disengaged, charging across the street, leaping through the window of the nearest building, the one next to where Alex now hid. A swarm of bullets followed him, and he felt one pierce his side before he landed on the apartment floor. A woman screamed, but Jaden ignored her. He sprinted to the door and out into the hallway. Behind him, he heard crashes and shouts as the Twisted followed him into the building.

Jaden readied himself in the hall and the first Twisted lost his head the instant he crossed the threshold of the door. The second crashed into the corpse of the first. His momentum carried him and he crashed into the wall on the other side. Jaden crouched as the third Twisted raced in. Each of his swords sprang out, snake strikes. One blade went up through the chin of the Twisted entering the hall; the other found the heart of the man who had crashed into the wall. Jaden stayed low and moved down the hall.

One of the doors opened and a man peeked out. Before Jaden could tell him to get back inside, bullets tore through the walls from the unit through which Jaden had entered. The curious man couldn't even get out a scream as his body was riddled with bullets. There was no time to mourn the man; Jaden kept moving toward the stairwell. The pain from his partially missing ear wasn't slowing him down, but he noted the blood soaking his shirt from the last shot. He knew that he needed to do better if he wanted to make it.

The gunfire paused for a moment, and he heard a radio somewhere behind him chirp to life. He immediately recognized Maryana's voice. "Bring that building down, now!"

Seconds after the command, the sound of breaking glass came from multiple directions, and he charged up the steps. In his earpiece, he heard Owl's voice. "The army is headed back to the city. They are coming for you."

He didn't have time to respond, or even think about what that meant. He forced his body to move up the stairs with all the speed he possessed.

He made it to the fifth floor before the first explosion shook the building. It was impossible to tell how many more explosions followed. The sounds were continuous, and they came from every direction. Jaden was racing past the door to the sixth floor, when it burst inward. Fire and shrapnel flooded the stairwell. The building was going up in flames, and quickly.

The flames raced upward as he continued his sprint for the roof. Despite his speed, the flames were gaining ground, and he felt heat nipping at his back. He was only one level below the roof now. He focused his will and continued upward. The stairs under his feet started to move as the building rumbled with more explosions.

He reached the exit as flames licked his legs, and he dropped a shoulder. The frame of the door gave way and the metal bent as he hit it at full speed. He thought he heard a bone crunch, but in his heightened state, he couldn't tell what had broken.

Jaden rolled across the roof, thankful that the fire hadn't engulfed him. The building shook as more explosions barked from below him. He ran toward the edge of the building, but when the sole of his boot hit air instead of the roof, he realized he was in free fall. The building was collapsing under his feet. An explosion blew a hole through the roof to his left, and a chunk of concrete slammed into his side. The bullet hole there screamed out in pain. Dust and fire shot up around him as he disappeared among the rubble.

31

Darkness surrounded Jaden. Normally, this wouldn't have been a problem. He could see perfectly fine in darkness, when it was caused by a simple lack of light, but this was something different. So much dust hung in the air that it was preventing even him from seeing anything.

One thing he knew—there was no light coming in through the dust, which meant he was buried under rubble. Not an ideal situation, but at least he could move. The debris covering him shifted fairly easily. It could have gone the other way. He might have been pinned under a few tons of steel until Maryana saw fit to have her Twisted pull him out...if she ever did. Still, it was impossible to deny that their plan wasn't exactly going smoothly. Alex was hiding in the next building over, ready to support him with her rifle. Ed was still hiding in the hills, and the rest of the GMT was somewhere on the ancient roads around the city. And all of them were screwed—and screwed for no reason—if Jaden didn't dig his way out of this mess.

He found a solid foothold and raised himself up, shifting the debris, worming his way upward. Since he'd been on the roof, he shouldn't have to dig himself out too far. Sure enough, before long, he shifted a piece of steel and a shaft of light peeked through. He was just about to head for it when his hand rested on something soft. Something unmistakable. A human leg.

He pawed his way along the body until his fingers found its neck, and he confirmed what he'd already suspected. The person was dead. A powerful wave of anger flashed through Jaden at that moment. How many people had been in that building when Maryana's troops had taken it down? Fifty? A hundred? And how many still lived? Maybe a handful? And all for the off chance that the explosions would kill Jaden. This went far beyond collateral damage. The carelessness with human life was beyond wasteful... it was inhuman.

Perhaps Alex was starting to rub off on him. He knew that most of these people would have been dead in twenty to forty years anyway, maybe sixty at the outside, but he didn't care. He simply could not abide Maryana's wanton disregard for the precious lives she'd just destroyed. Jaden emerged from the rubble with renewed vigor, eager to finish the mission and end Maryana.

No sooner had he climbed atop the rubble than he saw the first Twisted charging at him. He drew his swords and held his ground, feeling the precarious piece of steel he was standing on vibrate as the Twisted ran toward him. He flicked his sword outward, taking a tiny bit of pride in his economy of motion, and the sword slipped into the Twisted's heart, a quill slipping into an inkwell. Jaden pulled the sword out and flicked the blood off it, striding past, even as the Twisted collapsed.

The rest of the Twisted were not as foolhardy. Rather than charging him, they renewed their explosive assault.

Grenades flew through the air, landing near him, in the rubble under him. Each explosion compromised his already dangerous position in the ruined structure. He couldn't survive up there for long, with them chucking explosives at him. His eyes settled on his target far below—the entrance to the City Council building. Maryana hadn't come out, as he had hoped, but the Twisted had scattered to attack him. If he could get down there, perhaps the plan could get back on track. They hadn't failed this mission, yet.

As the grenades flew, Jaden danced over the rubble, cutting a path through the teetering structure, leaping nimbly from collapsed staircase to split windowsill, using the remains of the building to his advantage, staying away from bullets, explosives, and those Twisted who were foolish enough to come after him themselves. As he worked his way lower and lower, he tried not to think about all the dead in that building. Or all those clinging to life, who needed immediate medical assistance. He had to stay focused. He could do so much more for the people of *New Haven* by killing Maryana.

Finally, his feet touched down on ground level, and he could see it in front of him. His target. The entrance to the City Council building. He charged for it, but before he reached it, four Twisted stepped through the door, blocking his path. Four more came from his left side, and three from his right. He slowed, considering retreat, but a glance backward showed four more behind him.

Fifteen Twisted, and they had position on him. He was surrounded, and his enemies were inching toward him, closing their circle. He silently cursed, knowing he'd fallen into a trap. Jaden was confident in his own abilities, but he wasn't foolish. He knew he couldn't take fifteen enemies.

But that didn't mean he was going down easy. He raised

his swords and fixed his eyes on the Twisted between him and the door. If he was going to die, he'd do it trying to get to his target. He slashed at one, but the others were already on top of him. One grabbed his left arm. Another grabbed his right. He tried to yank them away, but two Twisted were on each of his arms, now.

Another Twisted stepped toward him, claws raised. He reached back his hand, ready to slash at Jaden's throat, and a bullet went through the center of his forehead.

ALEX LAY ON HER BELLY, staring out of the window as she worked the bolt on her rifle and fired again. One of the Twisted holding Jaden's right arm fell. She fired one more time, and Jaden yanked his right arm free. One sword was all he needed to regain the advantage. He quickly dropped two Twisted to his left, then spun toward one behind him.

Revealing herself, breaking the plan and firing before Maryana appeared, wasn't an easy decision, but there was no way she was going to let Jaden be torn to shreds in front of her.

She was just about to fire again, when she spotted a blur of motion. Pulling her eye away from the scope, she saw more Twisted approaching. A group of five was coming from the west, sprinting down the street toward the City Council building. No, not five. Ten. Make that twenty. More were coming from the other direction now, too. There had to be a hundred of them. She immediately understood that this was CB's group; the one that had been called back from chasing Owl. Jaden reacted quickly, leaping into the air. She didn't see where he landed; there were simply too many of them.

Rushing footsteps pounded along the floor behind her. Alex had just enough time to turn her head before rough hands grabbed her under the shoulders and hauled her to her feet, lifting her like she weighed nothing at all. She threw a punch, blindly lashing out at the enemy's midsection, but it was easily deflected. A set of hands grabbed her, pinning her arms to her side while another set of hands roved along her body, efficiently removing her sword, her pistols, and all three knives. In less than two seconds from the start of the attack, she was restrained and weaponless.

CB stood in front of her, a Twisted on either side of him. Another one was behind her, holding her arms. CB opened his hands and let Alex's weapons fall to the floor. "That was a nice try, drawing us away from the city, Alex." His voice was thick with sadness. "A very nice try."

"Didn't work for long, I see," Alex said. The words sounded dumb in her ears, but she needed to buy herself a moment to think.

"She called us back," he said, simply. "There are new orders. I have to take you to her, now."

With that, he turned and walked toward the door. The other Twisted followed. Alex squirmed, but the grip on her arms was like iron as the Twisted carried her.

"CB," she said as they reached the stairs and started down. "I know you're in there."

"Of course, I am. That's the real hell, isn't it? I'm in here, and I can't do a damn thing but what I'm told. I can't help my friends. I can't even visit my wife." He didn't turn as he spoke, keeping his eyes ahead of him.

"You can fight this!" she insisted. "You're the strongest-willed bastard I've ever met. If anyone can fight this, it's you."

Now, he finally turned, and there were tears standing in

his eyes. "You don't think I'm fighting? I've been fighting since the moment I was turned. Fighting with everything I have. You remember our old motto? I've been fighting. Fighting and preparing. Preparing and fighting! That's all I do. And now, I have to take you to her."

Alex stared at him blankly, wondering if maybe he'd gone insane. "CB, you're not making sense. Please, just try. Think of Jessica! She's out there and—"

"Keep her quiet," CB said to the Twisted holding her.

The Twisted changed position, one, holding her with one arm, while the other covered her mouth. She could move a little now, but not enough to get away. And she couldn't speak to CB.

They took her out of the building and through the street, carrying her past where Jaden had confronted the group of Twisted. She saw a half dozen Twisted bodies but, thankfully, not Jaden's. The Twisted watched as she was carried past, their expressions conflicted. The former badges didn't want to see Alex hurt, but the vampire slaves delighted at seeing their master's orders carried out.

They entered the City Council chamber. Maryana sat at the head of the table, and the full Council was seated around her. They were all Twisted, now. Alex felt like she was going to be sick.

Maryana's face broke out in a wide grin at the sight of them. "Go ahead and put her down. Pretty sure she can't do much against a room full of us." She turned to CB. "How's it feel to be the one to bring your star pupil to her execution?"

"Not great," CB said, softly.

"I'll bet not. But into every life a little rain shall fall, right?" She looked at Alex, who was standing on her own now, arms free. "So, you're the one I've been hearing so much about. The hero of *New Haven*." She tilted her head a little, giving Alex a close look. "I'm disappointed. You showed guts the first time we met, but I don't think there's much more to you than that. A lot of hot air in a sad, little balloon."

"Yeah?" Alex said, her voice quivering with anger. "How about I blow that hot air up your—"

"You know what?" Maryana said, holding up a hand. "It's been a long day and my spine is still sort of severed. I don't have time for this. You're more enjoyable dead than alive. CB, rip her head off."

In a flash, CB was on her. The fingers of his right hand wrapped around her neck, and he lifted her off the floor. Alex's eyes widened in shock and terror. CB had her. She was unarmed. What could she do?

Then she realized something—CB had her by the throat, but he wasn't squeezing. Every muscle on his face and neck was standing out in harsh relief, as if he were fighting with all his might. He was resisting, Alex realized.

"CB?" Maryana said, a hint of concern in her voice. "Chop-chop. We still have Jaden to deal with."

CB's arm was quivering now, and his eyes were turning redder by the moment. "Alex... I can't... for long.... you have to..."

He was fighting. Just like he'd said. How had he put it? Fighting and preparing. Preparing and fighting.

Then she got it. The team motto.

Ours is not to question why...

It had been so long since they'd used the unofficial team motto. Not since the discovery of Agartha. Not since Drew's death.

"CB?" Maryana called. "I want that head in my lap in the next three seconds. That's an order."

There was blood seeping from his nose, now.

She saw it then, sticking out as clear as day. CB's GMT knife, strapped to his combat vest where he'd always kept it. Her hand shot out and she wrapped her fingers around the handle. As she pulled it back, she felt its weight.

In Alex's mind, she saw CB as a young man, flying the away ship back to *New Haven* after his entire team had died in the streets of Toronto, knowing that he was the last of the GMT, and it was his duty to rebuild it.

Alex shoved the knife forward with all her strength.

She saw him sitting across from her, giving her the news that she had been selected for the GMT, and his not-quite concealed smile at her whoop of delight.

The tip of the blade sank into CB's chest.

She saw him on his wedding day. Every eye had been on Jessica as she walked down the aisle; every eye but Alex's. She'd been watching CB, and the love she saw in his eyes gave her hope for a better life to come.

Alex kept pushing until the knife pierced his heart.

Ours is not to reason why, just to be prepared to die.

The fingers around Alex's neck went limp and the life went out of CB's eyes. Alex's feet touched the floor, and CB's body collapsed.

For a moment, Alex went numb. Then the emotion came rushing back with an intensity she'd never felt in her life. She squeezed her fingers tight around the knife's handle and turned toward Maryana.

Maryana stared down at CB, wide-eyed. "What the... Somebody want to tell me what the hell just happened?"

Alex stepped forward. Before her foot hit the ground, the door shattered into an explosion of splinters, and Jaden charged through, sprinting at Maryana.

32

"Kill him!" Maryana screamed. She pushed her chair back from the table, putting more distance between her and Jaden. There was rage in her eyes at the site of Jaden, but Alex also saw fear.

The eleven remaining members of the Council sprang out of their chairs and lunged across the table. The two Twisted who'd been guarding the door raised their pistols, but Jaden sliced through them before they could level their weapons.

The Council attacked him as a mob. Jaden was able to put a sword through two of their hearts, but the close space worked against him, and he was tackled by the remaining members. They had no weapons other than their claws and teeth. They tore at his flesh as the chaotic mass of bodies fell backward.

The council had the strength and speed of the Twisted, but their minds were civilian. Alex's mind was hardened by battle. She knew that this moment, when everyone was focused on Jaden, was her one shot. Her target was twenty feet in front of her. She pushed hard off her back foot, propelling herself toward Maryana, gripping her knife tightly.

Maryana moved fast, considering she was dragging herself with only her arms. She pulled herself to the window and punched the glass with a short, lighting fast-hit. The window shattered, and she pressed her hands against the floor, preparing to launch herself out of the window.

Alex dove toward her, swinging her knife in a downward arc. The blade sank into Maryana's right calf, sliding all the way through the muscle and sinew and burying its tip into the floor below. Maryana tried to throw herself out of the window but she only moved forward a few inches, pulling her own muscle through the blade. She turned back, her eyes wild, and saw the knife in her leg and Alex holding onto the handle. She lashed out, claws extended toward Alex's arm. The motion was fast, but Alex pulled her arm back just in time.

Alex grabbed the knife's handle with both hands and yanked it out of Maryana's leg. Blood erupted from the wound, sending a stream of dark red into the air. Alex lunged forward, thrusting the knife toward Maryana's heart. But Maryana was moving just as fast. By the time the knife came down, she already had one hand through the broken window, and the blade missed its target, slashing harmlessly at the place where Maryana had been a moment ago.

Maryana gripped the side of the building with one hand and pulled hard. Her body dragged over broken glass and plummeted out of the window. Alex dove after her, her fingers clutching at empty air, missing Maryana by inches. She let out a scream of frustration as she lay with her arms and torso out the window, watching Maryana fall. She balanced there, inches away from tumbling out of the window.

The street below them was crowded with Twisted, every one of them looking up at her. One of them caught Maryana and gently set her down on the ground.

Alex turned back to see Jaden standing on a pile of mangled corpses that had been the City Council. The long table where they had held so many meetings and debates was covered in blood and tissue. Jaden held the last living council member by the throat. He wildly clawed at Jaden's arms and face. Jaden thrust his sword into his heart, ending the struggle. The Councilman fell to the floor, and Jaden bent to pick up his second sword.

Alex didn't know how much of the blood covering Jaden was his own, but he was clearly in bad shape. Strips of flesh were missing from his cheeks and neck, and his shirt had been torn to shreds. His torso was covered in bite and claw marks. She wondered how he was still standing. His eyes were filled with pure rage.

Jaden snarled and sprinted toward the open window.

"No!" Alex yelled. "There are too many of them!"

The words were still leaving her mouth as Jaden leaped over her and tumbled out of the window. He readied his swords as he fell toward the hundreds of Twisted waiting on the ground.

A small, familiar voice came from somewhere behind her. "Where are you, Alex?"

She turned and spotted her radio handset lying on the ground next to CB's body. She ran over and grabbed it. "I'm in the Council building, Owl. Jaden just jumped into the middle of a Twisted army. Get the team out of here, now!"

"I will. Right after I pick you up. I'm almost there. Get to the roof as fast as you can."

Alex could tell that she wasn't going to dissuade Owl. She grabbed the pistols off one of the dead guards and headed toward the stairs. As she left the room, she heard explosions from the street below.

The Council chamber was on the top floor of the building, so Alex only had one level to go to reach the roof. As she burst through the door, she spotted someone crouching there—Owl.

The four Twisted hot on her heels gave her no time to think about how her friend had beaten her to the roof. As she stepped onto the roof, she turned and opened fire. She dropped three of the Twisted before they stepped through the door. The final Twisted made it through, but he'd only taken one step before his head exploded in a mist of blood and the report of a rifle split the air.

"I see you picked up Ed," Alex said. "How the hell did you get up here so quickly?"

"Same way we're getting off."

"Jaden's down there!" Alex pointed to the edge of the building. They looked over the edge. The Twisted were jammed together so tightly that the street looked alive. Most of them were focused on something on the ground, but a few looked up and aimed their weapons at Alex and Owl.

"We have to go," Owl said. Before Alex could respond, Owl threw her over her shoulder and sprinted toward the opposite edge of the building. As the gunshots split the air, she leaped off the edge and soared to the building across the street.

JADEN REPLAYED the last few minutes in his mind. The moment he'd leapt from the building, he'd realized his folly.

Maryana's army was gathering around her, and she was screaming at them to capture him. Bullets tore through his legs and a grenade exploded next to him. Despite the long odds, he knew better than to give up. He pressed forward toward Maryana, striking at those around him with his blades. But there were simply too many. They piled on top of him and tore at his falling body. He heard gunshots and hoped that some of the GMT would survive.

Slowly, the chaos around him turned to order. The shouting and gunfire stopped, and enough Twisted cleared off to let Jaden see the fading light of the day. He relished that moment. He'd gone so long without seeing the sun.

Twisted held onto his arms and legs. He looked to his right and saw that his hand had been removed at the wrist. Blood trickled from the wound and the jagged flesh at the end of his arm. He felt strange, almost like he was floating. He wondered if there was any blood left in his body. His other arm was whole, and his left hand still clutched his ancient blade.

The Twisted pried the sword from his hand, and he was not able to put up much resistance. They dragged him into the building. Maryana was just inside the door, held aloft by two Twisted. Her legs dangled limply, blood still dripping from the wound in her calf.

She broke into a wide smile. "Hey, Dad. How's your day going?"

Jaden looked her in the eyes. "Give me a moment to catch my breath, and we can finish this."

"Hmm, I don't think so. You taught me a final lesson. There was a time when I would have let you heal, just so I could enjoy killing you at your peak physical condition, rather than as the worn-down husk you are now. I'm still tempted to keep you alive for the next few centuries, just to torture you. The only problem is, I would like to rebuild humanity, so I can rule them for the next thousand years. You got close to ending me today. As long as you're alive, you're a threat." She glanced at the Twisted standing behind Jaden. "Bring me his swords."

Jaden felt a wave of sadness as he looked at this monster—a monster he'd created. "You've proven your ability to destroy, but I think rebuilding may be beyond your limits. You turned the world to ash and were buried in the rubble for the last century and a half. The people who survived are stronger than you think. Your rule with be short."

Two Twisted came through the crowd and handed Maryana Jaden's swords. She took one in each hand, holding them out and admiring the glimmering edges. Blood still dripped from each blade. "Do you remember when I asked you to make me a set of these?"

Jaden looked up at her, barely able to lift his head. "I do. I told you that I would teach you to make your own when you were ready. I did not see the poison that filled you at the time. You will never gain the skills to forge weapons equal to those."

"I'll never need to waste my time with that, now. I've already got a set." She looked at Jaden's right arm. "I see you are not symmetrical at the moment. Let's see if these blades are as sharp as you say."

She brought the blade down in a flash, and Jaden's left hand fell to the floor. A trickle of blood dripped down from his wrist. Jaden kept his stare on Maryana. He did not make a sound.

"Wow, you really do great work, Jaden. I could barely feel that blade chopping through your bone. I'm going to use these blades to cut all of your vampires to pieces." She chuckled. "Oh, wait. I can't do that, because they are already dead."

"They are gone," Jaden said, his voice filled with sadness. "My time has passed and so has yours. The world is ready to move on. I can feel it. Both of us will soon be forgotten."

She snarled at him. "I will never be forgotten. I am the force that changed the world. My rule will be eternal. The last creature who could have stopped me has no hands and is about to die."

"No. You are a cancer that will be cleansed from the world. In the great expanse of time, it will mean nothing. You mean nothing." Jaden smiled.

"I'm going to kill every person in your city." Her voice rose to a yell. "I'm going to wipe out every record of you. Any tongue that speaks your name will be ripped out, until everyone who knew you is dead."

"As I said, my time has passed, but you will not be the one to remove my memory. The hole in your chest came from a man. The wound in your leg is the work of a woman. Your downfall will come at the hands of the humans. I see that, now."

"You don't see shit," she spat. "You are just trying to make yourself feel better before I kill you."

"I see how hideous you are, on the inside just as much as the outside. I hope you think of me when Alex takes your head." After a thousand years of fighting, Jaden drew his last breath, ready to finally rest.

"Nice try, but all your needling can't change the facts. I've won." Maryana swung Jaden's sword with all her might. The hum of the blade fell silent as it passed through his neck. The light left his eyes, and his head fell to the floor.

33

Alex's head bobbed from side to side as the transport rumbled and jostled along the road, but she didn't notice. She stared straight ahead, her face unreadable.

She couldn't believe it. The unthinkable had happened. CB was dead. She'd never talk to him again. Never hear one of his speeches. Never debrief after a mission together. He'd given her a shot at the GMT, he'd trained her, he'd put her in a position to lead when most commanders probably would have benched her. And now, he was gone. But she felt no guilt at being the one to drive a knife through his heart. It wasn't her that had killed him, it was Maryana. Alex had set him free.

The fact that he'd done the impossible and resisted Maryana's direct order to kill Alex made the loss even worse. Not only had Alex lost her mentor and her friend, but humanity had lost the strongest-willed son of a bitch alive. He'd proven that in his final stand, and now he was gone.

While CB's death was the biggest loss in Alex's world, it hadn't been the biggest loss to humanity as a whole. That had been Jaden. He'd protected humanity for a thousand years. By all accounts, he was the greatest of the vampires. Even Maryana respected and feared him. Hell, she'd brought down the world, partly to mess with him. Now, their greatest protector and weapon in the war against Maryana had been lost.

And for what? The mission had been foolhardy, to say the least, and they'd paid dearly.

Barely a word had been spoken since they started driving away from Agartha. Ed occasionally stood and glanced out the back windows to make sure they weren't being followed, but he did it in silence. Felix drove the truck, gripping the wheel hard, his eyes fixed on the road ahead. Somehow, Owl seemed to be the most shell-shocked of all of them. She'd been as close with CB as Alex had, and she had the added complication of being of Jaden's direct bloodline. Alex could only imagine what complicated emotions she must be experiencing.

They'd been driving for over an hour when Frank finally spoke up. "All right, listen. I know I'm not a warrior, like you guys. Not really. I fired my first weapon a few days ago and I killed my first Twisted in that same fight. I'm just some guy, who was in the wrong place at the wrong time. I dumbly volunteered to let myself be injected with vampire blood, and now here I am, living in a nightmarish future."

Alex looked up at him, her jaw clenched. Part of her was annoyed that he'd interrupted her quiet contemplation, but she also wanted to know where he was going with this.

"I may just be a random guy," he continued, "but I've seen some shit. I lived through the end of the world. I saw some of the toughest people I've ever met crumble, and I watched as some of the most unexpected people found a way to survive."

The beginnings of a frown began to form on Alex's face.

This wasn't the appropriate time for stories of the good old days, and she was quickly losing patience.

"You know what the difference was between the people who survived and those who didn't?" Frank asked. "After the worst had happened, some people found a way to get back up and keep moving. It's not that they weren't sad or shocked by what had happened, but they were able to keep going, you know?" He paused, trying to find the words. "I guess what I'm saying is, we have to keep moving forward. What happened today is one of the shittiest things I've seen in my long life, but Maryana isn't going to stop now. That means we can't, either."

Alex couldn't remain silent any longer. "We just lost maybe the two best warriors on planet Earth. They were our friends. Our brothers. Are you saying we can't take a couple of hours to deal with it?"

His eyes met hers, and she saw a determination in those eyes that she hadn't noticed before. "Yes. That's exactly what I'm saying. Every minute counts. Every second. Get on the radio to Agartha. Start planning. We need a way to take Maryana down, and feeling sorry for ourselves isn't getting us any closer to victory."

Ed shifted in his seat. "Frank, I think you should—"

"I should what?" Frank snapped. "I should shut up? I'm not going to. There's too much at stake. We have to step up to the plate and we have to do it now. And if you don't like that, you can kiss my ass. I'm going to kill Maryana or die trying, and I hope you all are with me on that."

"Uh, no," Ed said. "I was going to say you should act like this more often. You almost sound like a real GMT member."

As much as Alex hated to admit it, Frank was right. There wasn't time for sorrow. Not now. She pushed herself to her feet. Her body felt like it weighed a thousand pounds, but she forced it to keep moving. She went to the empty passenger seat and fell into it. Then she lifted the radio from the dashboard and held it to her lips.

"GMT to Agartha, do you read?" She waited ten seconds, then spoke again. "GMT to Agartha, do you read?"

"We read you, GMT," a female voice said. "What's your status?"

Alex squeezed her eyes shut. "We're...we're en route. I need you to put me on with Brian McElroy."

JESSICA STARED out of the window of a nondescript apartment in Sparrow's Ridge, careful to keep to the shadows. She'd been watching for a while now, and she'd noticed something odd. More and more people were heading out of the Ridge and toward the Hub. And she had no idea why.

She was considering this when she heard the sound of a key turning a lock. A moment later, Billy stepped inside, squeezing his bulky frame through the half-open door. As soon as he was inside, he eased the door shut and flipped the lock.

"Thank God, you're back," she said. "What's going on out there?"

He shook his head, as if overwhelmed. "I'm sorry I was gone so long. I only meant to gather a few people for our planning session tonight, and then..."

She took a step toward him. "What?"

Billy's large eyes were filled with sadness when he spoke again. "I don't know if it's true, Jessica, but people are saying the GMT tried to attack the city. They're saying that Maryana killed some of them, it's not clear who. Some say

Jaden, and some say Alex. I guess there's going to be some sort of parade through the Hub in a little bit. I don't know... it's all so bizarre."

She could see in his eyes that there was something else. "Billy, what is it?"

"I don't know if I should even... I mean, it's not confirmed in any way. But people are saying CB died during the attack. They're saying Alex killed him."

Jessica grabbed the windowsill, steadying herself through the wave of vertigo and nausea that followed those words. She waited in silence until it passed. "Billy, we have to go to that parade."

"I don't think that's a good idea," he said. "If you're seen—"

"It wasn't a question. We're going."

He looked at her for a long moment, then nodded.

They made their way through the streets as inconspicuously as possible. Jessica was dressed in the blue jumper of a sanitation worker, and she wore her hair up, hoping that would be enough to deflect casual eyes from recognizing her. They needn't have worried. The people were so nervous and concerned about the word-of-mouth summons passed from Twisted to human about the parade that they didn't pay much attention to their fellow humans. By the time they made it to the Hub, it was clear that the spectacle would be enough to deflect all attention from any individual attendee.

They arrived just as it was beginning. Lines of Twisted marched through the street in carefully orchestrated formation. Jessica saw new faces among them, non-badges who she knew for a fact had not been Twisted earlier that day. It appeared that the Twisted army had been replenished after the GMT's attack.

The crowd was somber and nervous as they watched,

waiting for their insane queen. Every person in that crowd knew she was capable of anything, and that knowledge left them on edge. In many ways, crazy was far worse than evil. Crazy couldn't be predicted, so none of them were safe.

After what felt like five hundred Twisted had passed, Maryana finally appeared. She sat in a chair carried by four Twisted, held aloft above their shoulders. She held something in her hands, but Jessica couldn't make it out clearly at first. When she finally did, she gasped.

It was a glass box, and within that box was Jaden's severed head.

"We've only begun!" Maryana shouted as they marched. "The parade is just getting started, and it doesn't stop until we reach Agartha. We're going to hold Jaden's head up high as we wipe his city from existence."

34

After an hour of debating in the cold conference room, the voices were starting to blend together for Alex. It was all just a drone of sounds.

The GMT and the leaders of Agartha were discussing how to proceed. There was no shortage of ideas. Cynthia proposed filling in the outer blast tunnel. Permanently closing the biggest way in and out of Agartha would leave them better protected. As others had quickly brought up, it would also leave them trapped.

The news of Jaden's death had affected the citizens of Agartha even more deeply than Alex had anticipated. Even after all the of other vampires died, the people had held out hope that Jaden would save them. Now, their savior was gone. The only thing they wanted to discuss was how to fortify the city and hide from Maryana.

Alex had tried to tell them that any number of turrets and traps would only briefly delay the city's downfall. Still, they'd ignored her and kept going around in circles about different configurations of explosives and traps.

Alex got lost in her own thoughts. She knew that there

was a solution to this riddle. One that didn't involve hiding under a mountain and waiting to die. She had all the puzzle pieces; she just needed to put them together. She decided to try making her point once again. "Look, I appreciate how scary this all is, but I still think we aren't going to be able to defend the city against Maryana's army for long. There has to be another way."

"So what are you saying?" Cynthia said, her frustration beginning to show. "Should we just open up the front doors and let Maryana walk right into the city? You may just give up on *New Haven*, but we have some backbone down here."

Ed stood up. "Watch your mouth. The people of *New Haven* are her prisoners, and you're hiding in this hole. Good people have died fighting against all odds for you. If you disrespect us again, you are going to find out how much backbone we have!"

Owl stood up and put a hand on Ed's chest, gently pushing him back toward his seat. "Fighting each other isn't going to help anything. I know we are all stressed out, but we need to focus."

Charles, the new head of Engineering, spoke up. "Maybe Maryana doesn't care about us now that Jaden's gone. You said she wanted him dead more than anything. Now that she's killed him, she may leave us alone."

Ed smacked his forehead with the palm of his hand. "Holy shit, that is the dumbest thing I have ever heard. Maryana wants pain and suffering for all. She isn't going to let us live happily ever after, just because she killed Jaden. She will come for us."

"That's why we are rebuilding the turrets," Cynthia argued. "If we put up a strong enough fight, they may give up. She already has four times the number of people that live here. Losing a bunch of them just to get to us may not be worth it."

Owl sighed. "I know this is hard, but you can't think logically when it comes to Maryana. I've seen her up close, and she is crazy. Smart, but crazy. If she has to kill forty thousand New Havenites to get the ten thousand people in this city, she will. In fact, I think that might make her happy. That's what makes her so hard to fight. She doesn't take the path you expect."

"Fine, she is coming for us. Then what's the plan?" Cynthia paused for a moment, letting the silence hang in the air. "We are going to fix the turrets, unless you think the five remaining GMT members can take out Maryana."

"We can't." Everyone in the room turned to Alex when she broke her silence. "There are at least one hundred Twisted for each member of the GMT. We've tried to sneak in and assassinate her. That failed, even with Jaden."

"See? We need to defend our position."

Alex held up a hand, silencing her. "Maryana is cruel in ways that make her seem crazy, but she still uses strategy. She always uses more force than she needs. She keeps the fights unfair, so that she comes out on top. Jaden told me a story of her creating an army of twenty thousand to kill a small group. Her forces almost took this city already. The vampires saved us, but if they hadn't been here, that army of two hundred would have done it. I'm guessing that the next time she comes, she'll bring at least twice that many soldiers."

"So, what do we do?" Owl asked.

"The unexpected. We bring the fight to her." Alex's mind raced as the solution was forming.

"You just did that." Cynthia said. "It didn't work."

"That's not the *we* that I'm talking about. Five soldiers

will never succeed. If we have an army of five thousand, it may work." Alex paused, taking in their confused expressions. "The most success we have had fighting her was during the ambush. We almost had her there, and we killed a lot of her troops. She will be expecting everyone in Agartha to be hiding and defending. You're proud of your backbone, Cynthia? Then use it. Let's bring every able-bodied man and woman to fight her army."

There was a long silence.

"Alex, they're just civilians," Owl said finally.

"They are more than that. I think Jaden saw it before he died. The people of this city are not just sheep that need us to protect them. They have the same drive and spirit that makes every member of the GMT fierce. We were all civilians until duty called on us to be better. This moment in history calls for *all* people to be better. They will rise to the moment. Each and every citizen of Agartha will fight for themselves. They will fight for their friends, their family. They will fight to save the human race from the plague that has kept us from walking on the surface for so long. They don't need to be saved; they need to be unleashed."

"So, we face the Twisted on the battlefield, outside of the city?" Cynthia asked as she crossed her arms.

"Better. We're going to attack. I have an idea of where it will work. We will use the element of surprise. If we do it right, the battle will be quick. All we need to do is kill Maryana."

The door to the room opened, and Brian and Stephanie walked in. "Alex, I've got something I need to show you."

FRANK AND OWL exchanged a nervous glance as Brian

prepared to fire the weapon once again. Brian and the rest of the GMT stood in the next room watching them through a window.

"That's perfect," Brian told them through an intercom. "Just pay attention to the effects. I want to know exactly how you feel."

"Do I have to do this again?" Frank responded. "Maybe Owl could just—"

"Don't be a baby," Brian interrupted. "I need to repeat the test to confirm the findings." He paused a moment as he tapped at his tablet. "Okay, going in three, two, one."

Brian touched his tablet and the two Twisted fell to their knees. In a moment, both were on their backs, crying out in pain. They toppled over and lay on the floor.

He pressed the button on the intercom. "Please try to stand up as quickly as you can."

"You're an asshole, Brian!" Owl shouted. She tried to lift herself off the ground with one hand but lost her balance and fell back down.

Frank did better than Owl. He was able to get to his feet. Owl's second try was more successful, and she was soon standing next to Frank. They wore expressions of pain on their faces, but they were starting to look steadier.

Brian touched the tablet again and the two relaxed. "Sorry about putting you through that. I just needed to verify the results."

"Are you ready to explain now?" Alex asked.

"It was Ed's idea." Brian nodded in his direction.

Alex's eyes widened and she looked over at Ed. "You came up with this?"

Ed looked from Brian to Alex. "Um, I think you finally mushed your brain staring at those equations, Brian."

Brian shook his head. "Don't you remember? In the cafeteria. You wanted a weapon that could shoot through walls and hurt only Twisted. This is it."

Ed smiled. "Yeah, I guess I did come up with that. So how did I do it?"

"We are using the strength of the Twisted's senses against them. It's actually really simple. I'm generating sound frequencies that are imperceptible to human ears. The combination of low and high ranges disrupts their balance. The frequencies can go through solid objects. The range isn't too far, but it is pretty effective, as you can see."

"How come they could get back up?" Alex asked.

"Think of it like opening a door and there is a jet engine on the other side. If you go from silence to maximum volume, it is painful and disorientating. It is an explosion of stimulation for your ears and mind. Like a flash grenade. But eventually your body starts to adjust and you get past the disorientation."

"How long will it last? And how close do we have to be?" Alex's mind raced as she asked the questions.

"Based on our very limited testing, it only takes fifteen to thirty seconds for the Twisted to acclimate to the noise. After that I'm guessing it will still be hard for them to concentrate, but they will be back on their feet. The range should be about one hundred yards." Brian smiled at his achievement.

"This is great, Brian, thank you. I need you to make as many of the devices you can, as quickly as possible. If you can increase the range, that would be even better."

Owl entered the room with the rest of the group. She rubbed her temples and glared at Brian. "I don't want to be around the next time you decide to test that."

"Would you have been able to fight with that noise going on?" Ed asked.

She considered the question. "I think so, but I would not have been at one hundred percent. It definitely caught me off guard when he turned it on."

"This is perfect," Alex said. "The only thing we need now is a way to monitor *New Haven*. I need to know when Maryana is coming for us."

"And how are we going to do that?" Owl asked.

"We may just have an ally still in the city. CB let something slip when he was taking me to Maryana. Jessica is still alive. Now we just need to figure out how to contact her."

35

Over the past three days the small apartment in Sparrow's Ridge had been transformed from an empty hideout to the secret headquarters of those New Havenites willing to stand up to Maryana. Jessica had worked tirelessly, gathering information, people, and supplies. Sleeping no more than a few hours a night, she'd planned and strategized. Still, there was so far left to go.

Wesley and Billy had approached about three dozen people, carefully selecting only those that they knew they could trust. They'd probably been overly cautious, but it would only take one wrong choice to bring their little operation to a very bloody end. So far, they hadn't done any actual fighting, but they'd done plenty else. Without electricity and the usual infrastructure, the people of *New Haven* were suffering. Jessica had heard stories of injured and ill people showing up at the hospital only to be turned away at the door. Apparently, Maryana had decided on a whim that only her Twisted should have the privilege of medical care, never mind that their undead bodies basically took care of healing themselves. Luckily, Billy knew a trust-worthy young doctor, and she'd been making the rounds, treating people in their homes, under the cover of night. Jessica's team had even done a little repair work, assisting people whose homes had been made unsafe during the various rounds of fighting.

But there was still so much left to do. The most pressing threat in Jessica's mind was the water supply. *New Haven* had collected most of its water from vapor in the clouds. That wasn't an option with the ship grounded, and the water supply was running dangerously low. And yet, Maryana's people had prioritized the public-address system. It was infuriating. If they didn't end Maryana's reign soon, a lot more people would die.

On the other hand, they didn't necessarily need Maryana to die before they could start changing things; they just needed her gone. And if she kept her promise of heading for Agartha, they just might have their chance.

But the most surprising development was that Owl had made radio contact with Jessica using the GMT channel, which, thankfully, Jessica was still monitoring. Apparently, Brian had figured out a way to boost the signal, so it reached from Agartha to *New Haven*. They kept their conversations brief for fear of discovery, but during their short talks, they'd formulated a plan.

There was another impact of the work that Jessica was doing. The more she concentrated on the big, almost impossible problems of their society, the less she thought about CB. It wasn't that she was trying to ignore her grief completely. It was just that she couldn't afford to let it hit her full in the face. If she didn't keep her mind occupied, she'd start thinking about how he must have felt when Alex drove a knife into his heart. About how he'd never have a proper funeral. About how she'd never again hold his hand.

She shook her head, clearing it of such thoughts. There'd be time for that later, assuming that later happened and she was alive to experience it. She looked across the table to Billy, who was scratching on a piece of paper. "What's the final tally?"

He let out an annoyed grunt. "I wouldn't call it final, by a long shot. More like a rough estimate, conducted in the least scientific circumstances possible."

"Okay, give me that, then," she said, dryly. One of the most important tasks the group had taken on was attempting to account for the size of Maryana's Twisted army. They did this by calculating the people who'd gone missing, both those reported officially at the Hub (one of their bravest members still worked there), and the much larger group not officially reported, but circulated through the rumor mill. People whose family members went missing tended to spread the word. As Billy had said, it was far from an exact science, but at least it gave them some vague idea of the numbers they were dealing with.

"We've got two batches of people who went missing, right? The ones the day after the GMT's attack, and the ones over the next few days. I'm thinking that first batch was just to replenish the Twisted who died in the fight. She wanted to bring her army back to the five hundred or so she had before that."

"Fair assumption," Jessica allowed. "How about the others?"

"Tough to say. Especially because they've been so spread out. A few dozen missing yesterday. A few more today. My guess is that she's just adding more on a whim. She's not exactly the most level-headed leader we've ever had. Could be she's eating some of them, too."

Jessica shifted in her seat, trying not to get annoyed. Billy had a way of talking around things and giving long, complicated answers to simple questions. "So, what's the number?"

He bobbed his head back and forth, considering. "I'm going with seven-fifty."

Jessica frowned. It was about what she'd expected, but the number sounded so large when she heard it out loud.

"How about your end?" Billy asked, turning to Wesley.

"We've got a dozen guys down in an empty part of the sanitation facility, putting together makeshift weapons. And we've got explosives. All the weapons for a small army. We're just missing the army."

Billy didn't respond to that. It was a major point of consideration. Perhaps they could recruit enough people to fight some small portion of the Twisted, but the moment they expanded their recruitment, they opened themselves up to discovery. The timing was going to be crucial.

"Let me ask you something, Jessica." From the sound of Billy's voice, it was clear he wasn't looking forward to the conversation that was about to happen. "If what they're saying about Alex is true, if she killed CB, are you going to be able to work with her? We're going to need the GMT to have a shot against Maryana."

Jessica considered the question. Logically, she understood that Alex hadn't really killed CB. She'd set him free. Her head knew that fact. But her heart was another matter. Jessica didn't hate Alex for what she'd done. A part of her was grateful. But she also knew she'd never be able to look at the woman who'd stabbed her husband in the heart quite the same way as she'd looked at her old friend,

Alex. "I'll be able to work with her. Don't worry about that."

"Good. Because the last thing we need is—"

A sudden squeal cut through the air, interrupting his words. Then Maryana's lilting, distinctive voice echoed through the streets of *New Haven*.

"Testing, testing. Hot damn, we're live. Hey, ladies and gentlemen, it's your old pal and beloved mistress, coming at you via our newly restored PA system."

"Good lord," Jessica growled. "She really dumped all the city's resources into fixing that thing just so she could hear herself talk, didn't she?"

"A lot of you were at my little parade the other day, and you may have noticed I was not exactly my usual spry self. I wanted to let you know I'm back walking, running, jumping, and eviscerating again. Vampire healing is a wonderful thing."

Billy's face fell, and Jessica understood why. It was tough not to feel like they'd missed their shot at Maryana. If she was fully recovered now, she'd be even tougher to beat.

"Many of you also saw my little glass box. The one with Jaden's head in it. I promised during that parade that I'd be taking it to Agartha, and I'm going to do just that. And I'm taking a few more boxes with me. One for each member of the GMT. Gotta catch 'em all." She paused to laugh at her own odd joke. "My army and I will be leaving in just a few minutes. But fear not! I'm leaving a couple hundred of my dearest friends behind, and I've given them strict orders. If anybody steps out of their homes, the Twisted are under orders to tear their throats out. I shouldn't be gone long. At least, you'd better hope I'm not. I also gave the Twisted orders to kill everyone in this city if I'm not back in three days. Just to give you a little extra incentive to cheer for your beloved leader. I'll see you soon. Until then, be good and stay inside."

They sat in silence for a few minutes after Maryana had signed off. Then Billy spoke. "I guess this is it. Our chance."

Jessica nodded. "We just have to wait for the signal, then we make our move."

36

Maryana gazed up at the billowy clouds hanging in the sky, indifferent to the events transpiring below them, and smiled. Walking in the light was still a thrill for her. She didn't know if it was worth giving up her formerly beautiful face, but it was certainly pleasant.

"What do you think of the sun?" She looked up at the glass case mounted on the pole she was carrying. Jaden's Twisted face stared blankly back at her. She paused, as though Jaden had responded. "Oh, you wish you could feel it, but your body is missing? That must be awful. It will probably feel as bad as watching me slaughter everyone in the city you spent so long protecting. Don't worry, you'll be able to savor the experience. I'm going to take my time."

She paused again. Jaden's head moved up and down as she walked.

"Hey, I'm not crazy. The world is crazy. And before I started my little mission, it was a big old mess. You gotta admit, Jaden, I fixed things. All the wars and fighting between countries is gone. The pollution, the nukes, global warming, border wars, that's all history thanks to me. I will let the people multiply after this. They will know that I am the absolute ruler of the world, and I'll keep everyone in line. If they screw it up again, I'll just shrink them back down."

The Twisted surrounding Maryana watched nervously as she continued her conversation with the severed head. The army accompanying her was five hundred strong. While the Twisted close to Maryana had guns, much of the army held pipes and other pieces of blunt metal. She did not have enough weapons for all of them. There were a few scouts out in front, but the rest of the army moved together. The terrain had become mountainous, and they were getting close to Agartha.

One of the scouts came running at full speed. He settled in by Maryana's side. "There is a vehicle heading toward us. We haven't seen it yet, but we can hear the engine."

Maryana smiled. "That's wonderful. I thought they would hide in their hole. Facing them in the open will be much easier." She yelled loudly enough for all her Twisted to hear. "Everyone take cover on the sides of the road. When the transport gets close, I want a full attack on it. Just remember to leave the GMT's heads intact. Do what you want with the rest of their bodies."

The army of Twisted scattered into the forest on the sides of the road and prepared to lie in wait.

Alex bounced up and down in the passenger seat of the transport truck. Owl was driving as fast as she could along the old road. The two of them were alone in the large vehicle, and every sound seemed to echo, accentuating the emptiness.

Alex's nerves were on edge as her body began to anticipate the coming battle. She thought back to a simpler time, when Owl was still a human, flying the away ship. They'd risked their lives on every mission, but the people back on *New Haven* had been safe, far from the battles. She'd wanted to make a name for herself as the greatest member of the GMT. Part of her missed that reckless girl who'd thought fighting monsters was a game. She hadn't truly understood what was at stake. The woman who bounced along the road had no illusions about the risk and the importance of the upcoming battle.

"Stop as soon as you feel them," Alex said. "We're only going to get one chance at this."

Owl nodded, her eyes fixed on the road ahead. "I've got it."

"I know you do. You're a kickass warrior. There's no one else I'd rather have by my side today."

"Right back at you."

Owl slammed on the brakes of the transport. Alex felt her seatbelt bite into her shoulder and pull her back to the seat as the truck stopped. She looked down the road as far as she could, but there was no army.

"They're here. I feel them." Owl put the truck in reverse and turned it around.

As soon as the truck started to change direction, Alex saw Twisted leap from the forest. She jumped into the back of the transport and flung open the back door. An assortment of weapons was waiting for her.

Owl floored it, sending them racing away from the charging Twisted army. Alex risked a glance up from the crate she was opening and saw that the first wave of them were getting close to the transport. She hoisted the missile launcher from the crate onto her shoulder. She aimed it at the Twisted in the front of the pack and fired. She felt immense pressure on her ears for a moment as the force of the rocket filled the truck. She saw the trailing stream of smoke and then watched a ball of fire explode in the middle of the road. One Twisted seemed to disappear completely, and three others went flying backward through the air.

"We definitely have their attention. Don't slow down!" Alex threw the missile launcher aside and picked up an automatic rifle.

Twisted raced through the thick smoke from the explosion as debris rained down on them. They did not stop to consider the damage to their fellow soldiers. They just followed their order to kill the GMT. Alex targeted her rifle at any Twisted that were getting close to the transport, squeezing the trigger and letting out short bursts of three shots. Each burst was aimed at center mass, ensuring that she hit her targets and killed their momentum. Some of the shots found Twisted hearts, leaving the targets in a pile along the road. Others bounced back up quickly, alive, but still slowed in their progress toward the truck.

Alex swiveled the weapon between targets, quickly knocking down one after another. She felt a dull click when her magazine fired its last round, and she quickly dropped the empty and slapped in a new clip. A Twisted flew through the air as he tried to jump into the back of the transport. Alex was able to chamber a round and shoot him out of the air just before he landed. Blood sprayed from his chest, and he rolled on the ground for a second. Then he sprang back up and rejoined the group running toward the transport.

She wondered if they would last long enough to reach

their destination. She saw an old familiar canyon appear in her peripheral vision. Her old teammate Drew had died in this canyon just before they found Agartha. That day had started a chain of events that led to this moment.

The army of Twisted followed the transport into the canyon. Alex continued to hold the front line back with a spray of bullets. The world seemed far away from her at that moment. The sound from her weapon and the roar of the engine were muted. She could see every flash of fire from the barrel of her rifle. Every fiber of her being was focused on keeping them alive for a few more minutes.

BRIAN WATCHED Alex and Owl enter the canyon on a monitor in the control room. The Twisted army raced behind them. Stephanie gasped at the hoard of Twisted so close behind the truck.

"I see them in the canyon. Can we engage?" Frank's voice shook with fear and adrenaline when it came through the radio.

"Do not engage!" Brian responded. "Wait for my signal." He turned to Stephanie. "Make the call."

Stephanie tapped her tablet and opened a channel to *New Haven*. "Jessica, do you copy?"

"I copy, Agartha." Jessica sounded clear and ready.

"Maryana is here. It's go time."

"Give them hell, and we'll do the same," Jessica said. The radio clicked to silence.

Brian held his breath as he watched the army of Twisted funnel into the canyon. He spotted something toward the far end of the army—the group of fifty well-armed Twisted surrounding a woman with two swords on her back.

Brian shook as he watched her cross into the canyon. He hit a button, opening all the radio channels. "Maryana is in. All teams, go!"

THERE WAS another dry click as Alex squeezed the trigger of her rifle. She reached for another magazine while she ejected the spent one. Then she heard a sound like a beast roaring to life. The hairs on her arms stood up as she spotted Frank charging at full speed toward the back of the Twisted army. Behind him, people poured out of the woods on the hillside. They filled the road, blocking the army's path of retreat.

Then a gunshot echoed through the canyon and one of the Twisted close to the transport fell to the ground. Alex glanced up and saw Ed standing forty feet above her on the edge of the canyon's wall. His rifle was pressed against his shoulder, and he fired again. A moment later, he wasn't alone. Men and women stepped up, filling the empty spaces beside him all along the canyon wall.

Alex glanced to the other wall of the canyon, and spotted Felix taking his place on the other edge followed by hundreds of citizens. They were armed and, backlit by the sun, they appeared more like a formidable army than a group of volunteer citizens risking their lives on a desperate plan.

She heard the rattle of an automatic weapon coming from in front of them. She glanced over her shoulder, looking through the front of their transport. Two more trucks, mounted with weapons, and an army of people were waiting in the road. They fired into the mass of Twisted.

The trap was sprung. Hope and pride filled Alex. There

was one last element left to activate, and she could end this. She expected that at any moment, Brian would activate the sound generator, and the Twisted would fall to the ground.

Unfortunately for the men and women of Agartha she did not get what she expected.

37

JESSICA AND BILLY huddled in the maintenance tunnel, surrounded by wires and electronics. Jessica lowered the radio and gave Billy a hard look. "It's time."

Billy just nodded solemnly. Though he looked more like a drunk than a warrior, Jessica had come to respect him over the past few days. He wasn't always the most direct individual, but he was tough as nails where it counted. And if it hadn't been for his connections in just about every sector, they wouldn't have gotten this far. Of their three dozen confidants, about thirty-three had come from Billy.

And now, hopefully, that thirty-six was about to become a whole lot more.

It hadn't been easy sneaking down here. Billy'd had one of his connections rig a small explosion on the other side of Sparrow's Ridge. Luckily, it had worked, drawing the patrolling Twisted away. With Maryana's kill order in effect on anyone found outside, the streets had been deserted as Jessica and Billy raced from the apartment to the nearest access hatch, three buildings away. They'd made their way to the correct junction under street level, set up their equipment, and waited for the go ahead from the GMT.

Now that it had come, there was nothing left to do but check the connections one more time to ensure that they were plugged into the citywide PA system. Jessica did so, and then drew a deep breath. This was it. A tiny shock jumped into her finger when she pressed the button to play the recording. She didn't know whether that was a good omen or a bad one.

For a moment, there was nothing. Then a familiar voice filled the streets up above, echoing down to the tunnels.

"Hi, *New Haven*. This is Alex Goddard. I know you haven't seen me in a while, and I apologize for my absence."

Jessica pushed her equipment aside and pulled out her revolver. She nodded for Billy to follow, then started down the tunnel. There was no reason to wait for this to be over before they began their brutal mission. If it didn't work, they were pretty screwed. Better to face the Twisted with their kill order than to stay in hiding and face the eventual wrath of Maryana.

"I left because I wanted to find a way to stop Maryana," Alex continued, her recorded voice echoing through the city. "I wanted to find a way to save you. That's my job. That's the GMT's job. We're here to save you."

Jessica reached a hatch, one that she knew came up in the heart of Sparrow's Ridge. She touched the handle and waited for her moment.

Alex paused before continuing. "Here's the thing, *New Haven*. I can't save you this time. Please believe me, I tried. I threw myself into it with everything I have. But it wasn't enough. This thing we're facing is just too big. A lot of people have died in this fight, including Colonel Brickman. CB was my hero. He was the toughest guy I ever knew. And maybe the smartest, too. He once told me that the one thing I should never underestimate is the people of *New Haven*. You are descended from the only ones who survived Maryana's infestation the first time around, and you're going to survive it again."

Jessica checked her weapon and tightened her fingers around the handle. It was almost time.

"I can't save you," Alex said, "but I don't have to. You're going to save yourselves. What I'm asking is not going to be easy. I know about the kill order. The Twisted are going to attack you the moment you step outside your door. But they won't kill all of you. Get a weapon. There are stores of makeshift weapons in thirty different buildings in every district throughout the city. Their windows are marked with orange Xs. If you don't see one of those buildings nearby, use whatever heavy objects you can find." She paused. "Look, I know I'm not going to motivate you with pretty words. That was Fleming's way. And I'm not going to scare you into it. That's Maryana's style. I'm just a *New Haven* kid who barely passed ninth grade Algebra, so I'm going to give it to you straight. Take your city back. Fight the Twisted. Show Maryana *New Haven* belongs to the humans. I'm proud of you. Now go kick their asses."

The transmission ended with an audible click. As it did, Jessica threw open the hatch and pulled herself up onto the street. Less than a block away, two Twisted stared at each other, confused looks on their faces. Then one of them spotted Jessica, and his face immediately changed. As Maryana's kill order took over, all control left his body, replaced by the furious need to kill the one who'd defied his master.

The Twisted started charging before his companion even noticed Jessica. She dropped to one knee and held the revolver steady, waiting until it got a bit closer. She didn't have to wait long. The creature moved with uncanny speed, and it was everything she could do to force herself to hold her ground. Even after seeing the Twisted wandering around the city so much lately, seeing one charging with the intent to kill was something different entirely.

She waited as long as she dared, then squeezed off three shots. It had been a long while since she'd fired a weapon, so she didn't trust her marksman skills enough to go for the head. She fired at center mass. On her second shot, the Twisted stumbled, falling on its face and sliding ten feet along the street, carried by its own momentum. The creature started to get up, but Billy was already in motion. He sprinted to within ten feet of the creature and shot it twice in the head.

There was no time to be pleased with their victory. That was only one of the two-hundred and fifty Twisted Maryana had left in the city, and so far, Jessica and Billy were the only humans in the street. Jessica's eyes shifted to the second Twisted, and she saw that he was running in the other direction. Toward people... There were other people in the street!

Just past the Twisted, Jessica saw a group of ten men and women. They let out a battle cry as they charged at the Twisted. Jessica glanced up and saw more of them pouring out of one of the buildings where they'd left the makeshift weapons. The orange X on the window gave it away.

Unfortunately, their weapons store didn't include many firearms. The first man the Twisted reached was carrying a board with a nail driven through it. The man swung it at the creature's head valiantly, but the Twisted easily knocked it away and drove his claws into the man's midsection. As he gored the man, the others piled on him, driving their knives into his body, chopping at his neck with their axes and beating at its head with blunt objects.

Five more humans paid with their lives, but it wasn't long before the Twisted fell, his body a bloody mess.

As Jessica watched, four more Twisted rounded the corner, running to help their fallen comrade. They were quickly followed by nearly a hundred citizens.

"It's working." Tears stood in Jessica's eyes as she spoke. "I can't believe it's working."

Billy let out a deep laugh. "After more than two decades running Tankards, the one thing I never doubted was that the people of *New Haven* knew how to throw a punch."

Jessica moved through the streets of Sparrow's Ridge, directing people toward any area where the Twisted seemed to be getting the upper hand. As she observed, the people seemed to be coming up with strategies on the fly. Those with blunt objects distracted the Twisted, while those with knives stabbed for their brains and hearts.

As she turned a corner she saw a man savagely drive a chef's knife into a Twisted's eye, pushing it through to the brain. The man looked up, and Jessica saw it was Wesley. He gave her a nod and a grim smile as the Twisted collapsed.

Many a human fell. Oh, so many. The human blood flowed down the streets of the city, while the speckles of Twisted blood were much rarer. But that was all part of the plan, God help them. There were two-hundred-fifty Twisted and forty thousand humans. Based on what Jessica was seeing, the average Twisted was taking out about twenty people before he was brought down. That was a terrible price to pay. It was also enough to defeat the Twisted.

After things seemed to be reaching a conclusion in Sparrow's Ridge, Jessica had a terrible thought. Yes, the hardscrabble folks of the Ridge had managed to overcome the

Twisted, but what about the softer people in the Hub, where there would likely be a higher concentration of Twisted? She turned on her heel and sprinted through the blood-soaked street toward the center of the city.

When she reached it, she was surprised to find it much like the way she'd left the Ridge. The fighting continued in small pockets, but things had quieted down a bit. There were more human bodies on the ground than in Sparrow's Ridge, but there were more Twisted bodies, too.

Near the City Council building, a woman stood at the center of a small crowd, her bloody knife held aloft and a wide smile on her face. "For *New Haven!*" she cried.

The crowd answered in an even louder voice. "For *New Haven!*"

Jessica stopped in her tracks as she recognized the woman. She hadn't seen her in years. She'd been Brian's former lab assistant and Fleming's greatest confidant. It was Sarah. Jessica shook her head, wondering if Maryana had decided to empty out the prison, along with the hospital.

She supposed it didn't matter, at least not for today. The people of *New Haven* had won the battle against the Twisted, and now they were cheering. Not for some great leaders or some military hero, but for themselves.

38

Brian watched on a monitor in Agartha's command center as the Twisted army moved into position. As soon as the canyon was lined with armed troops he hit the command to activate the sonic generator. He kept his eyes on the monitor, waiting for the Twisted to fall down, stunned, but nothing happened. His heart raced and color flushed his face. He looked at his tablet and saw the error message blinking there. *Power overload - section 238-16.*

"Oh, my God. Stephanie, we have a problem. We need to fix this, now!"

She jumped out of her seat and grabbed the tablet from Brian. "I can fix this. Just be ready to activate the weapon." She grabbed a radio and ran toward the electrical room.

Brian hit the button to open the radio channel to the troops in the field. "The sonic generators are not working. We are trying to fix it, but until we do, you are on your own."

Even with the gunfire coming from above, Frank heard

Maryana's voice echoing off the canyon walls. "Get up top! Break through their ranks."

Bullets ricocheted around the canyon, sending up puffs of dust as they hit the ground, or splatters of blood as they tore through Twisted flesh. The first-time soldiers of Agartha had terrible accuracy. They managed to hit some of the Twisted, but most of the shots were not fatal. When Maryana yelled her order, the Twisted sprang from the floor and began climbing the canyon walls.

Frank continued his charge from the rear, both of his hands wrapped around the hilt of a sword. An army of men followed behind him, but his vampire speed put him one hundred yards in front. He reached an injured Twisted soldier scrambling for the canyon wall, his right leg dragging behind him. The Twisted turned to face Frank with a pistol. Frank's instincts kicked in and he tracked the barrel of the weapon, moving just ahead of the shots. He charged at full speed, bringing his sword parallel to the ground. The blade passed through the Twisted's neck, and his head rotated as it flew through the air, spraying a line of blood against the rocks.

Frank scanned the ground and saw about fifty of the Twisted were already dead from the initial assault from above. Fifty more were injured and climbing the walls toward their attackers. He spotted a Twisted twenty feet away, starting her climb. He leaped toward her, kicking up dirt as he left the ground. He put his sword through her heart and looked for his next target.

Bullets and the sound of gunfire bounced around the canyon. The soldiers caught up to Frank and opened fire on the surviving Twisted. They'd successfully flanked the Twisted on all sides.

Frank heard a scream from the top of the wall. A quick

glance around the canyon told him that the Twisted there would be finished in moments. He began to climb.

Felix watched the Twisted reach the top of the canyon wall and launch themselves into the air. They shot up over the top of his troops and landed behind them, pressing them toward the edge. Twisted and humans were packed in shoulder to shoulder. Felix looked down the sights of his rifle, but it was impossible to get a clean shot at the enemies among his troops. He saw a Twisted rip out one of his soldiers' throats. The flesh stuck to the Twisted's hand as he pushed the injured man away and pressed forward toward more humans. A soldier unloaded a handgun into the Twisted. The shots tore into his back, but some of the bullets went wild, hitting other Agartha troops. The Twisted fell to the ground, and before he could get up, Felix put a round through the back of his head.

Felix heard screams to his left and pushed through the soldiers in that direction. He spotted a Twisted with five knives sticking out of his torso. The angry Twisted pushed forward, slashing at the soldiers around him. Each time he landed a blow, bones cracked loudly. The creature was moving quickly, and Felix couldn't see a way to get a clear shot at him. He charged toward the Twisted and pulled a knife out of his back. He jammed it upward into the base of the creature's skull. The Twisted looked like a marionette who'd had its strings cut. The limp body fell in a pile on the ground.

Movement in Felix's peripheral vision caused him to jerk his head up. He expected to see a Twisted, but it was a mangled soldier's body flying through the air. Felix's heart broke at the sight. The man couldn't have been older than twenty, but his young face was calm. The crooked angle of his neck suggested the calmness was permanent. Felix pushed forward in the direction from which the body had been thrown.

He broke through the crowd and saw a Twisted with his arm locked around a woman's throat. She swung wildly at the Twisted, but her hands bounced harmlessly off his body. The Twisted used her as a shield as he tore into other soldiers. Four bodies already lay on the ground behind him. Felix brought his rifle to his shoulder. He drew in a breath and held it as a bead of sweat ran down his face. The Twisted drew his arm back to strike the next soldier, giving Felix an angle on his head. Felix squeezed the trigger, and the bullet flew true.

The Twisted collapsed on top of the woman. Felix pushed the body aside and pulled the woman to her feet. She had a glassy look in her eyes, and he could tell she was in shock. "You okay?"

Instead of answering, her eyes widened as she stared past him.

Felix turned, following her gaze, and saw Twisted holding an automatic rifle, spraying bullets into the crowd of tightly grouped soldiers. He felt a sudden pressure in his abdomen and staggered backward, barely keeping his feet as the soldiers around him fell. He raised his rifle, but it felt much heavier than it should have. Still, he managed to squeeze the trigger, hitting the Twisted in the arm and body. None of the shots were fatal. Pain was starting to radiate his midsection, and he felt hot, wet blood spreading across his stomach. The Twisted's rifle barrel moved back toward him.

Another Twisted burst through the line of soldiers. This one wore a GMT uniform and carried a sword. Frank lunged forward, driving the tip of his blade through the first Twisted's head. Felix watched the rifle drop to the ground, and Frank pulled his sword out of the creature's skull.

Felix dropped to one knee and then fell backwards to the ground. His rifle dropped next to him. Frank ran over to him. He ripped Felix's shirt open, revealing a hole in his lower left side. Blood pumped out of it. Frank used the torn shirt and pressed down on the wound.

"It doesn't look that bad," Frank said, his face grim. "Just hang on and we'll get you some help."

Felix smiled weakly as the color drained from his face. "You couldn't have shown up thirty seconds earlier? I mean, I'm glad you came, but you're as slow as Tino Martinez." He let out a little laugh, but he grimaced in pain.

"I don't think this is the time for baseball or jokes," Frank said, watching blood soak the fabric under his hands.

Felix drew in a shallow breath. "I think now is the perfect time for baseball and jokes."

A half-smile formed on Frank's face as tears blurred his vision. "You want to know when the Cubs finally won the Series?"

"Yeah. I think I'd like that." A light smile stayed on Felix's lips.

"2016. Your boys won maybe the greatest game seven in World Series history."

"Ah. I would have liked to see that."

"They were celebrating in the streets of Chicago for days. Even I had to admit, it was something special."

"Thanks, Frank. You're an okay guy, for a Cardinals fan." Felix eyes drifted shut, and his head rested on the dirt of the mountain under a blue sky.

The Savage End

ED HELD his ground as the Twisted raced up the canyon walls, shooting Twisted out of the sky as they jumped over him. He let out a fierce battle cry as he fired his weapon. His screams gave strength to the green soldiers he led.

"Go for the head and the heart!" he shouted.

While most of the Twisted were charging up the walls, a large, well-armed group remained in formation on the canyon floor. Ed knew who was in the center of that group, and he led his troops toward them. His only goal was to find Maryana and put a bullet through her head.

He kept his eyes on the fighting to his left, watching for Twisted. He saw one grab a soldier and swing him by his head, killing the man and using him like a club to knock back other troops. Ed skidded to a halt, bringing his rifle to his shoulder. He knew his shot was true as soon as he pulled the trigger. The upper right portion of the Twisted's head exploded, and Ed was running again before the body hit the ground.

Ed heard explosions of gunfire and knew that was where he needed to be. He pushed through the troops and saw Maryana and her soldiers forming a wedge and firing into the troops around them. Bullets sprayed into the tightly packed humans. The soldiers who had guns fired back at the Twisted. They were not efficient with their shots, but the volume was high enough that Maryana's troops were dropping. Ed aimed at a Twisted standing over a pile of bodies. He put two quick rounds into the monster's chest.

As Ed advanced, two bodies rose from the pile of bodies. They wore Agartha uniforms, but they were Twisted. He saw a flash of a familiar monster through the chaos. Maryana sprinted from soldier to soldier, biting them and then tossing them aside. She was turning more into Twisted as fast as she could.

The two newly-made Twisted rushed the soldiers around them and attacked. Ed pushed forward and shot each of them as he tried to reach Maryana. She was pushing through the line toward the back. Soon, she would be behind them with a clear path to escape.

Ed spoke into his radio. "Maryana is almost through the back line on my side of the canyon."

"We're almost there," Alex responded.

Then Ed saw Maryana jump through the air toward the forest behind the lines. He raised his rifle so fast that he thought the muscles in his arms might tear. While he was taking aim, Owl jumped after Maryana. She held Alex in her arms and the two chased after her. Ed fired at Maryana, and his round hit her in the side, causing her to spin in the air. He lost sight of her as he was knocked off his feet by one of her Twisted.

He crashed to the ground and rolled, trying to raise his weapon to defend himself. He cried out as pain shot through his left arm. He glanced down and saw that it was bent at an odd angle. Another broken arm. But that was about to be the least of his worries. The Twisted who'd knocked him down pulled back his clawed hand and focused on Ed's throat. Ed looked his killer in the eyes and thought of Patrick.

Instead of striking, the Twisted dropped to the ground, his hands over his eyes.

"The sonic generators are on!" Brian shouted through the radio. "You have fifteen seconds!"

Ed grabbed his pistol from his right hip and put a bullet into the Twisted's skull. He stood; his left arm dangled limply at his side. He started to move in the direction where Maryana had disappeared.

ALEX AND OWL made their way across the battlefield with only one objective—to find and kill Maryana. They raced down the middle of the canyon, killing injured Twisted as they went. They'd almost reached Maryana when she suddenly shot into the air, leaping over the last of her Twisted. Owl didn't hesitate. She grabbed Alex around the waist and jumped after Maryana.

Alex held onto Owl with her left arm and kept her pistol in her right, ready to take a shot at the first opportunity. As Maryana flew through the air, a bullet struck her. She spun wildly and landed hard on the forest floor.

Owl and Alex landed thirty yards away from her. The forest was thick with pine trees and brush. Alex turned to Owl. "Don't wait for me! Go!"

Owl took off at full speed. She'd crossed half the distance to Maryana when she tumbled to the ground.

Alex could still see her when she fell. Brian's voice came through her radio "The sonic generators are on! You have fifteen seconds!"

Now, Alex sprinted through the woods. Though she couldn't see Maryana, she knew she'd be lying on the ground, but she wouldn't be there for long. Alex charged past Owl, who was slowly picking herself off the ground. Then, just ahead, Alex saw the blood. There were splashes of it in the pine needles were Maryana had landed. The spray was thick enough that Alex could move quickly while tracking it. She knew that she didn't have much time.

Alex ran through the brush and into a clearing in the

pines. Small brush grew out of the rocky ground, and the area was bathed in warm sunlight. In the middle of the clearing, Maryana was pushing herself to a standing position. Blood trickled down her side and her face was scrunched in a painful expression.

Alex fired with one hand as she pulled the sword off her back with the other. The report of her pistol broke the momentary silence of the forest. Maryana reacted quickly, diving forward onto the rocky ground. Alex put four rounds in her, but she couldn't tell whether she'd hit the heart. She got her answer a moment later as Maryana sprang toward her, a blade in each hand.

Alex immediately recognized the ancient blades, even as they hummed through the air. If she hadn't anticipated the attack, they would have sliced her in half. Time slowed for Alex as she dodged and swung her own blade toward Maryana's neck. Hope sparked in her as the sword neared its mark, but Maryana countered, parrying the strike with inhuman speed. The blades collided an inch from Maryana's neck, sending a flash of sparks into the air.

Somehow, Alex's blade kept moving. For a moment, she thought she'd landed the blow, but then she saw that her blade had been cut in two. All that remained of her sword was the hilt and six inches of protruding steel.

Maryana grinned as she spun toward Alex, both her blades in motion. Alex had seen Jaden perform this move a dozen times, and that was the only thing that saved her. She dropped to one knee, avoiding the first blade by centimeters. The blade whizzed over her head, slicing through her hair rather than her skull. She twisted her body to the left as the other blade sliced past her shoulder. She brought up her pistol and fired off rounds as quickly as she could. The bullets tore into Maryana's wrist and thumb. The combination of the power and the proximity to the weapon tore her hand to shreds. The sword and the hand flew past Alex and clattered to the rocky ground.

To her credit, Maryana was a true warrior, and the destruction of her hand barely slowed her attack. She spun, landing a kick to Alex's ribs before Alex could fire again. Alex flew backward and landed on her side, sending pain shooting through her cracked ribs.

Maryana stood up, looking at the stub where her hand had been a minute before. "You stupid little bitch. You just couldn't go down easy, could you?" She stepped closer to Alex. "You want to make things difficult? Fine. You're going to be the new leader of my army. You are going to rip your friends' throats out, and then you're going to spend the next thousand years bowing to my every whim."

Alex tried to draw a breath and shuddered in pain. She pushed herself onto her hands and knees. A small cough escaped and blood splashed the leaves below her. The sunlight flashed off a piece of steel three feet to her right.

She stood up, drawing in a painful breath. She swayed on her feet and raised her fists. Blood trickled out of the corner of her mouth. "The only thing I'm going to do is kick your ass."

Maryana let out a yell and charged, but Alex was already in motion. She pushed the raging pain away as she dove toward Jaden's sword. She hit the ground and rolled, snatching up the weapon. The sharp rocks cut into her shoulder as her broken ribs dug into her lungs. The pain was so sharp that it severed all thought from her mind. She found her feet just as Maryana reached her. Alex thrust the sword upward as Maryana slammed into her, and the steel rammed through Maryana's sternum and into her heart.

The two entangled bodies flew backward, slamming into

a pine tree. Stars filled Alex's vision as the back of her head bounced off the tree trunk. She felt blood trickle down her neck. She used the last of her strength to push Maryana off of her. Through the pain, Alex smiled as Maryana's body fell limp and lifeless to the ground. Darkness filled her vision and her last thought was that the war was over.

39

THE TRANSPORT VEHICLE was five miles outside *New Haven* when the rain started to fall. It began as a light mist but quickly transformed into heavy drops that splattered against the windshield like tiny explosions.

"Can you see okay?" Alex asked. "If we all died in a car crash a week after taking out Maryana, it would be a very bad look."

Owl shook her head sadly. "After all the stuff I've piloted us through, you think I'm going to crash going forty-five miles an hour on some old road?"

"You did get us shot down that one time," Alex pointed out, "so there is some precedent."

Alex glanced toward the back of the transport just in time to see Ed elbow Brian.

"You gonna be okay, buddy?" he asked. "Cause if you want to cry or something, go right ahead. I'll make fun of you for the next decade, but go right ahead."

Brian looked up slowly as if he was waking from a dream. "What? No, I'm fine. Totally fine. Stephanie's going to be coming to *New Haven* in a week with a supply shipment. I can make it until then."

Frank shook his head and chuckled. "Love is one hell of a drug."

Alex laughed. Though she'd spent much of the time since the battle with Maryana in and out of various states of consciousness and in large amounts of pain, one of the bright spots had been Brian and Stephanie. The two were madly in love, and they weren't afraid to show it.

"Hey," Owl said, suddenly perking up. "That's it, Alex. Maybe you'll finally have time to date now. I mean, there hasn't been anyone serious since Simmons, right?"

Alex frowned at that. Ever since she'd woken up to the new status quo, people had been speculating about what she should do next. Now that there weren't vampires to fight, everyone seemed to assume she'd be having some existential crisis about what to do with her life. Mostly, she just wanted to rest and heal. And, with the way eighty percent of her body was covered with cuts and bruises, dating was the furthest thing from her mind. "Yeah, well, Simmons is a tough act to follow."

"That he is." Owl paused. "Can I tell you something? I sorta dated him for a bit. Before you joined the team."

Alex's eyebrows shot up in surprise. "And you never thought to mention it?"

"It was, like, two weeks! And it never went anywhere." She paused again. "I mean, it definitely went somewhere, but it was never serious. You know what I mean."

"I do, and I'd love it if we could stop talking about this.
"

They rounded a curve and *New Haven* came into sight. Alex didn't know if she'd ever get used to seeing it like this, resting on the ground. But she supposed this would be the way it would look forever now. There was no reason to try to get it into the air again.

As they got a bit closer, Alex spotted something else. She turned and glared at Brian. "You radioed ahead, didn't you?"

Brian shrugged sheepishly.

"I told you—"

"I know! I know!" he said. "It's just... I thought the people deserved the chance to give you a proper welcome."

Alex sighed. "I wish you guys would have left me in my hospital bed and come back by yourselves."

Ed crouched down between the two front seats and grinned. "What? And have you miss out on all this?"

The people of *New Haven* stood gathered in front of the city. Thousands and thousands of them. And though the rain poured down on their heads, there was a smile on every face. They cheered with glee as the transport pulled to a stop at the edge of the crowd.

"Toughest part of the job," Ed said with mock discomfort. "These hero's welcomes are not for the faint of heart." He hopped out of the back of the van, his arms raised in victory as he took in the shouts of excitement. Frank followed him out, as did Brian.

Alex put her hand on the door handle, but she stopped when Owl spoke.

"I wish they were here with us to see this," Owl said. She didn't say who she meant, but she didn't need to. They'd lost so many in the war that had led up to this moment.

"Me, too. But if they were here, it might not have happened. *New Haven* is sitting on the surface, completely safe, and without their sacrifices, who knows if that would be the case?"

Owl turned and looked her in the eyes. "Alex, we need to talk."

Alex felt her heart sinking; she knew what Owl wanted to discuss. "We will. But later. I don't think the thousands of people out there would appreciate us sitting here having a heart-to-heart while they wait in the rain."

Owl looked almost relieved. "Okay. Later, then."

Together, the two women opened their doors and stepped out into the rain. Alex steadied herself against the truck, doing her best to hide her new-found limp.

At the sight of them, the crowd roared, and even though Alex had expected it, based on the reaction to the others, it still nearly unmoored her. These were the people for whom she'd fought so hard for so long. They'd been through so much, and now their lives were changed forever. They walked the Earth, just as their ancestors had. Rather than being cramped in tiny living quarters on a ship, they were free to live where they wanted. They could chart their own destinies. Seeing all of them gathered like this and imagining that every face she saw represented a life of limitless possibility was almost too much to bear. Tears sprang to Alex's eyes. She threw a fist into the air, acknowledging their shouts and cheers.

Jessica stepped out of the crowd, her arms crossed and a smile on her face. "Welcome back, strangers. "

Alex wiped her eyes and met her friend's smile with one of her own. "Thank you, Councilwoman."

"It's *Acting* Councilwoman," Jessica corrected.

"Sure it is." Alex knew that it would be very difficult indeed for Jessica to step down from leadership now.

After she'd helped the people take out Maryana's Twisted, Jessica had immediately gone to work, enlisting volunteers and doing the tasks Maryana should have been doing from the moment the city-ship landed. Within a few days, she'd restored power and had begun plans to construct some farms near the city. It was hardly surprising that the people had asked her to temporarily lead the new City Council until elections could be held.

Alex swallowed hard and felt her tears returning as she looked into Jessica's eyes. "I'm so sorry about CB."

Jessica nodded, her expression of understanding saying more than words ever could. She squeezed Alex's arm. "Me too. I'm sorry you had to be the one to do it. But thank you."

Alex blinked and tears ran down her cheeks. She suddenly remembered something. "Oh, I have a gift." She drew the sword strapped to her back.

Jessica looked confused. "A sword... thanks, I think. Unless you're planning on stabbing me with it."

Alex held the sword out, laid across her hands. "It's for *New Haven*. The sword was Jaden's. I left the other one in Agartha. They're going to hang it over the main entrance. Sort of a reminder of the price they paid to protect their city. I thought maybe we could do the same."

Reaching out, Jessica carefully took the sword. "We will. It's an honor." She turned to the rest of the GMT. "What do you say we get out of the rain?"

With that, they entered *New Haven*. They were home.

ALEX PULLED herself forward with her arms, lungs burning as they begged for oxygen. Her legs scissored, driving her upward. She broke the surface of the water and drew a sweet breath as the sun hit her eyes.

It took her a moment to notice the woman standing on the lake's shore. Alex paddled leisurely toward her. When she finally exited the water, she glared at the woman. "You know, one thing I like about living on the ground? When I get sick of all the people, I can just leave for a while. I came out here to be alone."

Jessica cocked a thumb toward the rover parked nearby. "Then you shouldn't have taken a vehicle with a tracking device."

Alex sat down in the grass, letting the water roll off her skin, enjoying the feel of the warm sun on her face. Ever since she was a little girl, she'd dreamed of swimming. For the past three weeks, she'd done it nearly every day in this lake, ten miles outside *New Haven*. "So, what's so important that it couldn't wait until I got back?"

Jessica sat down beside her. "Honestly, I kind of needed a break, too. This job never ends." She paused and looked at Alex. "Have you thought about what you're going to do next?"

Alex laughed. "You know, people keep asking me that."

"Well, you are kind of a celebrity."

"The other thing I've noticed," Alex continued, "is that people who ask that question always have an idea of what they think I should be doing. I take it this is no exception?"

Jessica shrugged. "There has been some talk on the Council."

Alex groaned. "Okay, tell me."

"A lot of the people who have left the city in the past couple weeks are heading east to a valley twenty miles from *New Haven*. Based on our tests, it's going to be great for farming. People are setting up out there, trying to build homes, making a life away from *New Haven*. They're even starting a little centralized settlement to take care of some of the logistics."

"A new city," Alex said, a little surprised. She'd assumed it would happen eventually, but not this quickly. "Let me guess, they want to call it something cheesy like CB Town."

Jessica grinned. "The name Brickman Station has been thrown around."

Alex groaned. "Ugh, that's the last thing he would have wanted."

"It's more for them than for him," Jessica said. "If they want to remember him, I'm not going to stop them."

Alex picked up a rock and inspected it for a moment before skipping it across the water. "So, what's this new settlement have to do with me?"

"Well," Jessica said, "the Council was thinking you might want to lead it."

Alex just stared out at the water for a long moment. "Huh."

Jessica raised an eyebrow. "Any thoughts?"

"CB suggested I should get into politics. I've been trying to ignore that memory, but maybe he was right. I've had enough adventures to last a lifetime. Maybe it's time to serve in a different way."

Jessica shrugged. "Sure, if that's what you want."

Alex tilted her head, surprised at the response. "Well that's why you're here, right? To convince me to run this new settlement?"

"I didn't say that," she said with a grin. "Look, CB was a genius when it came to warfare, but he was an idiot when it came to politics. If you want to lead this settlement, fine, do it. But don't do it out of some weird sense of duty. And definitely don't do it because CB said you should go into politics."

Alex shifted in her seat. "Okay... If you don't want me to take that job, why did you come out here?"

"I have another job offer for you."

The former members of the GMT met at Tankards that night. Alex was the first to arrive, and she paused on the way to their usual table. She nodded hello to Billy, who stood behind the bar. "You bartending tonight?"

"No choice," he answered, sourly. "Most of my employees left. Seems like everybody wants to be a farmer or some shit, now."

Alex looked around, noticing for the first time that the bar was oddly sparse for that time of night. "Maybe you shouldn't have done such a good job fighting off the Twisted."

He chuckled at that. "You kidding? A lifetime of bartending is a small price to pay for getting to see my people defending their city the way they did. That was something." He shook his head as if he still couldn't believe it.

Alex took her seat, and it wasn't long before Owl, Frank, and Ed joined her.

Ed shook his head as he sat down. "So this is what true Resettlement looks like. An empty bar on a Thursday night. It's a sad state of affairs."

Billy set a round of beers in front of them. He looked at Owl and Frank awkwardly. "Not sure if you two drink beer, but I wanted to buy you one anyway. In fact, none of you ever needs to pay for a beer in this place again."

Ed's grin was so wide it nearly stretched off the sides of his face.

When Billy had gone, Alex raised her glass. "Guys, I want to say something. It's taken a while for this to really sink in, but we did it. We did the impossible. We stopped Maryana, and we saved *New Haven*. And I want to say thank you. Here's to the GMT."

"To the GMT!" They clinked glasses, and they all drank to their victory.

After they'd set their glasses down, Owl leaned forward and glared at Alex. "So, Alex, you gonna tell me why you're avoiding me?"

Alex raised an eyebrow. "Avoiding you? We had lunch yesterday."

"With three other people. Ever since we got back, you've been avoiding being alone with me. I'm thinking maybe it's because I said I wanted to talk with you about something."

"That might have something to do with it," Alex allowed.

"Okay. If you don't want to have the talk in private, we'll do it right here." Owl drew a deep breath before continuing. "We know from Maryana's example how this vampire thing can spread. It's too dangerous to exist. Even one Twisted is too many, and you've got two sitting right here."

"Owl—" Alex started, but Owl cut her off.

"Frank and I are both direct progenies of Jaden. That means we can make new Twisted. And that can't be allowed. Frank and I have talked, and we've agreed. We need you to do us one more favor, Alex. End it. End the vampire line. End our lives."

Alex looked her friend in the eyes for a long moment. Owl's face was earnest and filled with sorrow.

"I've got a better idea," Alex said.

Owl and Frank exchanged a surprised glance.

"Come work for me. You too, Ed."

Frank crossed his arms. "Work for you doing what, exactly?"

"Just what Owl said." Alex smiled. "Ridding the world of vampires."

Ed's face scrunched up. "Am I the only one who's confused?"

"Look," Alex said, "Owl's right. Vampirism is too dangerous to be allowed. And this isn't the vampires' world anymore. That story is over. But there are still vampires out there. We don't even know if the virus has reached every continent. So, we start with that. Then we swing back around and look for Twisted. Jaden says Maryana had followers all over the world. As long as they exist, *New Haven* and Agartha aren't truly safe."

"You're talking about putting the GMT back together," Ed said, his voice filled with awe.

"No," Alex said. "This is something new. Something different. Jessica is having a ship built for us. But I'm not talking about a quick, one day trip and then back to the city. I'm talking about a mission that could last months. Maybe years. I'm talking about wiping every vampire off the Earth." She looked at Owl. "When that's over, we'll have this talk again. But not before."

Owl stared down at the table for a moment, then nodded.

Ed frowned. "Just so I'm clear, you're asking us to leave *New Haven* right after Tankards promised us free beer for life?"

Alex took a deep breath. "Look, I don't know about you guys, but the past few weeks... Don't get me wrong, I'm thrilled Resettlement happened, but I've got this hunger inside me. After everything we've been through, I don't think I can just sit in this city working a normal job. As long as there's something threatening humanity, I have to fight it. It's who I am." She paused, a slight smile creeping onto her face. "And I'm thinking it's who you are, too. So who's with me?"

"How beauteous mankind is!" Ed quoted. "O brave new world, that has such people in't!"

"Is that a yes?"

"Hell, yeah, it is," Ed grinned.

Frank sighed. "I never considered myself a warrior, but I'll fight in your war, Alex."

"You're going to need a pilot," Owl added. "It would be irresponsible of me not to go."

"Good," Alex said. "I expected no less."

She felt a weight lift off her chest at their words. She'd been fighting beside Owl since her first day on the GMT. Ed had been part of her first command. Frank had only been on the team for a little while. But these were the heroes who'd brought humanity safely home, and she'd never stop fighting by their sides.

Alex pushed her beer aside and smiled. "Let's get started."

AUTHORS' NOTE

Thank you for taking this six-book journey with us. We hope you had as much fun with this story as we did.

We had some debate about how to leave things with Alex, but in the end, we knew she needed a life of adventure. Though her story ends here, her journey probably never will. She'll keep fighting for what's right until she draws her last breath.

While Alex's story is over, we may not be done writing in this world. We have another story we'd like to tell here. It's going to be a bit before we are able to tell that one, but if you'd like us to drop you a line when we do, click here to join our email list.

Once again, thank you for reading. It means the world to us that you spent this many hours with us and our characters. As far as we're concerned, every one of you is part of the GMT.

Jonathan and P.T.

Printed in Great Britain
by Amazon